DATE DUE

12/6		
F 09		
12-31		
2-7		
GAYLORD		PRINTED IN U.S.A.

RIDE TO GLORY

A Western Quartet

*Also by T. T. Flynn
in Large Print:*

Death Marks Time in Trampas
The Man from Nowhere

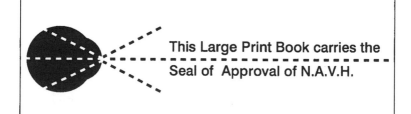

This Large Print Book carries the
Seal of Approval of N.A.V.H.

RIDE TO GLORY

A Western Quartet

T. T. Flynn

Thorndike Press • Waterville, Maine

This Large Print edition is published by Thorndike Press, USA and by Chivers Press, England.

Published in 2001 in the U.S. by arrangement with Golden West Literary Agency.

Published in 2001 in the U.K. by arrangement with Golden West Literary Agency.

U.S. Hardcover 0-7862-2129-1 (Western Series Edition)
U.K. Hardcover 0-7540-4720-2 (Chivers Large Print)
U.K. Softcover 0-7540-4721-0 (Camden Large Print)

The text of this Large Print edition is unabridged.
Other aspects of the book may vary from the original edition.

Set in 16 pt. Plantin by Minnie B. Raven.

Printed in the United States on permanent paper.

British Library Cataloguing-in-Publication Data available

Library of Congress Cataloging-in-Publication Data

Flynn, T. T.
    Ride to glory : a Western quartet / T. T. Flynn.
      p. cm.
    ISBN 0-7862-2129-1 (lg. print : hc : alk. paper)
    1. Western stories. 2. Large type books. I. Title.
PS3556.L93 A6 2001
  813'.54—dc21   00-067207

Table of Contents

Ghost Guns for Gold

Street & Smith's *Western Story Magazine* under the editorship of Jack Burr had again become foremost among Western fiction pulp magazines. T. T. Flynn had proved very popular with readers of the magazine, and Burr solicited him to submit more short novels. "Ghost Guns for Gold," as Ted Flynn titled the short novel that follows, was completed in April of 1939 and bought for $360.00 (at the top rate of 2¢ a word) on April 15th. It appeared in the issue dated August 27, 1938 with the title changed to "Ghost Gold for Gringo Guns." The author's original title and full text of the story as he wrote it have been restored for its first book appearance.

1

"A DESPERATE PROMISE"

Breck Benson sat in the stuffy little court-room at Valdone and watched the only man he had ever hated enough to want to murder him. The courtroom was crowded. Specta-tors were standing against the back wall when Judge Hardcastle rapped for order, got heavily to his feet, and peered sternly over his glasses at the prisoner.

Somebody coughed and the sound was like a shot in the sudden taut silence. Madge Morrison's small cold hand caught at Breck's big one. Breck squeezed her fin-gers. His throat was dry and tight as he stole a glance at Madge's pale face marked with the hurt, the fears of the past weeks.

"Has the prisoner anything to say before sentence?" the judge inquired.

Jail nights and days had put pallor on Clem Evans's face, had gaunted him, changed greatly the dashing young man who had ridden up from Mexico to talk business with Madge Morrison — and had stayed to turn her heart topsy-turvy in one swift week. But pale as he was, Clem Evans still was wiry and handsome, and as good-looking as ever, judging by the way Madge's brown eyes clung to him.

The lawyer who had defended Clem Evans spoke smoothly to the judge. "My client wishes to throw himself on the mercy of the court, Your Honor."

"Is that all?" the judge asked dryly.

"I believe so, Your Honor."

Judge Hardcastle blew his nose, drank from his water glass, and frowned.

"The court's mercy has been worn out lately," he said bluntly. "This defendant was found guilty by fair trial of killing a man without provocation. No witness was produced who saw the victim reach for his gun as the defendant claimed. The defendant could not prove the dead man had threatened in El Paso to shoot him on sight. The jury weighed the evidence and found him guilty. Clem Evans, as an example to other gun-toters, the court has decided to hang you. The sheriff will. . . ."

Madge Morrison moaned softly and fainted against Breck's shoulder. Old María Trujillo, the girl's childhood nurse, muttered compassionately under her breath as she started to chafe Madge's wrists.

"Pobrecita . . . poor little girl. My little dove. *Aie . . . chica. . . ."*

They took Clem Evans back to his cell. The courtroom emptied. Madge Morrison walked out to the buggy with Breck in stricken silence. Not until Breck drove the matched bays out of the courthouse square, away from curious eyes, did Madge break down again.

"Breck, I can't stand it! I'll die, too!"

"I'm sorry, honey. Everything possible was done."

"They can't put a rope around his neck and kill him, Breck. They *can't!* What can I do?" she cried wildly. "Oh, Breck, were you ever in love?"

"Who would I ever be in love with?" said Breck huskily. "Madge, don't look like that. I'll fix it for you. I'll get him out."

"You know you can't, Breck. And you don't like Clem."

"I like him if you like him. Leave it to me."

"If I could only believe you, Breck. . . ."

"I never busted a promise to you, did I, Madge?"

"N-no."

"I won't this time," said Breck. "But Evans won't ever be able to come around

11

these parts again. What'll you do after he's gone?"

"Take that offer I had for my ranch," said Madge without hesitation. "I'll go down into Sonora, to that *hacienda* near La Jarita that my brother bought just before the Yaquis killed him. La Jarita valley is beautiful, Pete wrote, when he sent me the papers to keep. Clem said the same thing when he came up here to rent the *hacienda* after Pete was killed. I was already planning to go down there, Breck."

"I know," Breck nodded. "You never did tell me what made you set on going down there in the Yaqui country for a visit."

"I didn't tell anyone," Madge said, "not even Clem. Before Pete was killed, Breck, he found gold hidden on that old *hacienda*. Gold bars. I'm sure they're still there. Pete wrote me there were reasons why he couldn't move them for a year or two. He told me where they are, Breck, I was going down to get them."

"Are you sure Pete wasn't tryin' to make you feel good when he wrote a yarn like that?" Breck asked mildly.

"Pete wasn't even excited," Madge insisted. "His letter sounded worried, if anything, as if he expected trouble."

"Pete *was* pretty level-headed, even if he

was kinda wild," admitted Breck thoughtfully. "He tell you anything else about the *oro*, or any trouble he might've been having?"

"No," said Madge. She caught her lip under white teeth for a moment, then gulped, burst out: "Oh, Breck, if Clem could only get safely across the border, nothing would ever be wrong again. But I know it can't be. They've got him now . . . they're going to *h-hang him*."

Breck took that small hand again, and grinned reassuringly. Seemed like, he thought, he'd been just a sort of helpful big brother to Madge ever since he'd known her. Times he'd almost said things that were in his mind, but somehow he never had — and now it was too late. One thing he could say.

"Who said it can't be done? Watch that *hombre* Breck Benson throw a mean loop an' drag you plenty happiness, Madge. Stayin' around here ain't helpin' you any. You pack up an' git down there to this town of La Jarita, an' look that *hacienda* over . . . an' get set to be happy. I'll tend to the rest."

Madge searched his face again. Her small sigh of relief was barely audible. But some of the tense fear left her. The look in

13

her eyes, and her wan smile of relief were worth any promise, Breck thought.

"I've got to believe you, Breck. It's all the hope I've got. And for even trying to help, I'll love you forever."

"Sure you will," said Breck. His smile was crooked. "You'll name the first kid after me, won't you? Stop blushin'. I'm gonna take you back to the courthouse now an' get my horse. I've got plenty to do if Clem Evans ain't gonna hang."

The train was whistling in the far distance when Breck rode a lathered horse out of the pines above Forty Grade station. And the saddled horse at the end of the lead rope had run as hard. Unshaven, haggard, red-eyed from lack of sleep, Breck threw up his head to the challenge of those distant peaks, swore huskily under his breath, spurred down to the rutted road and the small red station beyond.

Forty Grade was made up of the station, the agent's tiny house on the other slope, the side track, and a rough dirt road heading up over Forty Grade Pass. Eastbound trains came off the mountains with brakes smoking; westbound trains got clearance orders before entering the high, looping grades.

Breck dismounted behind the station, tied his horse to the short wooden rack, snatched pigging strings from his saddle, and made for the station platform. A telegraph key was chattering inside an open window. Steps sounded inside the station. The gaunt Forty Grade agent came out carrying a looped bamboo stick with train orders stuck in a cleft. He stared suspiciously at the unshaven stranger.

"You want something?" the agent asked.

Breck's gun slid from the holster. "Plenty. Anyone else around?"

The agent gulped. His black alpaca coat hoisted around his middle as his hands shot up. "N-no," he stammered.

"Going to stop that train?"

"Nope."

"This time," said Breck, "you are."

"I'll have to set the signal from inside," gulped the agent.

"You ain't got much time."

When the red stop signal was set above the station, Breck took the black alpaca coat off the agent and hog-tied him on the office floor with quick jerks of the pigging strings.

The train's rush was singing on the rails outside. The whistle blared acknowledgment of the signal as Breck changed into

15

the agent's coat. Too small, but the buttons fastened in front, covering his gun belt. Breck clapped on the agent's green eyeshade, and smiled bleakly at his reflection in a piece of broken mirror on the wall.

"A hell of an agent, but mebbe I'll do. Lie there an' keep quiet."

Bitterly from the floor the agent warned: "They lock up the mail and express. Too many hold-ups have been tried on the grades above here."

"No harm in trying again," Breck grinned.

He caught up the bamboo stick with the flimsy train orders attached. The low thunder of the train was close as he tossed sombrero and coat out the back window of the waiting room and hurried out front.

Safety valve sending out a white plume of steam, brake shoes grinding, side rods clanking heavily, the engine rumbled past the platform. The engineer leaned down and caught the bamboo hoop from Breck's hand.

"What'n hell's the idea of a red board?"

"Trouble!" Breck yelled.

Baggage and express car rolled past. The smoker would be next. Breck swung up to the platform, stepped into the blue-

16

gray smoke haze inside.

Half the seats were full. Several men were moving along the aisle. The first men Breck met asked: "How long we going to be here?"

"Not long. Where's the conductor?"

"Back in the coaches somewhere."

Toward the rear of the smoker two men sat together. Clem Evans, next to the window, stared listlessly through the glass. Tom Platte, the Valdone sheriff beside him, saw the black alpaca coat and eyeshade, and spoke to Breck.

"What's the stop for?"

Then Platte saw the haggard face, dusty pants, scuffed riding boots and spurs, and snatched inside his coat.

Breck's gun flashed out. "You lose, Sheriff! Walk out with him!"

The jerk of Clem Evans's right hand moved the sheriff's left hand, for they were handcuffed together. "Breck Benson! By God, it ain't true!" Clem ripped out.

The sheriff's face was livid. For a moment he seemed to shake, but it was only the chattering brake shoes bringing the coach to a dead stop. The opposite seat was vacant. The man in the seat behind had not seen Breck's low-held gun, or realized what was happening.

Platte, Valdone's sheriff for a decade and a half, saw the red-rimmed bitter eyes, hard with threat, and started to obey. You didn't pack a sheriff's badge many years before you learned when to be brave and when prudent.

Clem Evans gritted — "Wait a minute, Platte." — and snatched a revolver from the sheriff's coat, his handsome young face suddenly snarling. "Quick, Benson, while we got a chance. I thought it was the noose. Now I won't be stopped. Watch 'em behind. I'll clear a way in front. And I'll gut-shoot this dirty law wolf if he holds back."

"Damn you, keep your head," warned Breck. "Horses are behind the station."

Sheriff and prisoner stumbled into the aisle. Breck turned his back to them, following at their heels and covering the front of the smoker, where other passengers were suddenly aware that something was wrong.

"Hold it, gents!" Breck warned.

Clem Evans snarled at the men he was passing: "Get them hands up, you skunks!"

Breck was the last one out, and, when he slammed the door to the cinder platform, Clem Evans was already jerking the sheriff at a stumbling run around the end of the station.

18

Three coaches back, the conductor stood by the steps staring in astonishment. Passengers who had gotten off did not seem to realize what had happened. When Breck reached the hitch rack behind the station, Clem Evans was jabbing the sheriff with the gun.

"Unlock 'em before I trigger you!" Evans's voice cracked. He cursed the sheriff in a low, venomous voice.

Tom Platte's mustache jerked with rage. "Keep this fool quiet," he told Breck. "I'll unlock him if he'll keep his hand still."

The handcuffs snapped open, and Clem Evans crouched, menacing the sheriff, who stepped back against the station wall.

"God, I've thought how it'd be to corner you with a gun. Platte, you dirty. . . ."

Breck knocked the gun up. "None of that! Start ridin'!"

"Thanks, mister," Tom Platte said coldly.

The sheriff stalked around the end of the station. Breck hit the saddle as Clem Evans spurred across the road. A handgun in one of the train coaches opened up after them. Two other guns joined in, but the racing horses made poor targets.

Breck looked back as he rode into the trees. Smoke and steam were rising above the engine. Passengers were swarming out of the coaches — and at the front of the station a tall bitter figure was standing alone, staring after them.

It was not hard for Breck to realize that Platte was thinking of the day when they would meet again.

2

"HACIENDA OF MYSTERY"

The scrub foothill pines whispered in the wind, the mountain jays screamed raucously at the passing riders, and in the twilight Breck and Evans came to a long-unused cabin, and a corral that held two sleek black horses.

"I had to take a chance the horses would still be here for us," said Breck, dismounting. "We can ride all night now. Ain't a posse'll have a chance to catch up."

Fatigue lines were cut deeper in Breck's face as he took the saddle to the corral gate, dropped the bottom pole, ducked through with his rope.

Clem Evans was still pale, but wiry and handsome as ever as he shaped a cigarette. "I'm still trying to figure it out, Benson. Took plenty of planning, didn't it?"

"Plenty," said Breck, shaking out his loop inside the corral. "I was ready before you went to trial. There wasn't much doubt the jury'd find you guilty, and the judge'd sentence you to hang. That meant they'd have to take you to the pen for the hanging. Forty Grade station looked like the best place to get you off. The rest was finding out at Valdone what train the sheriff usually took to the pen, an' what day he'd leave with you. I had to get these horses ready. Better slap your leather on this one."

The two dead-beat horses had wandered away, no longer needed or wanted. Clem Evans saddled in silence. Quickly they stood by the horses' heads, finishing cigarettes before riding on. Evans's manner was strained, wary as he said: "I ain't clear why you did it. Last time we talked. . . ."

"Last time we talked," said Breck evenly, "I called you a dirty card cheat, and had a gun out first. Well, mebbe I was wrong. We all make mistakes. It ain't any of my business why you shot that man White in cold blood in front of the Valdone bank. Maybe White did say in El Paso he'd shoot you on sight, and then went for his gun, like you claimed at the trial. All I've got on my mind now is a promise I made. I promised you wouldn't hang, an' would be ready to travel fast if there was any human way possible. So we're traveling."

Breck swung up into the saddle. Clem Evans followed, and, as he gathered up the reins, he asked: "Who'd you promise?"

"You've got a damned good idea, Evans. It was Madge Morrison, with her heart busted, loving you to hell an' high water, no matter what you'd done. She believed me when I said I'd get you off. She sold her ranch for what it'd bring, so she could leave for good."

Clem Evans cleared his throat. "Where's she going?"

"South," Breck said without expression. "South over the border, Evans, to that little *hacienda* her brother bought down near La Jarita."

Clem Evans shook his head. "She can't go there. Too dangerous. That's why I came up here in the first place, to rent the place from her. I knew she'd never be able to use it. No white folks near. Indians, *mestizo* Mexicans . . . Gallegos, the local *commandante*, is three-quarter Yaqui with a garrison of Yaqui soldiers that he bought off from hell-raising by giving them army guns and army pay."

"You wanted the place bad enough to ride a week to rent it."

"I'm not a white woman!" Clem Evans snapped. "I can get along with Gallegos. If Madge'd give me the papers to that place, I'd settle there and maybe send for her."

23

"You'll dust south of the border or hang here," said Breck. "And Madge can't turn back now."

"She'll *have* to turn back. That's final, Benson."

"Nothing," said Breck curtly, "is ever final. Not even dying. Pete Morrison's letters said that *hacienda* was something to sing about. When the lovemaking started between you an' Madge, you sang the same tune. Madge believed it. She's on her way to the *hacienda* now . . . and she'll marry you there."

"Madge is headed for La Jarita *now* . . . to marry me?"

"That's right."

Clem Evans slowly nodded. The thoughts behind that handsome face were not readable, but the sudden flash of his agreeable smile fanned the old rage in Breck. "Fine, Benson. All I want now is a chance to make the border."

Breck's smile was hard. "I thought you'd see it that way. The sheriff wants me as badly as he does you. So I'll just mosey along an' be best man at the wedding. Let's get going. You can bet Platte ain't losing any time."

A week later an ancient trail, worn

deeply into the rock, brought them out of the harsh desert country through the first purple-peaked Sonora mountains. Breck and Clem Evans were dusty, unshaven, trail-weary. On little water, less food, a blanket apiece, they had traveled hard through the cactus-studded border deserts. And once the line had been crossed, Evans had reverted to the swaggering, arrogant fellow who had ridden north to Valdone and Madge Morrison. Eight days — and still under the surface, seething, gnawing, was the knowledge they would always be enemies. Neither referred to it.

Along the trail now old abandoned mine shafts and tunnel mouths were visible.

"Must've mined plenty through here," Breck commented.

"Still do a little," answered Evans. "Two hundred years ago this La Jarita district sent out shiploads of gold and silver. Three families and the Church owned most of the mines. They say officials in Mexico City used to jump when La Jarita families talked turkey."

"How do the families stack now?"

"Died out, sold out, wiped out," said Evans. "The Gallegos family was the last to go. Yaquis got 'em. Killed every

25

Gallegos man, and carried the women into the mountains."

"The local *commandante*'s called Gallegos?"

Clem Evans grinned. "His grandmother was one of the Gallegos women the Yaquis got. He's three-quarter Indian. Likes to think of himself as Colonel Don Ramón Gallegos, who'll make 'em jump, too, in Mexico City like his namesakes did."

"Will he?"

Evans shrugged. "He'll be top dog around here for a long time, anyway."

"Know all about him, don't you?"

"I've been drunk with him." Evans shrugged again.

Breck mused: "Madge should have arrived days ago."

"Gallegos will know," said Evans.

"You always come back to this damn' Gallegos."

Clem Evans grunted. "Most things in La Jarita district come back to Gallegos. He's the big rooster . . . as long as the Yaquis back him up. If you get along with Gallegos, you're all right at La Jarita. If you don't get along . . . it ain't so good."

Around a bend ahead, half a dozen riders galloped in single file, and stopped, bunched up, at sight of the strangers. They were Indians in blue cotton trousers, barefooted, armed with revolvers, rifles, cartridge bandoliers over their shoulders, and they rode straight up, scowling and arrogant.

They were Yaquis, Breck saw, those bloodthirsty fighters that Mexico City hadn't been able to whip in three hundred years. They'd been slaughtered, deported to the Yucatán fever jungles, driven deeply into the Sonora mountains. And always they'd boiled out again, fighting, raiding, slaughtering, hating all men not of their own blood. Now the lowering faces that blocked the trail wore no look of welcome.

"I'll handle 'em," Evans murmured. "It's a damn' good thing we don't look like money."

The big swarthy-skinned leader had greasy black hair spilling from under a high-crowned sombrero. He stared fixedly as Evans greeted him in smooth Spanish.

"*Buenas tardes. Coronel* Don Ramón Gallegos had word we come?"

A grunt answered. A scowl surveyed them. In silence the big Yaqui reined aside. The others followed suit. The trail was open.

Breck didn't look back as he rode on with Evans. By the unbroken silence behind, he knew the Yaquis were watching the strangers out of sight.

"A bunch of them south of La Jarita held a friend of mine in front of a fire and roasted the bottoms of his feet," Evans said. "They turned him loose to walk thirty miles over hot sand."

"Did he make it?"

"Six miles. Gallegos and some of his men found the body a few days later and backtracked to the campfire." Clem Evans grinned faintly. "I always figured Gallegos had a hand in it. There was a girl he had his eye on. He had her in a week after Steve Lucas was killed."

"This is a hell of a place to be bringing Madge!"

"I tried to stop it, Benson."

Breck nodded reluctantly. "You can always tally up on that. Just the same, it ain't a place for Madge to settle."

"Maybe you got ideas what to do about it?" Evans said.

"No," said Breck. "Not yet."

Evans's quick look was challenging. Breck lapsed into silence. They rode on with antagonism like a bitter cloud between them.

The valley of La Jarita River was some ten miles wide. From the descending trail, the river looping through the valley was blue and beautiful. The low, small, white-walled *hacienda* to which they presently came was set among lime and orange trees, and banked with roses whose beauty seemed incongruous for the khaki-clad soldiers lounging there by their horses.

"The army," said Breck, eyes narrowing. "Your Colonel Gallegos, huh?"

Clem Evans nodded, an uneasy look on his face.

The small rock *hacienda* house had been built in recent years — ten years ago, perhaps, judging by the growth of the lime and orange trees. Seen close, the white color was weathering from the stone, the roses were a wild tangle, the trees unpruned, and weeds and brush were taking over the place.

Breck noted a soldier who stepped to the door and knocked with news of their coming. They were not challenged as they dismounted. A natty young officer with lighter skin than the Yaquis sprang forward with a delighted smile.

"Don Clem! Son-of-a-beetch!" Then in rapid-fire Spanish: "The devil himself must have chased you. The Guaymas and Hermosillo girls would cry in their *rebozos* if they could see. *¿Madre mio . . .* where is our *caballero?* Never has he looked like this!" White teeth flashed in laughter.

Clem Evans grinned, also, as he dismounted. "Worse than the devil, Felix, I almost got a rope around my neck. Gallegos is here?"

That drew another flash of teeth. "Oh, *sí,* my friend. The *coronel* is always here . . . or there . . . with his gallant respects."

"The *Señorita* Morrison has arrived?"

"With her servant," the officer nodded, and sighed. "That maid! *¡Dios!* A woman to terrify even my *coronel.*"

Breck understood it all, sketchy as was his Spanish. And these two understood each other, it seemed, like thieves who had robbed the same pockets.

Clem Evans thought to introduce him in English: "Captain Felix Paredo . . . *Señor* Breck Benson."

"*Señor* Benson . . . ees pleasure."

"Same to you," said Breck noncommittally.

The house door flew open. Madge ran out into Clem Evans's arms.

"Clem! You made it! Oh, I was so worried! Did anything happen to you? You both look half dead. Oh, Breck, thank you!"

The Yaqui soldiers were grinning. A sly

30

smile on Captain Paredo's face vanished as Madge's visitor came striding out with silver spurs jingling.

Stocky, almost as dark-skinned as the Yaqui soldiers, Colonel Gallegos's black hair thrust up in a stiff pompadour. His face was only slightly less Indian-looking than those of the Yaquis, lighted although it was by a smile of welcome.

"*¡Amigo!*" he cried to Evans. "The *señorita* has been inconsolable! I have tried to welcome her, to reassure her, with small success, I fear."

Gallegos shrugged regretfully. Strong broad teeth flashed white as his hand fingered the bone handle of one of the two big side guns he wore.

Probably, Breck thought worriedly, a knife hidden somewhere about him. That puffed chest. Like a stocky strutting turkey cock — for Madge's benefit. And Gallegos looked as ruthless as the Yaquis who soldiered under him. Easy enough to believe the colonel knew about those roasted feet and terrible miles over hot sand to death.

But Madge, pale, worried despite her happiness, held Breck's attention. Madge should be all happiness now. But something had happened. New fear had come to Madge Morrison since she had left Val-

31

done. She couldn't have slept much last night by the weariness around her eyes.

"And who is this?" Gallegos asked expansively, turning to Breck.

Evans introduced Benson.

The colonel's stubby hand was muscular, hard. Strength there, endurance — trust the Yaqui blood for that. Stabbing black eyes looked Breck over, dropped to the big single-action .45 Breck wore. Then the broad white teeth flashed another smile of welcome, and Gallegos turned and bowed to Madge.

"*Señorita,* I leave you weeth your happiness, no? Command *Coronel* Don Ramón Gallegos at your pleasure."

A sound from the house doorway ruined that gallant speech. Gallegos bit his lip. Breck looked there and grinned. María Trujillo, Madge's old nurse, fat, formidable in her somber black dress and *rebozo,* had probably just coughed in the doorway. But it had sounded more like a snort of disdain for the strutting colonel.

Gallegos beamed again at Madge, gave old María a venomous look, and swung up on the big white horse one of the soldiers held for him.

"*Adiós, señorita. Señor* Evans, *mi amigo,* I will expect you in La Jarita tonight."

Captain Paredo and most of the soldiers galloped off after the colonel. Five of the Yaquis remained. Clem Evans turned to the nearest man and said in Spanish: "Why do you stay here?"

"It is ordered."

"Colonel Gallegos insists it may be dangerous here," Madge explained. "La Jarita is seven miles away, and the mountains are near. He refused to hear of my staying here alone until armed men that could be trusted are working on the place. Clem, is it really so dangerous?"

Clem Evans shrugged, frowning slightly. "Maybe." He added something unintelligible under his breath.

"When Gallegos heard I was in La Jarita," continued Madge, "he called at the hotel to ask if there was anything he could do. When he heard I was Pete's sister, and going to open up the *hacienda*, he was astounded. He had known Pete." Madge smiled at Evans, "I think he guessed we were going to be married. Anyway, he tried to help. The *hacienda* had been closed. He sent men to open it up, and since then he's kept soldiers here for protection."

"How about the armed workers?" asked Breck.

"I haven't needed them," Madge said.

"You two come in and look around before you eat and rest."

Breck paused in the doorway and grinned at old María. "How is it? Better than Valdone?"

María's stern face did not break into the smile she usually had for Benson. "*Señor* Breck," she mumbled. "I am afraid."

The couple ahead had turned into a room on the right. Breck stopped.

"What is it? Why are you afraid, María?"

"*¿Quién sabe?*" shrugged María. "Thees is no place for my leetle girl, *Señor* Breck. Why you let thees baby of mine you loff come here?"

"Whoa," Breck muttered. "None of that. Them two are gonna be married an' be plenty happy."

María sniffed. "What she know of loff? So leetle, so jus' a baby! Any man what sing to her of loff, she believe. I tell you so. An' you go seeck in your bellee an' don' tell her nothing. Thees all *your* fault. Now what you do?"

Breck patted María's hand, and shrugged as he smiled. "Damned if I know, María. Think about it for me."

34

3

"HAUNTED GOLD"

The low-ceilinged living room that Breck entered had carved ceiling beams, colorful with blue, red, and yellow patterns. Over a stone fireplace at one end of the room hung the head of a magnificent mountain sheep. Tawny mountain lion skins lay on the floor. The furniture was handmade, covered with soft, native-tanned leather, patterned with brass-headed nails.

Clem Evans was looking around idly as if thinking of something else while Madge talked.

"Beautiful, isn't it, Breck? Pete bought it just like this. Colonel Gallegos told me a German mining man, interested in the old mines around here, bought this tract of land about eight years ago and built this place for his young wife. But he died a year or so later."

"What happened to the wife?" Breck asked.

Clem Evans threw a quick look at him.

"The colonel didn't say. Breck, all this

land was in his family once. Over by the river the colonel showed me ruins of old houses and a church where the Gallegos family once lived. They owned mines, were incredibly rich. Now look at him, only an Indian soldier." Clem Evans laughed shortly. "The Gallegos family owned some land an' mines . . . but now Gallegos owns everything around here. If he wants it bad enough, it's his."

"So you're beginning to believe that, too," Breck murmured.

"Better believe it," Clem Evans said, staring at him. "You'll keep healthier."

Madge changed the subject. "Are you riding into La Jarita this evening, Clem?"

"I'll be back tomorrow sometime, honey."

"Colonel Gallegos said they were having a *fiesta* tomorrow. Breck and I will ride in and meet you at the hotel," Madge decided.

For the briefest instant, Evans looked annoyed, and then he shrugged agreement. Two hours before sunset, he rode off to La Jarita, keeping to himself any reason why Colonel Gallegos might want to see him.

The supper María Trujillo served Breck was a banquet after the hungry trail days, but in the candlelight Madge's face was wan, worried in unguarded moments.

"What's wrong?" Breck asked finally.

"Wrong, Breck?"

"You're worried."

"I didn't think it would be like this," Madge confessed after a moment. "I thought, if Clem came here, everything would be all right. I thought you and Clem would make everything all right, Breck. But now . . . I don't know. Clem went to La Jarita as soon as he was ordered. . . ."

"Gallegos is worrying you," Breck guessed.

"Yes, he is," Madge said swiftly. "Breck, from the hour Colonel Gallegos came to see me in La Jarita, I've felt like a prisoner. I can't move without his men watching me. His eyes are cruel. There's something behind his smile. Breck, do you think he suspects what . . . what Pete found?"

Breck had washed, shaved, donned a clean black suit out of an old chest holding some of Pete Morrison's clothes. They were eating at a small table in the living room. The big mountain sheep head over the fireplace was staring sightlessly at them through the candlelight — as it must have stared many times at Pete Morrison.

Pete had been a broad-shouldered, laughing, happy-go-lucky young fellow who thought the world of Madge. What would he have thought of Breck's helping his sister come into this La Jarita region where Gallegos and his Yaquis dealt life and death as they pleased?

Under his breath, Breck asked: "Where's the gold?"

"Pete found the key in Spanish on the flyleaf of an old, old book, and mailed me the translation and explanation," Madge said. "I carry it with me. Turn your head a moment, Breck."

Paper rustled as Breck looked away.

"Here," said Madge, unwrapping a small packet. She unfolded a sheet of paper and handed it across the table.

In ink Pete Morrison had scrawled:

> From Cross to Cross
> We Fight in Misery
> Our Crosses Cross
> God's Golden Treasury
>> In God's Faith,
>> Don Tomás Gallegos

Take 948 steps downslope from the mountain cross, bee-lining for the chapel altar steps by the river. Dig under the loose rocks just below the two-eared quartz rock. They buried it deeper but the topsoil washed. Hide this and forget it, Sis, unless you get proof I'm dead.

Pete

"I've heard of such things," Breck muttered, putting the paper down and staring at it. "Pete must have known what he was talking about. He must've dug down there an' looked. That verse an' date were written in an old book?"

Madge nodded. "Over by the river, among the ruins, are the remains of an old chapel. The altar steps are there, and a little of the lower part of the marble altar. When you stand on the altar steps and look over toward the mountains, you can see a great rough-hewn stone cross there on the crest of one of the foothills. I could just barely make it out. I didn't dare look more than once or show any interest. Colonel Gallegos was standing there, watching me." Color had come into Madge's face, low excitement in her voice. "Colonel Gallegos has told me enough so I can understand that verse, Breck. Don Tomás Gallegos wrote it the day the Yaquis killed the Gallegos men and carried the women off . . . over a hundred years ago."

"Plain enough," Breck agreed. "They

must've fought between those crosses. Maybe it started up in the mountains an' they fought back toward the houses, or they fought outta the houses and tried to make the mountains."

"And they'd already buried the gold in that hiding place. . . ."

Breck bent over the table, read aloud from the paper: *"Unless you get proof I'm dead. . . ."*

"Pete expected trouble, didn't he, Breck?" Madge said huskily.

"Looks that way. Madge, you ain't got any more chance of getting the gold away from here than Pete had."

"I see that now."

Breck indicated the paper. "Did you show this to Evans?"

"I thought I'd surprise him with it after we were married."

"It'll be a surprise, all right," said Breck dryly. "Did he ever mention gold to you?"

"No," said Madge, surprised.

"Did Gallegos?"

"Only to tell me how rich the Gallegos family used to be. Breck, why do you suppose Colonel Gallegos wanted Clem to ride into La Jarita this evening? Why couldn't they have talked their business over right here?"

Two of the four candles on the table flickered slightly from an air current, and Breck casually pushed his chair back as he said: "Maybe Evans'll tell you about it. . . ." Breck spun out of his chair, diving for the window behind him. With an audible little thump the window abruptly settled into place. Breck's hand swept the curtain aside, and only the window glass and the blackness of the night were outside.

"Breck, what is it?" Madge's voice was low and anxious.

"One of those damned Yaquis! Eased the window up with a knife or somethin' to hear what we were saying. I'd have tried to slip out and catch him, if he didn't have the others hanging around out there, too. I don't want a knife in my ribs tonight."

Madge drew an unsteady breath. "They watch day and night, Breck."

Breck sat down again, growling: "I wonder how much he heard. Better burn that paper, Madge. You don't need it now. Tomorrow we'll try to cut sign and find out what kind of cards are being dealt in this game." Breck grinned crookedly. "Maybe Evans will know after he's through playin' *compadre* with Gallegos."

Fiesta. In the mid-morning when Breck

41

and Madge reached La Jarita, gaily clad natives were thronging the old plaza and narrow streets nearby. The plaza had lost its century-old dinginess, cluttered now as it was with little homemade stands selling tacos, enchiladas, fruits, cakes, and candy. Vendors of cigarettes, herbs, charms, rosaries, and jewelry wandered through the noisy, gaily-dressed crowd of Mexicans and Indians.

Mountains and valleys a day's ride away must have emptied of people for this La Jarita *fiesta*. Men, women, children, and babies, Mexican and Indian, talked, called, laughed, and shouted against a background of gay music from a platform in the plaza.

Madge was delighted when the sorrel horse Gallegos had put at her disposal carried her into the plaza.

"Breck! I didn't expect all this!"

"Fiesta," Breck chuckled. "Even those buzzards Gallegos left watching you will loosen up before the day's over. Here's the hotel an' . . . an' . . . great snakes! Look at Evans! Ain't he the *caballero?*"

The old hotel was built around a stone-floored patio, open to the street. A balcony came out over the sidewalk. In the shadows under the balcony Clem Evans was standing. Valdone would never have recognized the tall, wiry *hombre*, dressed in a tight-fitting, swaggering *charro* costume with silver buttons down the front, a black felt hat hung with little colored tassels around the rim, and a tiny dark mustache the barber had left from ragged face stubble.

"Clem, you . . . you look like a Mexican!" Madge cried as Evans helped her down.

"Had to wear something, honey," Evans answered. "I've got a room for you. The *fonda*'ll take care of the horses. Hello, Benson. You got some new clothes, too, I see."

"Pete Morrison's," Breck said, giving his reins to a Mexican hostler. "I'll walk around a little an' catch you two later."

Breck lifted a hand and vanished into the passing crowd. He wanted to be alone quickly before anyone could follow him. Minutes later, he backed into a doorway and watched. There was no sign of anyone trailing him. Rolling a cigarette, Breck moved off to inspect La Jarita.

Guitars were strumming inside crowded *cantinas*. A trio of *señoritas* walking arm in arm giggled, whispering something about the *Americano*. A little black-robed priest moved past, smiling at the tall stranger.

43

Smells of chili, of unwashed bodies, perfume, cheap black tobacco, sour-sweet *pulque* and *tequila* permeated sunshine and shadow. . . . Suddenly a violent disturbance inside a shabby *cantina* was punctuated by a wild yell that drew Breck through the doorway before he stopped to think.

Girls were screaming, men were swirling, crowding around the plank bar, fighting, tangling, falling over themselves as they tried to reach a young giant in a black sombrero fighting furiously with his fists and feet and cursing them in angry Spanish and English.

They were twenty to one, and more were rushing in when Breck hit the back of the crowd, hurling men aside, jamming, elbowing himself through.

Knives were out, fury, hatred of the *gringo* had flared in those dark Mexican faces.

"Come on, yuh gabbling monkeys!" yelled the stranger. And in Spanish: *"¡Burros! ¡Cerdos! ¡Cabrónes!"*

His big fists were clubbing them down. His booted feet were kicking back men with knives. A sweep of his long arm grabbed a bar bottle and smashed one contorted face into a bloody mass as Breck fought his way close.

A gun came up ahead of Breck — and Breck whipped out his gun, smashed the armed Mexican behind the ear, elbowing the falling body aside as he leaped in against the bar beside the stranger.

"Kill the gringos!"

A whoop of welcome greeted Breck.

"Hey, stranger! Pick yore meat an' hang it!"

Twenty to one — thirty to one, for more were crowding in from the street now as the cry rang louder: *"Kill the gringos!"*

Breck clubbed a *peon* down with his gun barrel. A knife slashed at him, and he broke a flashing wrist with a savage chop. Another knife slashed through his coat and nicked the skin before the young giant's foot kicked the man back into the crowd.

That great lusty, bawling voice lifted again, cursing those who were shoving the leaders closer.

"Where's your gun?" Breck yelled.

"Snatched it outta my holster, the knife-throwin' sons-of-bitches!"

"Is there a back way outta here?" Breck shouted above the din.

"Yeah!"

"Head there then, before they get us both down!"

Breck fired at the ceiling. Those men close to the gun flung back, trying to get away. For the first time the fighting giant seemed to realize it was time to get out. He lunged back along the bar, knocking men out of the way. Breck fired again, and men fought back away from them as they reached the rear of the room in a rush.

A gun roared behind them. The bullet shattered glass in a picture frame on the back wall. Breck fired again over their heads and followed the stranger through a doorway, through a back room, into the sunlight flooding a littered alley.

"This way, *amigo!*" the big fellow yelled.

They ran along the alley, cut into a passageway between two buildings, and entered a dirt-floored courtyard where half a dozen burros were tied. The big man motioned Breck into a shabby little room that held a cot, a table, and a chair. Inside, he caught a whisky bottle off the table and offered it to Benson.

Breck drank and passed it over. His companion upended it and let it gurgle for a moment.

"Hah! That gits yuh clean to the toes! Thanks, friend. That was close. I kicked one of them monkeys outta my mine a month ago. Thought he'd take it out pottin' at me with a rifle from the hills, but he figgered him an' his *amigos* could do it

46

just as well here in town. Three of us have been runnin' a busted-down mine south of here. We stopped by to drink a little before we headed back over the border into white man's country. I'm Paso Smith. What's your handle, stranger?"

"Name's Breck Benson. Don't you like it here?"

"Country's all right . . . but it's run by a skunk I'm half minded to look up before we leave."

"Colonel Gallegos," Breck guessed.

"I see yuh've met the dirty snake." Paso Smith drank from the bottle again, wiped his mouth, and lifted a warning finger. "Friend, if yo're down here to make money, don't tarry. You'll just be working for Gallegos. Two years we busted our hearts out in that damned mine . . . an' we're lucky to get out with our skins. Taxes, bribes, an' Gallegos's dirty Yaquis raidin' when gold was shipped out kep' us flat. Yo're licked before yuh start around here."

Paso Smith squinted over the bottle. Older than he looked at first sight, lines of worry and work were bitten in his face. But he smiled again as he put the bottle down and shrugged. "What business did yuh say yuh was in?"

"Friend of mine named Pete Morrison got killed down here. His sister's opened up the *hacienda* he owned. I drifted in for a visit."

"Who said Pete Morrison was dead?" Paso Smith demanded. "We heard he'd closed up an' gone north."

"Where'd you hear it?" Breck rapped out, all attention.

Paso Smith scratched his head. "Damned if I know," he confessed with a sheepish grin. "Seems to me, Smoky Henderson, one of my pardners, heard it around town. We had troubles enough of our own an' never thought any more of it."

"Word was brought north the Yaquis had killed him."

"Who brought it?"

"Fellow named Clem Evans."

"Never heard of him."

"Colonel Gallegos backed it up."

Paso Smith cursed Gallegos long and bitterly in two languages. "Those Yaquis don't kill *Americanos* unless Gallegos gives the word. Plenty of the Yaquis are all right. Gallegos uses the worst of 'em for his dirty work. I'll show yuh where yuh can get the truth."

Paso Smith stepped out the door and pointed over the roof top to the spire of the old church on the plaza, thrusting its cross toward the blue sky.

"Go back of the church, where the priests live, an' ask for Father Ramirez. He speaks English. If there's anything to know about this Pete Morrison, yuh'll get it there."

"I'll walk over now," Breck decided instantly.

"Come back an' tell me what yuh find out," urged Paso Smith.

4

"A STRANGE MESSAGE"

A young pink-cheeked priest opened the door of the small house behind the big church. He nodded at Breck's request, leading the way back into a walled patio behind the house and church.

Father Ramirez turned out to be the little, graying, black-robed priest who had smiled at Breck on the plaza.

"So we meet again," chuckled Father Ramirez in English only slightly accented. "I hope this garden has more welcome than some of the *cantinas*."

Breck laughed, instantly liking this twinkling-eyed little priest who evidently knew all about the *cantina* fight.

"A man named Paso Smith told me I could get all the news about Pete Morrison from you," said Breck after he introduced himself. He saw the twinkle go out of the priest's eyes and a calm, searching scrutiny look him over.

"Who are you, *Señor* Benson?"

"A friend of Morrison's. Word was

brought to his sister that the Yaquis had killed Pete."

"Ah, then you know the sister?"

"I came here to see her."

"I heard she had come to La Jarita. It is said that Colonel Gallegos is interested in the young lady."

"Kinda," admitted Breck grimly. He had a feeling that those calm eyes were reading his innermost thoughts. The faintest of smiles flitted across the old priest's face, and was replaced by a troubled look. Father Ramirez sighed, murmured half to himself: "Ramón Gallegos has brought so much evil into this country and little good." Then the priest said earnestly: "My son, if you care for this girl, return her to her people. She should not stay here."

"The man she's gonna marry'll have the say about that," Breck pointed out.

"And who is this man?"

"Calls himself Clem Evans."

Father Ramirez shook his head. "I do not know him. But this Ramón Gallegos I know, and the girl is not safe if he has shown interest in her."

"Will you tell her so?"

"Gladly, if you think she will listen."

"She's in town today," Breck urged. "Evans got a room for her at the hotel.

How about her brother? Is he dead?"

"I cannot say." Father Ramirez fingered the cross on his chest, and his voice was low and troubled. "Sometimes, *Señor* Benson, the ways of God are slow. Ramón Gallegos lives outside the Church. We can do nothing with him, or expect little more mercy than other unfortunates whom he oppresses. I have tried through my bishop to have the man removed, or restrained, but so far Mexico City has not seen fit to take action. I suppose because Gallegos has kept a measure of peace among these Yaquis he knows so well."

"What happened to Pete Morrison?" persisted Breck.

Father Ramirez shook his head. "Dead perhaps. *¿Quién sabe?* The body has not been brought in. There is no one who knows. I have asked."

Hope of some news had lifted brightly for a little. Now disappointment showed in Breck's face.

Father Ramirez saw it and shook his head sadly. "What little I can tell you will do no good, my son. One of the faithful has brought me a report of a prisoner who is held in the cells under the fort. Not even the soldiers are allowed to see him. They whisper among themselves that he is an

American. Only Gallegos sees him. There have been nights when screams have been heard."

"You don't know who it is?"

The little priest shrugged silently.

"Seems like you oughta have done something."

"Screams are not new in those dungeons," said Father Ramirez heavily, "I have done all that a simple priest can do. Gallegos would deny anything, would dare to drag me down there himself if it suited his pleasure. And I have not been certain of anything."

"If you hear anything more, I'd like to know it," Breck said. "Better not mention them screams when you see Miss Morrison."

"Some screams she should know of," said the priest gravely. "They may make her willing to leave quickly."

The two partners of Paso Smith were in the shabby little room when Breck returned. John Greeley was bearded and massive. Smoky Henderson was slender as a whip, younger than Breck, with restless eyes and nervous movements. They listened silently as he recounted his interview with the priest.

Paso Smith ripped out an oath when he

heard of the cries underground. "Sounds like Gallegos. I'll hang that dirty Indian by the thumbs an' find out."

"Paso, we ain't lookin' for more trouble," John Greeley warned gruffly. "That noise might've been some fat Mex shop owner Gallegos has took a grudge against."

"Might not, too," snapped Paso Smith.

Smoky Henderson was prowling restlessly about the room. He looked out the small window — and suddenly jumped for the door and plunged outside.

Breck followed, the others after him. In the hot bright sunlight by the adobe wall, Smoky Henderson was holding a gun on a slender, cringing young Mexican. Across the patio three little girls were staring. They turned, ran into the nearest doorway as Smoky Henderson snarled: "I seen those kids pointin' over here. *This* was edgin' along the wall with one ear spread to ketch any talk comin' out the door. *Vamos* inside, you!"

And inside, Smoky pushed the Mexican down on the cot and stood over him with cocked gun. "Who ordered it?" he gritted in Spanish.

The prisoner cringed. "I know nothing, *señor.*"

"So yuh speak English?" Smoky spat. With a quick movement, he holstered the gun, drew a knife off his hip. "It won't make so much noise to cut yore throat!"

"Ah, *Dios* . . . no! *Señor* Montana Blue. . . . hees tell me queek to run watch thees man."

Paso Smith whistled softly as the gesture indicated Breck. "Benson, how come yo're crossed up with Montana Blue?"

"Who's Montana Blue?"

"Dirtiest renegade white man Sonora's seen in years. Owns the Blue Angel *cantina,* where most of the gambling done around here is done. Buys gold, women, an' stolen cattle. Runs cattle both ways across the border. Gits behind a murder when it'll do him any good. Nobody's ever proved he splits profits with Gallegos. But nobody doubts it, either."

Knife in hand, Smoky Henderson stood before the cowering prisoner and eyed Breck. Hot suspicion had flamed in his sharp young face. "Gallegos wouldn't let Blue get away with all that if there wasn't plenty of blood in the meat Blue was cuttin'," he rapped out. "Mister, yuh reached La Jarita this mornin'?"

"That's right."

"An' already Montana Blue is havin' yuh watched."

"I'd say so," Breck agreed. "Maybe I look like easy *dinero*. But this Montana Blue is a new one on me."

John Greeley had been stroking his short, dark beard and frowning. "I heard today that Montana Blue has been away for weeks. Mebbe you've run across him somewhere else, Benson."

A chill of premonition ran down Breck's spine. "Is Montana Blue about my size, good-looking? Got a little black mustache, an' is wearin' Mexican clothes today?" he demanded excitedly.

"I haven't seen him today," disclaimed Greeley. "But he wears Mex clothes a lot. You there on the cot . . . does that describe Montana Blue today?"

"*Sí, sí,*" the terrified Mexican agreed.

Breck nodded bleakly. He could feel the heavy pounding of his heart and a crawling feeling of dismay and apprehension under his belt.

"I know him," Breck admitted slowly. "I came across the border with him." His harsh laughter filled the room. "He called himself Clem Evans, an' he was hand-cuffed an' headin' for state prison with a sheriff . . . to be hanged. I held the train up an' took him off, an' helped him get over the border. Gents, take a look at the biggest damned fool you'll ever have a chance to see!"

"Well, I'll be damned!" Paso Smith drawled.

They were looking as if not sure whether to believe this fantastic statement. Even the cowering young Mexican on the cot was staring with mouth open. The suspicion was still on Smoky Henderson's face.

"Better tell us all about it," John Greeley said gruffly. "That little speech you just made takes in a heap of ground."

Breck told them, leaving out mention of the gold. They stared at him, then looked at one another.

"John, gimme that second gun yo're packin'," Paso Smith said finally. "I don't think right with an empty holster."

Reaching for the gun, Paso Smith began to curse Montana Blue and Ramón Gallegos in a gritting monotone that had the bite of acid, the cut of sharp steel as he tested the weapon and slid it in the empty holster.

"I reckon we know who made Pete Morrison disappear," he flung at them. "That was bad enough. What we've took off Gallegos has been plenty, too. But none of

it stacks up beside goin' north after Morrison's sister. Montana Blue's got one wife
here in La Jarita. He didn't have to go
north to rent that *hacienda*. It was here for
them to take if he or Gallegos wanted it.
"What's the answer?"

Breck knew the answer, but for the moment it didn't matter. "Montana Blue's
married?" he said in a dry, choked voice.

"One of the purtiest little Mex wives
around here. He treats her like dirt,"
Smoky Henderson supplied.

Breck's face was stiff as he tried to grin.
"That's enough for me. I should've let him
hang. Now I've messed everything up. I'll
try to get Madge back home. If I tangle
with Montana Blue, an' get killed, I'm
askin' you men to see that she gets back
over the border."

John Greeley nodded. "No trouble about
that. Haven't you got an idea why Blue
took the trouble to look her up?"

"He wanted some papers Pete Morrison
mailed to his sister. Couldn't have been
anything else. Maybe he thought marriage
talk'd help him. The way it worked out,
Madge came on down here. I'll try to find
her now."

"I'll tag along somewhere behind yuh,"
said Smoky Henderson. "Paso, tie this

58

Mex up. We don't want him bustin' out with all this."

"He won't," promised Paso Smith grimly.

The hot sun now hung straight overhead. Grimly pushing through the noisy plaza crowd, Breck wondered how Madge would take the hurt he was bringing her. Pride and heart would be smashed, he was afraid.

The shadows under the hotel balcony were cool. In the hotel a dapper Mexican clerk lifted his eyebrows when Breck asked for Madge Morrison.

"In her room, *señor*. Who it is?"

"Benson's the name."

"Ah . . . thees way."

They climbed a narrow stairway to the second floor, where old floorboards creaked underfoot. The clerk knocked on a massive room door, opened it himself, and said in a loud voice: "*Señor* Benson ees here!"

Breck stepped in, and the door closed behind him.

"Hello, Benson," a voice cold as ice greeted him.

Breck's gun hand held rigid for a second, then lifted overhead slowly. Four guns were covering him. Two dark-faced Yaqui soldiers were looking at him as if they wanted an excuse to shoot. Captain Felix Paredo was smiling broadly, and Tom Platte, the Valdone sheriff, faced him with a hard, threatening look of satisfaction on his face.

Captain Paredo sprang forward and took Breck's gun.

"*Amigo* . . . veree bad, no?"

"It ain't exactly good," admitted Breck. "Hello, Platte. I didn't think I'd see you down here so quick."

"Kinda thought it'd surprise you," Platte said curtly. "I asked some questions, found Miss Morrison had sold out an' left for Mexico, an' figured Evans must be fixin' to meet her. It wasn't hard to follow her trail on the railroads an' stagecoaches. Everybody remembered her."

"Where is she?" Breck tried to keep the anxiety he felt out of his voice.

"She and Evans left town, they tell me. Gone to Hermosillo to get married. There's a stagecoach leavin in an hour. We'll take it."

"Somebody's lyin'! A couple of hours ago the lady didn't have any idea of goin' to Hermosillo."

Captain Paredo laughed, and then he raised his hand in a slap that cracked like a whip against Breck's face. "My frien', give thanks to God you go north alive."

Tom Platte looked embarrassed. "A hell of a situation I run into," the Valdone sheriff complained. "Colonel Gallegos says Evans is his friend. The colonel's washin' his hands of it. What luck I have over at Hermosillo is up to me."

Platte believed that. Captain Paredo was smiling broadly, and his gun was cocked. No need to wonder if Gallegos sanctioned *ley del fuego* — the law of flight — for troublesome prisoners who looked as if they might be attempting escape.

The wonder was why Paredo hadn't shot when his man stepped through the doorway. Probably because Platte was present. They must want this American sheriff to go home with his mind free of questions. A prisoner to take back would help. Platte would probably decide the escaped Clem Evans and the girl who had traveled down here into Sonora to meet him were living happily in some other part of Mexico.

It was asking for a shot in the back from Captain Paredo to tell Platte now the truth about Montana Blue. Later there would be a chance. Breck rubbed his cheek, and nodded. "Looks like I'm going back with you, Platte. Let's go."

"Next time," advised Platte grimly,

"don't get in my way when I'm takin' a prisoner to the pen."

They left the hotel by back stairs and a back door. Smoky Henderson would be waiting at the front, might not know for days what had happened to Breck Benson — or to Madge Morrison.

They led Breck through great iron-studded wooden doors into the walled fort Father Ramirez had described. Breck thought of the old priest's story, and looked keenly about as Captain Paredo and the two armed Yaquis conducted him inside.

They went along a stone-floored corridor to a cell-like room with benches around the walls. Sheriff Platte had cut off by himself to arrange the departure for Hermosillo. Breck had no chance to speak to him alone. Now Paredo was genial as he stood inside the doorway for a moment.

"We leave shortly, *señor*. Colonel Gallegos sends to you his sorrow that thees happen."

"*We're* leaving?"

Captain Paredo nodded. "I go to Hermosillo to make sure thees sheriff 'ave no tro'ble."

The natty captain waited for a reply, got none, shrugged, and went out, bolting the door on the outside. Breck stared gloomily out into a sun-drenched courtyard.

Madge gone — Montana Blue out of reach — no chance to talk to Tom Platte. Paso Smith and his pardners had been left up in the air. The little priest would be helpless to do anything for Madge. And he, Breck Benson, was the fool responsible for all of this.

Breck promised the silence: *I'll be back! I'll bring hell these Yaquis never heard of!*

But that was an empty threat, when each minute might mean new horror for Madge. Breck rolled a cigarette with fingers that trembled. There seemed no end to the hour before the door rattled again.

Paredo was back with the same two soldiers, and Tom Platte was outside the fort, beside a four-horse stage that had a trunk and carpetbags lashed in the boot, and two Mexican women and a man as passengers.

Platte held heavy handcuffs connected with a chain. He locked them on his prisoner's wrists. Breck was seated between Paredo and the sheriff. The driver yelled to the horses, cracked the long lash, and the stage started with a lurch, rolling south out of town, plunging down the steep river-bank to a rocky ford, and up the other side to a rutted, dusty road that led west across the valley toward a gash in the foothills and the frowning mountains beyond.

Tom Platte was pleased with himself. Captain Paredo ignored the scowls of the man opposite and ogled the younger of the two women. Breck rode silently, after a covert glance down at the gun on Paredo's hip.

Might be a chance to reach that gun with a quick grab, get in a shot or two before Paredo and Platte went into action. There was a chance darkness might still find the stage somewhere in the mountains ahead. That would be the best place. Meanwhile, Breck would try to save the women opposite from a burst of wild shooting.

Presently they were in the foothills, and then rolling noisily into a mountain ravine through which a small stream poured. The cañon walls grew higher, the road rockier and narrower as it skirted the steep stream bank.

Once they pulled out to let another stage pass, heading toward La Jarita. Another time they passed around a string of freight wagons. Occasionally they met scattered parties of Indians riding toward La Jarita. But for the most part the road was deserted, wild, lonely.

Breck was as startled as the other passengers when the stage brakes were slammed on, and gun shots started a thunderous tattoo. Armed, masked riders whirled horses alongside the stage. The two women started to scream hysterically.

5

"RESCUED"

The captain snatched for his holstered gun — and Breck slapped his manacled hands down on the soldier's wrist. Swearing in Spanish, Paredo struck wildly at Breck's face with the other hand and fought for the gun. The two women were cowering in the other seat as the stage jolted to a stop.

Platte had made a quick move for his gun, then settled back on the seat and lifted his hands. Paredo saw a leveled rifle at one side of the stage, a six-gun on the other menacing him, and went limp, panting.

"Give 'em yore money, Paredo," Platte said disgustedly. "They got the jump on us. Might as well get it over with."

"You three in the back seat . . . get out!" came a curt order from behind the rifle.

Breck had already recognized the speaker's hat. His manacled hands pulled the gun from Paredo's holster. Smiling at the terrified women, Breck assured them in sketchy Spanish. "There is no danger . . .

66

see, we leave you."

Platte heard that as he was stepping out. He turned angrily. "Damn it, Benson, is this some of yore doin'?"

"Maybe you can figure how I had the chance," Breck said, coming out also. He holstered Paredo's gun at his side and held out his ironed wrists to the sheriff. "Unlock 'em, Platte. You and Paredo can have a turn."

One rider had stopped the horses and covered the driver. He waved the stage on now.

"Don't stop this side of Hermosillo, *hombre!*" he ordered the driver. "When you change horses, say that the bodies will be back in the mountains. *¡Vamos!*"

The driver's slashing whip sent the stage racing on its way, and Paso Smith, John Greeley, and Smoky Henderson pulled their masks down and grinned at Breck.

"That's a damned good hold-up for three hard-rock miners," Paso Smith chortled. "Hello, Paredo, *amigo mío.* I never thought I'd have the fun of meetin' yuh this way."

Captain Paredo bit his lips and glared.

Tom Platte had sensed the inevitable and reached for his handcuff key. "Who are these men, Paredo?" he growled.

"*Yanqui* miners that *Coronel* Gallegos will take care of when he hears about thees," Paredo spat.

Paso Smith smiled grimly. "Yuh always had a greasy smile on yore face when yuh brought us bad news. Try out that smile now, Paredo, while *you* git some real bad news. Git over there an' git handcuffed to that other gent. Who is he, Benson?"

"He's the sheriff I took Montana Blue away from. Followed us down here," Breck said. "Gallegos told him Blue an' Miss Morrison had gone to Hermosillo to be married, so they grabbed me, an' Paredo came along to see that I got as far as Hermosillo."

"Who's this Montana Blue yo're talkin' about?" Tom Platte snapped helplessly as Breck handcuffed one wrist, and snapped the other cuff on Paredo's wrist.

"Don't he know about Montana Blue?" Paso Smith gasped.

"I didn't have a chance to tell him. Paredo stayed too close. They wanted to get the sheriff an' me back across the border peaceably, I guess. An' there wasn't much doubt what'd happen if I let on I knew all about Blue."

Captain Paredo's face was a study in astonishment and rage as he listened. His face wore an uneasy look as Breck went on.

"Platte, I was a damned fool when I took your prisoner away from you. But you came down here an' were just as big a damned fool when you let Gallegos pull the wool over your eyes. Your Clem Evans is called Montana Blue down here . . . an' here's what really happened. . . ."

The Valdone sheriff's face grew hard and grim as facts were thrown at him.

"How about it, Paredo?" he barked at the man handcuffed to his wrist.

"What can I say?" Paredo shrugged his shoulders. "I am helpless."

Platte's savage jerk on the handcuff chain brought the captain lurching against him. With a club-like fist the sheriff sent the Mexican sprawling on his knees.

"Unlock me from this double-crossing, two-faced snake!" Tom Platte bawled. "I'll kill him myself for makin' a fool outta me while they was double-crossing a trustin' American girl."

Smoky Henderson showed his teeth in a delighted grin. "Don't kill him here in the road, Sheriff. We got some horses up a little draw a couple of hundred yards ahead. Let's get ready to travel before you have yore fun."

Breck freed the Valdone sheriff, amused in spite of himself at the outraged jerking of Platte's long mustache, the smoldering threat on the sheriff's face. But Breck's voice was curt as he warned: "Paredo's my meat, Platte. Don't forget it."

Paso Smith climbed down from the saddle, walked beside Breck as they followed the others toward the horses tethered nearby.

"Yuh got clean away from Smoky, an' we didn't know what to do," Paso said under his breath. "Father Ramirez got word to us. He tried to find Miss Morrison, an' she was gone. He didn't find out where she was, but the hotel clerk told him Paredo an' an *Americano* had holed up in her room an' grabbed you. The clerk had waited outside the door an' heard they was gonna take yuh to Hermosillo on the next stage. Not bein' able to find Miss Morrison an' Blue, we got extra horses an' come out here on the road to get yuh off the stage. Grabbin' you in La Jarita would've brought Gallegos an' fifty Yaquis boilin' around our ears. Benson, ain't yuh got any ideas where the girl is?"

"Not in Hermosillo. This Montana Blue and Gallegos have got her somewhere around La Jarita." Then Breck added

70

evenly: "Paredo ought to know. He'll talk. . . ."

Paso Smith looked at Breck, and nodded. "I guess Paredo'll talk, all right," he agreed soberly.

Stunted trees and bushes clung to the rocky slopes of the little ravine. Six saddled horses were tied there, and Smoky Henderson made his macabre joke. "We thought we'd pack the bodies away an' let 'em guess what happened. Suit you, Paredo?"

"I'll handle him," said Breck coldly. "Which is my horse?"

"Any one of them three with the stirrups tied up," John Greeley told him. "We didn't know where yore horse was in town, an' had to get one for yuh."

"Bring Paredo here."

"What you do?" Paredo gulped as Breck unlocked one handcuff, passed it through the stirrup straps, and locked it back on the Mexican's wrist.

"I'm riding back to La Jarita fast," said Breck coldly. "When you get ready to talk, yell out, and I'll stop and listen. Stand back an' let me get a foot in this stirrup."

"I have not'ing to talk!" Paredo wrenched out wildly as he tried to keep up with the horse's jump when Breck

71

swung into the saddle.

Snorting, stepping uneasily, the horse rolled eyes back to see what was fastened at his side. A little more fright would send him into a bucking, kicking panic.

"Let's go!" whooped Paso Smith, forking leather with the others. "Drag that damned monkey clean to La Jarita!"

Here was death in a few minutes. They all knew it. Paredo knew it. A gray look had come to his swarthy face. Desperately he ran, steps getting longer as Breck led the trotting horse out onto the cañon road. A hind hoof kicked wickedly out at Paredo.

"*¡Madre de Dios!*" he cried in anguish. "I talk! Anytheeng!"

Breck fought the frightened horse to a standstill and looked down at the gasping man. "Talk fast," he said coldly. "Where's Miss Morrison?"

"Weeth Montana an' *Coronel* Gallegos."

"Where?"

"In *el castillo*."

"The fort?"

"*Sí*."

Paso Smith began to swear. "I knowed it'd be somethin' like that. No chance of gettin' at her."

"What do they want with her?" Breck asked the man locked to his stirrup.

72

"*Señor* . . . how I know?" wailed Paredo. "Gallegos don't tell me hees mind."

Breck began to smile. When Paredo looked up at that smile, he licked his dry lips. "And you don't know why Pete Morrison's being held under the fort?" he said almost genially.

Captain Paredo's face split in a tight, awed grimace. He looked around at the stern-faced men sitting their horses there in the road and began to tremble.

"How do you know *that?*" he asked hoarsely.

Smoky Henderson cried out in rage and drew his gun. "So it's been Morrison screaming nights down in them damned cells? And it might've been us instead of him. Let him go, Benson. I'm gonna kill him."

"Then what'll you do?" Breck snapped. "Ride north?"

"Hell, no! But . . . but. . . ." Smoky's sharp young face looked baffled. "What'n hell *can* we do?" he appealed.

The thought of that massive-walled fort of La Jarita held them hesitant, silent.

"No more chance of cracking that fort than a calf bustin' a bull-fight fence," Breck said gloomily. "You men have done plenty already. Ride north now and you'll

73

make the border. You've got a right to try and make it safely. I won't think hard of you for goin'."

"Benson . . . yo're talkin' damned foolishness," Paso Smith drawled. "What are yuh aimin' to do?"

"When I reach La Jarita, it'll be gettin' dark," said Breck at last. "I'll take Paredo. We'll make it ahead of any warning from the stage. I'll be free to look up this Montana Blue an' Gallegos. Might be I'll have a chance to get into the fort an' look around."

"That'll be a fool stunt," John Greeley warned. "Yuh won't last five minutes after one of those Yaquis gets a look at yuh."

Tom Platte jeered at them impatiently. "Cut out the backin' and fillin'. Yuh know yo're goin' back with Benson. Let's get started."

"I was about to say it when you butted in," Paso Smith complained. "Git that skunk on his horse, an' we'll talk while we ride."

John Greeley's bearded face parted in a slight smile. "I just wanted to make sure everyone knowed what was ahead. Chances are some of us'll stay in La Jarita for good. Ride it, boys, and see who draws lucky an' who's unlucky tonight."

Paredo rode in their midst with his feet tied in the stirrups. A gray, dazed look of disaster was on his face. Questions were thrown at him, and he answered mechanically.

Pete Morrison had been brought in at night by Gallegos and trusted Yaquis. Only Gallegos saw Morrison. There were times when the colonel came up from the underground cells in wild rages, but Morrison had not been killed.

"Tortured?"

Paredo shrugged graphically. His knowledge of Morrison's sister was equally vague. She had come to the fort with Montana Blue. They had been laughing, talking. She might still be at the fort, might not. Paredo swore he had no knowledge. Montana Blue and Gallegos were friends. Blue had been away for weeks. Who could say what it was all about? By the Holy Virgin, the saints, his mother and father, Paredo swore in a harsh, dry voice, he knew nothing more.

"Sounds like the truth," Breck decided.

"He wouldn't know the truth," Paso Smith bit out.

"I got a reason for thinkin' this is the truth."

"Trot yore reason out, Benson."

"It ain't mine to tell you. Later, maybe."

"It don't make sense," grumbled Paso.

Breck kept his thoughts to himself. The story of those buried gold bars would make it sense. Gold bred cunning, ruthlessness. If Gallegos and Montana Blue were working together, why should they share news of gold with an army captain, there to take orders and do as he was told? Use him, let him know as little as possible, he would not have the story to tell further.

"If Paredo knew much, he'd know what Gallegos wants with Pete Morrison," Breck pointed out.

"Gold, women, an' power are all Gallegos wants from anyone," John Greeley stated. "Which one's he after from Morrison?"

"He's got Miss Morrison," Tom Platte put in.

"He'd never seen her before," Paso Smith growled. "Ain't in reason Montana Blue'd travel that far after a woman they'd never seen. An' kill a man an' nigh get hanged. What'd he kill the fellow for anyway?"

"Claimed this man White had threatened his life in El Paso."

"White?" Smoky Henderson exclaimed. "Wasn't that the name of the hook-nosed *Tejano* who used to deal faro in the Blue

Angel? The one that knocked Blue over the bar one night an' run for the border while he was still healthy?"

"This White that was killed in Valdone had a hooked nose," Tom Platte explained. "Blue must've killed him to even the score, or to shut his mouth. But I still ain't clear why Blue, sittin' purty down here, should come to Valdone, callin' himself Clem Evans."

"A lot of things ain't clear," Paso Smith grumbled. "All that's worryin' me is what's gonna happen in La Jarita."

The buried gold would have explained a lot, but that secret belonged to Pete Morrison and Madge. Breck found himself hating that long-buried gold, thinking of the directions left by a man who knew he would soon die.

From Cross to Cross
We Fight in Misery. . . .

Misery, death, unhappiness that gold had brought. Buried on a Sonora mountain slope, it still had the power to strike at men's lives. It had reached out hundreds of miles to blight Madge Morrison's life. It was sending these hard-faced men toward their death.

The afternoon hours passed quickly as they rode back through the foothills. They had passed a lumbering freight wagon, and the lazy driver had only stared idly at the *Americanos* and the army man who rode among them.

The valley slope rolled down toward the river and the jumbled buildings of La Jarita. They were nearing the river as the sun dropped out of sight and the swift dusk began to fall. They reached the river half an hour after black night closed in. Blazing rockets soaring skyward told that the *fiesta* was in full swing.

The horses splashed through the ford, the shod hoofs rang on the rocks of the opposite slope, and out of the night ahead of them a low voice hailed: *"¿Americanos?"*

Breck grabbed for the gun he had taken from Paredo. Other guns cocked around him as the horses were reined in abruptly.

"Who is it?" Breck called gruffly.

Great relief was in the reply. *"Señor* Benson, I have been waiting here at the ford for your return. This is *Padre* Ramirez."

6

"GALLEGOS'S PRISONER"

"I'll be. . . ." Breck caught himself, and dismounted quickly as the shadowy figure of a man moved toward them. "What made you think I'd be back tonight?" Breck demanded.

"I thought you would come sooner, my son," Father Ramirez said ruefully. "Hours I have waited. Your friends had gone after you. I knew when you were free you would come fast."

"You must've been pretty sure of it," said Breck dryly.

Padre Ramirez chuckled. "A man does not leave the woman he loves."

"What about her?" asked Breck, his voice suddenly husky.

"She is in the fort," the little priest said. "In the rooms of Gallegos. Word was brought but an hour ago that she still was in the fort."

"Where's Gallegos?"

"*¿Quién sabe?*" Father Ramirez shrugged. "He has been busy with affairs of the *fiesta*. This Montana Blue has been

79

at his *cantina.* Many of the Yaquis from the fort have been in the streets making *fiesta.* There is no more I can tell you."

"You've helped plenty," said Breck. "There ain't much I can do to thank you."

"Go with God, my son." The black-clad figure of the little priest vanished in the night.

"Paredo heard him," Paso Smith warned gruffly. "It'll go hard with the *padre* if Gallegos gets word of this."

"I'll remember it," nodded Breck. He swung back into the saddle and spoke to them soberly. "Last chance to cut off an' be safe. The town's full of soldiers. And the border's a hell of a long way off."

Smoky Henderson only growled: "How we gonna handle that fort?"

"I've been savin' Paredo to get us in and show us around inside. Like old friends, eh, Paredo?"

The captain groaned helplessly. "*Por Dios,* no! Gallegos take my skeen off in strips."

"Too bad we won't have time to wait around an' watch it," Breck regretted. "Right now, Gallegos ain't here . . . and I am. What about it?"

Paredo was silent a moment, then hopelessly he mumbled: "I am dead now . . .

what I care? What you weesh?"

Rockets were still shooting skyward as they tied their horses in the black shadows at one side of the fort. The barred windows showed no bit of light. Silence brooded over the thick stone walls, barely visible in these black hours before the moon would rise. But when they walked around to the front, all La Jarita seemed to have drifted toward the *fiesta*. Strings of colored lights on the plaza looked uncomfortably near. Gay music pulsed through the soft cool air. The noisy, swirling crowd seemed only a few steps away.

Then the open gate of the fort loomed before them. A lone Yaqui stood guard in the dim light of an overhead lantern.

Captain Paredo had accepted the inevitable. His voice had the brusqueness of command as he spoke in Spanish. "Is *Coronel* Gallegos here?"

"No, my captain," answered the man stolidly.

"Bueno," said Paredo, and led the way through the arched entrance into the great courtyard.

Half a dozen lanterns on the courtyard walls spread dull illumination. A soldier stepped out of the shadows nearby and stared.

"You are not needed!" Paredo snapped. He waited until the man turned away, and nervously muttered: "Thees way ees door to *Coronel* Gallegos's rooms."

Paredo was leading them toward the right side of the courtyard when Breck stopped him. "What's that back there at the gate?" he asked huskily.

They had all heard it — the sharp creak that rusty hinges make in moving. Then the dull thud of closing doors.

Back there in the tunnel-like entrance inside the gate a loud laugh saluted their backs.

"*Amigos,* you forgot the man you left behind and gagged! I 'ave been waiting for your visit! Myself, I will cut the heart from that dog, Paredo!" That was Colonel Gallegos calling to them, mocking them — lifting his voice in a shout to men they could not see. "Soldiers . . . kill the *gringos!*"

"Down!" Breck yelled over his shoulder.

Rifles snapped and spat back there near Gallegos. Guns smashed flame and sound from the roof edge above, so that the night seemed one long wild explosion of gunfire. Paredo had dropped to his haunches, ducking low as Benson went down.

Gripping the captain's shoulder, Breck

82

kept his gun against the shaking body as lead sleeted around them and struck the hard earth on all sides. "Where's that doorway to Gallegos's quarters?" he whispered.

"Ahead," moaned Paredo.

"This way!" Breck yelled, forcing Paredo up into a stumbling run.

It was a gauntlet of death through the black shadows, without a chance to see who followed. The firing became wild and ragged as the hidden gunmen tried to stop them with a hail of bullets.

A spurt of flame licked out on the roof edge ahead. Up there against the vague starlight a dark figure could barely be seen. Breck fired twice at it without much hope. A shrill death wail rang out through the gunfire. A clattering rifle and then an inert form landed heavily just ahead. Breck and his prisoner had to jump over the body to reach a dim open doorway that showed a faint glow of light.

A tall Yaqui with a rifle appeared in the narrow passage inside the door. Then a racing figure passed Breck and his prisoner and plunged at the doorway with six-gun roaring. The Yaqui tried to bring up his rifle. A .45 slug tore through his body, doubling him up as he fell back.

Paso Smith waved his six-gun with a wild yell, snatched up the rifle, and charged on into the main corridor two steps beyond. Paso was hatless, and blood was running down his face as he swung about in the corridor and yelled back encouragement. "Come on an' clean out this Yaqui nest! There ain't enough in Sonora to stop us! Benson, let go that monkey! I'll gut-shoot him!"

"Don't kill him," Breck snapped, hurling the terrified soldier ahead of him into the stone-floored corridor.

Half a dozen paces to the right the corridor ended in a heavy wooden door. A wall lamp there threw yellow light on steps leading down underground. Another staircase led up.

Breck indicated the door with his gun. "That leads to Gallegos's private rooms?" he panted to Paredo.

The captain nodded dumbly. His chest was heaving, his eyes were bulging, and he had the pasty look of a man already dying inside.

The swearing, stamping rush of the others boiled in from outside. Smoky Henderson, left arm hanging limp, had blood dripping from his sleeve. John Greeley was stern and formidable. Tom

Platte, of Valdone, was hatless, grim, and belligerent as he blurted: "Hell's shore boiled over! Did that priest bait us on?"

"We left a Mex tied up in a locked room," grated Henderson. "He got out, or they found him. The *padre* didn't know about it."

Breck was knocking back a heavy iron bolt that held the door closed. "Keep them back, men! We've got as much cover now as they have!" he called over his shoulder. "Paso, watch this feller!" Breck kicked the door open and dived into the room beyond.

The low-ceilinged room, lighted by a single lamp, held a long table, chairs, a desk, and gun racks on a wall, but there was no sign of Madge.

Breck spun around as Paso Smith drove Paredo into the room. "Where is she?" Breck roared.

Paredo held his hands out, palms up, choking his denial while his eyes stared in horror at Breck's pointed gun, and Breck suddenly stood motionless, listening. Fists were beating on the other side of a door at his left.

"Breck! In here! Hurry!"

Breck knocked the door bolt back — and Madge's scream burst through the opening door. "Breck, look out . . . !"

Her words were choked off — and a blasting gun met Breck's plunge through the doorway. A bullet tore the flesh of his left arm; a second shot nicked his ear. Hot powder particles stung his face. Death was there, close and certain.

Three Yaqui soldiers were across the room, guns out. Gallegos was backing toward them with an arm crooked around Madge Morrison's neck. He was dragging Madge back with him, shooting past her shoulder. Her struggles had thrown those first shots off the target. Now Madge pulled away, spoiling a third shot as Breck burst into the room.

The Indians could not shoot past Gallegos — and the colonel was safe behind his human shield. The man's short black hair seemed to bristle behind Madge's blonde head. The dark face was working with fury as Gallegos choked the girl into helplessness with his crooked arm.

Madness caught Breck — madness that blotted out the Yaquis, the smoke-filled room, the death blasting in his face. Only Gallegos remained — Gallegos and Madge and a red mist of fury.

Only a madman would have tried that rush. Gallegos had not expected it. The dark face looked stupefied for an instant, then suddenly fearful. Madge's arm knocked another shot wild — and Breck's rush was almost to them. Gallegos shouted to his men, leaping back for room to use his gun.

Breck shouldered Madge aside. It couldn't be helped. His gun crashed, blasted again. Gallegos was staggering from the first shot when the second bullet tore in under an eye. Then Colonel Ramón Gallegos was dead, collapsing to the floor as Breck knocked him out of the way to get at the Yaquis. The soldiers hadn't been able to shoot until their colonel fell. Now, suddenly, they had no stomach for the *gringo* death this *Americano* madman was bringing. They fought to escape through the doorway. The last one went down as the last bullet in Breck's gun sped on its lethal way.

Another gun took up the hell of fire. Tom Platte, of Valdone, was there, triggering a roll of roaring death that dropped a second Indian and splintered lead through the slamming door. Powder smoke swirled thickly in that stonewalled room which Breck saw was furnished with the lavishness of a wealthy man. Shot-deafened ears could hear little as Breck turned back out of the red haze, reloading mechanically.

Gallegos was lifeless and bleeding on the floor. Tom Platte was reloading, also, smiling grimly. "Purty good, Benson."

But Tom Platte could wait. Madge stood there, dark-eyed with grief, with fright, hurt.

"Breck, they told me you were dead."

Hours of weeping had made Madge's eyes red and swollen. A blue-black bruise was ugly over one cheek bone, but, as Breck caught her close for a moment, unbelievable happiness was in Madge's voice.

"Pete's alive, Breck. He's in a cell under us. Colonel Gallegos took me down there. They've tortured him. Ah, Breck, he's suffered terribly. But he's alive."

Paso Smith yelled with joy though the doorway: "So yuh got the king monkey! Some work! Hurry up outta there! We're in a wasp's nest, an' it's gettin' worse!"

Hard to believe men still fought beyond this room, but the guns were crackling outside, and men were shouting.

As Breck sided Madge into the next room, Paso bit out: "The boys are keepin' them out so far! Better git plenty of guns off the wall there! Might need 'em!"

Breck ran to the wall racks, jerking down a rifle, two cartridge belts and guns, and a bandolier of cartridges for the rifle. He thrust one of the gun belts and its gun at Madge. "You'll need this if we don't make it outta here."

Madge nodded. She knew what he meant, but her hand was steady as she took the belt.

From the corridor, Smoky Henderson yelled: "Man alive, come on! They're closin' on us!"

The gun belt was too big for Madge. She held the belt in one hand, the gun in the other, and her pale face was set. "Breck, I can't leave Pete."

"I'll try to get Pete out," Breck promised. "Go with these men. They'll get you away, if there's a chance."

"Who said we'd run and leave anyone behind?" Paso Smith blared.

"I'll not leave until Pete does," Madge said firmly. "Breck, I can show you where he is. I know where the key is." Madge caught from a desk drawer two big iron keys held together by a leather thong. "Down the steps outside that door, Breck."

Breck caught the keys. "Stay up here, Madge. Paso, watch Paredo. I'll need the light outside there."

7

"ONE AGAINST AN ARMY"

In the corridor, Breck snatched the wall light from the bracket and made for the stone stairs, circling down narrow, damp steps. Fifteen or twenty feet below there was a door held by great hinges, covered now with the rust of generations. Breck had to try both keys before the lock turned heavily to a mighty twist. Beyond the door, blackness had the damp, musty feel of death, the stench of horror, corruption, the rotting of souls and hope.

The light glinted on gray-green mold over the stone walls and ceiling. The rock underfoot was slippery. On one side of a shoulder-wide passage were little cells hewn out of the rock and barred with rusty iron. Straw covered the cell floors. Shadows lurched and danced on the walls and bars as Breck held up the lamp and called Pete Morrison's name.

"Here," a grating voice replied.

Pete was in the third cell, blinking, turning blinded eyes away from that feeble light. Bearded, filthy, emaciated, Pete Morrison clung to the bars and hoarsely demanded: "Who is it?"

"Breck Benson!"

"God, Breck! Gallegos brought Madge down here an' said you were dead."

"Can you handle a gun?" Breck demanded as the rusty lock grated and the cell door swung open.

"Can't see much. I'm damn' near blind from the dark. But I ain't as weak as they think. I've exercised all I could."

Three fingernails were gone and half-healed scars were livid on the hand Pete Morrison put out for the gun.

"What have they done to you?" Breck asked thickly.

Blinking, squinting against the light, Pete Morrison managed a ghastly smile. "Most of the Yaqui tricks that make men talk," said Pete Morrison. "Gallegos stopped just short of killin' me. I couldn't talk then. He kept thinkin' he could make me talk."

Pete Morrison's laugh was wild, harsh. Breck's nerves crawled at the thought of what he must have suffered down here underground.

"Was Gallegos after that gold?" Breck asked over his shoulder.

"Crazy to get it. Sure I'd tell him where it was. As if I didn't know the dirty wolf'd cut my throat if I told him. I knew him, see! Couple of years ago in Yuma I met the wife of a German who'd owned the *hacienda* I bought. The German had been murdered. Gallegos had got hold of the wife. She was a honky-tonk dancer when I met her . . . an' at nights, when she dreamed about La Jarita, she'd wake up screaming. She gave me the flyleaf out of an old book her husband had dug up. They'd both been sure there was gold around the *hacienda,* but they'd never been able to locate it.

"I found it," Morrison continued. "I cut some chunks off one bar and covered the place up again. An' one of my Mex servants stole the pieces of gold an' tried to sell 'em for gambling money at the Blue Angel *cantina,* run by a white son-of-a-bitch called Montana Blue. He must've taken the gold to Gallegos. They rode out to question me. I didn't have a chance from then on. Eighteen small bars of it, Benson. Four or five hundred pounds of gold . . . an' I'd die a thousand deaths before I'd let those dirty swine get their hands on it."

Morrison threw that out harshly as he

followed Breck up the stone steps.

"Gallegos is dead," Breck told him soberly, "an' I've got a bill to settle with Montana Blue."

Then they were above ground in the corridor, and Pete Morrison and his sister were in each other's arms.

A crackle of gunfire outside sent several bullets slashing into the narrow entrance passage. Tom Platte and Smoky Henderson answered his voice. They were on their bellies behind the dead Yaqui guard in the passage, firing at gun flashes out in the courtyard. John Greeley had climbed the ascending flight of steps and was sweeping that stretch of the fort roof with his guns.

"That Montana Blue's here, tryin' to run things in Gallegos's place, Benson," Smoky's cold young voice said. "He's at the gate with a bunch of Yaquis, makin' sure we don't get out that way! He's been tryin' to bait us out. Listen."

Through a lull in the gunfire the loud arrogant voice of Clem Evans rang persuasively. "I'm givin' yuh another chance. Come out with your hands up, an' I'll see that yuh get to the border. If yuh don't, you know what to expect from these Yaquis."

"If I could only get me a bead on that

snake," Smoky gritted.

The fort was built four-sided around the courtyard. They were on the north side and their horses were on the south. The only way out was through the front gate. By now the hundreds at the *fiesta* would be crowding near, nervous, curious, panic-stricken at this wild gun battle inside the walls.

"Paredo, their colonel's dead," Breck said. "Order them to put up their guns."

"*Señor*, they weel not!"

"Try it!"

Paredo's shout reached throughout the courtyard. "*¡Soldados!* I . . . *Capitán* Paredo . . . commands you now. I command an end to this! I, *Capitán* Paredo, will decide what to do."

"Yo're wastin' breath, Felix!" Clem Evans shouted. "They know yuh got to do what you're told! They want that bunch that killed Gallegos!"

An Indian yell of anger backed him up. Guns across the courtyard roared an answer to Paredo.

"Hold 'em off for a few minutes. I got an idea," Breck gritted.

He groped back into the darkened room where the gun racks lined one wall. A dozen or so gun belts hung beside the

94

guns. One by one Breck jerked the belts down, fastening the stout strap of one belt to the buckle of another, until he had eleven fastened together. Through the last big brass buckle he thrust a rifle barrel, and swept the heavy load off the floor as he ran back into the corridor.

"Paredo?"

"Here he is," said Paso Smith, just ahead.

"Knock him over the head!" Breck snapped.

"How about shootin' him?"

"No! We're not Yaquis!"

Paredo's babble of protest was cut short by a heavy thud.

"Couldn't have done it better if I had a light," Paso's voice said out of the blackness. "Clean over his ear."

"Didn't want him to hear what I say," Breck declared curtly. "We're trapped here, and we might as well face it. Not a chance to fight our way out with Miss Morrison an' her brother. Every minute makes it worse. There ain't any use saying what'll happen if those Yaquis get us. Paso, listen to what I'm tellin' you now. . . ."

They listened.

"You can't do it, Breck," Madge sobbed. "You know they'll kill you."

"Don't make it harder," Breck snapped. "Dying one way's as good as another."

"Might have an ace-deuce chance your way," Paso decided. "You take the belts, Benson. I'll handle this end of it."

"Damn you, do as I tell you! There ain't time to argue! You're needed worse to help look after Miss Morrison!"

Death was too near, too certain to waste words. Paso let it stand.

"Breck," Madge said. Her voice was low and steady now, clear and beautiful and unafraid. "This is good bye, Breck. I know it's good bye . . . for always. I caused this . . . and I know now I never really loved anyone but you. I'll never be able to tell you again. Ah, Breck, my darling, I c-can't let you go like this."

The gunfire outside mocked them as they clung together in the dark.

"I never could get my lovin' out in words," Breck wrenched. "But I'd take hell an' the Yaquis with a grin for half of this. No matter what happens, dead or alive, honey, I'll find you."

"Dead or alive, my dear, I'll be waiting," Madge choked.

Then she was gone in obedience to Paso Smith's low-voiced command, taking those steep stone steps to the roof in company with the others.

Smoky Henderson came out of the narrow side passage, muttering: "Ain't any reason why I couldn't stay an' do it."

"Shut up and keep goin'," Breck said.

The Valdone sheriff came out of the passage. His hand dropped on Breck's shoulder, his gruff voice hid his feeling. " 'Luck, Benson."

Then they were gone, and Breck had the passage to himself — and the bullets he triggered out the doorway drew an answering storm of shots. When the shots lagged and his voice could be heard, Breck called: "Evans, you dirty skunk, this is Benson! I'm gonna gut-shoot you before this is over! Hunt yore hole an' hide so those Indians can't see the yellow in your heart!"

Clem Evans cursed him. "Big talk, Benson!"

Breck repeated it all in Spanish, calling on Montana Blue to step out with his gun and show himself a man. That was something the Yaquis could understand, could listen to silently while they waited to see what would happen.

Furious, Clem Evans shouted at them to close in on the *gringos*.

Breck shot at the sound of the voice, and

every gun in the courtyard opened up again at the doorway. Bullets slapped, smashed around the doorway, and back in the passage.

Prone behind a dead Yaqui, Breck emptied one gun, picked up the rifle and triggered shots as fast as he could sight on gun flashes, then pushed the rifle aside, and crawled out the door with a gun in each hand.

Lanterns around the courtyard had been shot out. The darkness of death hung over that walled space under the stars. Gun flashes were all that betrayed taut, watchful men.

Yaquis were posted around the courtyard. Some had climbed to the flat fort roof on the east, west, and south sides of the courtyard. John Greeley had shot them off the north roof. Most of the guns seemed to be near the gate where Clem Evans was waiting.

Now Breck edged to the left, toward the turn of the courtyard and the east wall pierced by the gate entrance. The wounded arm was stinging him with pain, but it could still be used. He gripped a cocked six-gun in each hand. Two more loaded guns weighted heavily inside his belt, and another two were in the holsters against his legs. He had taken the extra guns from the belts he had fastened together, and carried them now for quick use.

Firing began to slacken as the *gringo* guns fell silent. Did the Yaquis suspect that the *Americanos* were crawling over that north roof toward the back of the fort, where the walls dropped to the rocky riverbank and a guard was not needed?

Heart pounding, nerves tight, Breck was jumpy with tension. Each step might meet a yell of discovery. Any second, guns on the back roof might open up. And any way you looked at it, Breck Benson was a dead man.

If he kept his feet long enough, there was a chance for Paso Smith and the others to drop that string of gun belts through one of the rifle slits in the back parapet. The crossed rifle at one end should hold the rope of belts for the six to descend.

A hell of gunfire at the front gate would give the others a chance to reach the river rocks and get to the horses south of the fort. If the horses were gone, they could scatter in the dark streets and hunt other horses at La Jarita's hitch racks.

Clem Evans's shout was mocking. "Running out of cartridges, Benson?"

Getting no reply, Evans cursed and warned his men: "The *gringos* are tricky."

Two quick shots from a fort roof sent Breck a little nearer his death. He ran out from the wall toward the gate, guns in his hands spitting fire. And more guns opened up over the courtyard, blotting out all other sounds. Raw lead and roaring death took the saddle.

Breck's guns went empty — he threw them down and drew two more, triggering so fast there was little break in the storm of lead that sleeted before him. Screaming bullets couldn't be heard; men couldn't be seen. The muzzle flashes at the gate guided Breck's rush. That ghost rush of flaring guns might have been many men instead of one — many men rushing the gate with desperate fury. The Yaquis began to scatter from the entrance in which they were suddenly trapped.

A man bumped into Breck, yelled once with fear before he died. It all happened while a man could draw a dozen breaths — and then Breck plunged into the mouth of gate passage, as safe in the confusion as the Yaquis were.

Men had stampeded into doorways to right and left. Thinly in ringing ears Breck caught the bawling voice of Clem Evans, yelling to the men to stand and fight. Breck bumped another Yaqui and shot him down, and jerked his last two guns from the holsters as Evans's voice lifted just ahead.

"Evans, damn you!" Breck roared.

The blast from Evans's gun drove powder particles in Breck's face, missed his head by the width of a finger — and left Clem Evans a close and open target.

There he died, Clem Evans of Valdone — Montana Blue of La Jarita — in the blackness of the trap he had tried to spring. And Breck whirled to the great wooden fort doors and found them closed by a heavy wooden bar.

Yaquis were shrieking — "That mad *gringo!*" — as Breck wrestled the bar over.

The gates swung open. Breck plunged out to the left, to the north, away from the horses they had tied. Six horses had been tied, and six people were trying to escape. Breck Benson would have to find his own horse.

Panting, Breck ran, half dazed by the fact that he still lived. A leg was bleeding, his side was bleeding, blood was sticky and wet on the wounded arm — but he still lived.

The *fiesta* crowd was milling toward the

fort. Now the nearest ones were scattering, women screaming, men shouting as word flashed that the shooting was now outside the fort. Breck laughed as he ran. Out here in a panic-stricken night one lone running figure would quickly be lost.

And it was so. The Yaquis were boiling out of the fort, shooting wildly, as Breck lost himself among the nearest houses to the north. Scattered shots were still echoing when Breck neared the plaza by a roundabout way through alleys and the dark streets.

Here people did not yet know what had happened; here in the almost deserted streets near the plaza there was no one to stop a man from picking two stout horses and riding off — and, if it was horse stealing, it was a fair trade for the lives La Jarita had tried to take.

Breck rode north out of town, leading the extra horse, reloading, stopping the bleeding as best he could from wounds that were not quite crippling. He rode fast, tense with anxiety for those six who had gone over the fort roof. No way of telling what had happened to them, no way of finding them now. If they got away, they were to circle La Jarita to the *hacienda* to get Madge's maid, while the others headed for the pass in the mountains through which he and Clem Evans had come to La Jarita. They would have a night's start before their tracks could be followed.

But when Breck reached the dark *hacienda*, María was not there. Nor was there any sign of what had happened to her. One of the six might have come for her, or Gallegos might have had her taken to La Jarita during the day. It might be good news or bad news.

Swearing huskily at the uncertainty, Breck changed to the spare horse and rode hard for the mountain pass. If Madge and the others were ahead, he could catch them.

He was in the mountains when the moon rose, and the rocky trail was empty. Hour after hour the trail stayed empty. Midnight passed, and the hours dragged into the gray dawn. The way now was through a cañon descending out of the mountains, and Breck and the two horses were alone in the vast night. Fatigue, hopelessness came down like a bitter cloud. Was he, Breck wondered, the only one who would be coming back to Valdone?

In the gray dawn a deer poised off the trail, staring, and near enough for two gunshots to drop it. Breck carried the carcass to the first high rise of a foothill and butchered the meat there where he could see the trail both ways. He built a tiny, smokeless fire of dry sticks, scorched a piece of the meat, wolfed it, and felt better.

He rested the horses an hour, while the sun rose, and was packing the deer haunches for travel when a file of riders showed for a moment on the trail a mile back. As Breck waited, guns ready, he made them out, and galloped back along the trail.

They were six, and the sixth was María Trujillo, riding clumsily, miserably.

"They got Smoky through the head before we started down, the devils," Paso Smith said soberly. "The horses were there. We took Smoky's horse for the lady at the *hacienda*."

"She was gone when I got there," Breck said.

John Greeley nodded. "We got away clean, an' I burnt leather gettin' to her, an' met the others over by that big white cross to the east."

Pete Morrison still looked like a scarecrow, but a boyish grin erased some of the lines the months in La Jarita had engraved on his face. "We stopped an' got that gold, Breck. See them saddlebags? Lucky the bars was small, even if they do weigh heavy. *Look!*" With an effort, Pete Morrison dragged a small yellow bar of metal out of a saddlebag and rested it across his lap. "Everybody shares in it," Pete said. "I reckon we all earned it."

Tom Platte had not said a word. Now Breck stared at that stern, unyielding face and tried to read it. That face was as impossible to fathom as a Yaqui Indian's, but suddenly the Valdone sheriff broke into a grin.

"Nobody'll care much, I reckon, on which side of the border Clem Evans . . . or Montana Blue . . . cashed in his chips, but if you ever try takin' another prisoner away from me, Benson, I'll. . . ."

Tom Platte wasn't used to talking to empty air, so he stopped in mid-sentence and watched Breck Benson guide his horse over to Madge's and whisper to her.

Madge had no hat. The wind had blown her hair, and the rising sun touched it with gold. She had never looked so beautiful to Breck Benson.

"Dead or alive . . . ," Breck said huskily, and suddenly there was nothing else that need be put in words.

Madge reached out for his hand, and then Breck's two arms went around her.

"Breck . . . oh, Breck," she sobbed with happiness, "we won't have to wait, after all."

María Trujillo groaned as she shifted in her saddle. "Kees her queeck, *Señor* Breck. Tha's what she wants. Then take me where I can rest. What I care about gold an' loff an' keeses. I hurt on these so-damn' saddle. Ah . . . look out, *señores.* Everytheen ees all right for my little girl . . . for everytheeng. *¡Gracias a Dios!*"

Half Interest in Hell

T. T. Flynn was living in Santa Fé when he became good friends with Roark Bradford. The two men traveled together to New Orleans where Bradford kept an apartment, and it was there that Flynn met Bradford's niece, Helen Brown. They fell in love. Because Helen was twelve years Flynn's junior, her father, a country doctor in Tennessee, objected to the difference in their ages and what he perceived as Flynn's "bohemian" character. This notwithstanding, they were married in the autumn of 1934 in Halls, Tennessee. Following this marriage, Flynn gave up his living quarters in Santa Fé altogether and lived and traveled extensively with Helen in a large Chrysler Airstream trailer. Part of the year the Flynns lived in the trailer in Pojoaque, New Mexico, parked outside Fred and Butch Glidden's home. Fred wrote Western fiction as Luke Short, Butch as Vic Elder. In 1937 Fred's brother Jon Glidden with his wife Moe moved to Pojoaque and bought a nine-room adobe across the road from Fred and Butch. Jon wrote Western stories as Peter Dawson. Another part of the year the Flynns lived in a little cabin near Los Alamos, and the rest of the year they spent in Helen's hometown of Halls. For a time the Flynns acquired a white frame house in Halls, and it was there they lived, outside of trips, until the outbreak of the Second World War. The house was then sold and the Flynns moved in with Helen's parents for a year or two before moving to Memphis to a duplex at 4042 Park Avenue. One side of this duplex was used for living quarters, the other side for Flynn's office and writing area. By this time the Flynns had two young sons. "Half Interest in Hell" was written at the duplex in Memphis.

1

"TROUBLE FOR SALE"

He banked most of the gold in Tecalone, where tall cottonwoods and brown adobe walls were friendly on the wide and broken range. This was a hard day's ride north of the border, and a man could finally sleep peacefully. But first there was a little celebrating to do.

Matt Landis woke up the next morning with a headache. Memory of the night before was foggy. Mart stood up and stretched. He inspected the belted gun hanging at the head of the iron bed. The gun was clean, oiled, unused.

His pants pockets were stuffed with money. Matt counted the money, his blond hair tousled, his hard but limber figure relaxed as he stood barefoot beside the bed. He whistled softly at the amount and recalled more about a poker game with some strangers. The play had been high. One young fellow had been ugly after losing. Trouble had balanced on a hairline. The knuckles of Matt's right hand still had the

109

feel of the blow that had headed off trouble.

Matt rubbed the knuckles slowly. He had hit, quick and hard. Bystanders had dragged the young stranger out back, and so it had ended. Matt remembered buying drinks all around. That was all — just an evening of good fun.

While he dressed, Matt considered his plans to ride on to Black Spring today. Chris Fraser had hurried out of Mexico almost two years ago, planning to buy a small ranch near Black Spring. There had been a girl Chris couldn't get out of his mind. By now Chris might have a baby. Twins even. Matt laughed softly at the idea of Chris with an armful of baby. There never had been a better trail partner than Chris Fraser until the girl had pulled Chris north across desert and mountains, like a drought-starved bull after cool water and green grass.

It was characteristic of Matt Landis that he went first to a barber shop for a shave, and then to breakfast. Black coffee pushed away the last of the headache.

Matt walked toward the livery barn, smiling again at the thought of Chris with a baby. It was queer what a girl could do to a man. It was downright sad. Matt had seen it happen time after time. Stout fellows, ready for anything, men to ride with, fight beside, suddenly were grinning foolishly and prancing like yearling colts. Sometimes they went off their feed and moped around. They had the look of wanting to howl at the moon. Then one day you caught them calling on a preacher. After that, you watched the end with amused pity.

Those reckless trail riders always looked pale, weak, scared at the end. The girl always had a firm and happy look, pretty as spring over a meadow stream, with shining eyes not at all afraid of the corral bars going up. Matt chuckled with the sheer joy of being outside a corral with new and exciting trails ahead. He glanced across the street at a small crowd before the courthouse steps. The sheriff was standing on the top step, reading rapidly from a legal-looking paper. The sheriff finished and raised his voice.

"This is a public sale, gents! No offer turned down! Somebody make the first bid!"

Matt strolled across the dusty street, rolling a cigarette. He had lost interest in the sheriff. His attention was on three men — no, four men — who stood with casual purpose on the fringe of the small crowd. If Matt had ever sized up trouble correctly, he was watching trouble now in those four men. The small crowd knew it, too. There was a massed expectancy of waiting for something. The four men had belt guns peacefully holstered — but each of the four had a lounging, business-like look, watching, waiting.

The auctioneer bawled: "Lon Taggert opens for six thousand! I got six thousand bid for half-interest in the Block and Star ranch!"

The sheriff had a drooping, rust-colored mustache. His vest was open, he wore red sleeve bands, and he called loudly for another bid with uncompromising indignation.

"Seven thousand."

Everyone looked at the new bidder. The auctioneer seemed surprised. "*You*, Ab Tanner? You bid seven thousand . . . *cash?*"

"Yep."

Ab Tanner was a small, thin man. Matt had to stand on his toes to see him, near the center of the crowd. But in a moment there was space around Ab Tanner, and Matt could see the young woman there with him.

Matt looked a second time. Ab Tanner

was middle-aged, stooped, meek-looking, and the girl was everything that Ab Tanner was not. She was a handful of angry determination; the anger was in the set of her shoulders, the lift of her head, and in every line of her soft and set profile.

The sheriff turned his head and spat. "I got seven thousand bid. Who'll raise it?"

"Eight thousand!"

"Lon Taggart goes to eight thousand! I got eight thousand bid! Eight thousand. . . ."

Lon Taggart was about Matt's size. He was near enough to show a lean-hipped, deep-chested figure. Matt guessed the man was something of a dandy. He had on a gray, wide-brimmed hat and dark coat, and an unlighted cigar rolled carelessly in one corner of his mouth. He had raised Ab Tanner's bid as if not greatly interested.

Matt saw something else and watched intently. One of the four men had moved into the crowd. He was edging forward aimlessly, as if wanting to see better.

"Nine thousand!" Ab Tanner called.

The edging man stopped beside Ab Tanner, and the small man gave a quick, frightened look and seemed to shrink.

"Ten thousand," Lon Taggart bid carelessly.

"I got ten thousand bid for half the Block an' Star! Ten thousand! It's still dirt cheap! Some gent will get a bargain if he acts quick! Make it eleven! Who'll bid eleven?"

Ab Tanner stood silently. Matt saw the girl speaking under her breath. Ab Tanner shook his head. She seemed to be pleading.

The gunman beside Ab Tanner had rolled a cigarette. He lighted a match. He had not spoken that Matt could see, had not looked at Ab Tanner or the girl. But Ab Tanner gave a furtive look toward the girl and shook his head to whatever the girl was saying.

The tight expectancy in the crowd became more evident. Men looked at Ab Tanner and the girl. Lon Taggert did not turn his head. Matt noticed one of the other gunmen grin. This one had a round, flat face, wind and sun-reddened. Furtive humor seemed to seep across the flat face from an unpleasant reserve inside.

"Ten thousand bid! Fair warning, gents! This is an open sale! I got to sell! Half the Block an' Star going for ten thousand! Goin' . . . goin'. . . ."

"Eleven thousand!" Matt called in a clear, loud voice.

Lon Taggert turned quickly. Almost everyone else looked to see who had bid. Seen full face, Lon Taggert had a clean look of hard flesh and muscle. He was not unhandsome, except for a livid weal across the left side of his face. It was not a scar. It looked like the mark of an angry blow — like a whip mark that had cut hard and recently and had not healed.

The auctioneer was surprised. He seemed uncertain. "What's your name, mister?"

"Never mind the name. I'm bidding eleven thousand."

The man beside Ab Tanner had turned, as if caught off guard. He stood scowling.

The girl with Ab Tanner had looked around, too, and Matt was startled by the blaze of dislike that leaped at him from the clear triangle of her face. She had surprisingly fair skin, and her anger was a rosy glow.

"This here is a cash sale," the sheriff warned.

Matt turned his attention to the business he had started on impulse. "I heard you say it was cash."

"Twelve thousand," Lon Taggert called.

"Thirteen," Matt said.

The three men on the outskirts of the

crowd began to move toward him. The man beside Ab Tanner moved, also. The girl saw it, too, and watched, lips parted expectantly. As Matt backed away two steps for room, he had the grim and amusing thought that the girl hoped trouble was closing in on him.

"I got thirteen thousand bid now! Thirteen. . . ."

"Sheriff!" Matt called, and, when the sheriff looked at him, Matt asked: "Is this a free and open sale?"

"Sure thing, stranger."

"You'll stop anyone who tries to keep me from bidding?"

"No one'll do that. This is a lawful sale."

"I wanted to know," Matt said amiably. "I like the law on my side if shooting starts. And Sheriff, if anyone around me pulls a gun, there'll be shooting. I'm touchy that way this early in the day."

"No one's pulling a gun around here, mister."

The four men had stopped. They had him bracketed right, left, and in front. But they were uncertain. Their orders, Matt guessed, had not covered a situation like this. One by one they glanced toward Lon Taggert.

"Thirteen thousand bid! I got to sell if

there ain't another bid. Thirteen thousand . . ."

Lon Taggert took the cigar from his mouth. "Sell it?" he snapped. "I won't be pushed into a fancy bid and then get caught with it. Sell it, Dagley, for cash."

"*Sold* . . . to the stranger there, for thirteen thousand! An' that means cash!"

Men opened a way to the steps as Matt advanced. He recognized a face or two from last night. Men who'd been friendly, last night, and now were not friendly.

It was a queer thing. Just as the tight expectancy of the crowd could be sensed a few minutes ago, now disapproval, unfriendliness could be sensed. Lon Taggert must have packed this gathering with his friends.

Lon Taggert moved over and fell into step beside him, and they walked up the courthouse steps together.

"Looks like you outbid me on purpose," Taggert said mildly.

"You could have raised."

Taggert's smile was something more than a smile as they followed the sheriff into the courthouse. The smile had a thin, frosty edge. It seemed to cover knowledge and reservations. "Mind telling me why you bid?" Taggert asked.

"Wanted to see what would happen."

Lon Taggert's thin smile came again. "You saw," he said, and pulled the cigar from his mouth with an abrupt jerk of decision. "How would a two thousand dollar profit suit you, mister? Cash, right here?"

They stopped as the sheriff walked in an office ahead of them. They were measuring each other.

"It's a good offer," Matt admitted. "You came to bluff out everyone else. Then you got bluffed out, and now you'll settle like a gentleman."

The weal on Taggert's face was an ugly crimson. Seen close, it looked more than ever like a quirt slash, and, if it was, Matt wondered if the other party were dead. There was a promise of cold, lurking hell back in Lon Taggert's gray eyes. He was not a soft man. He waited now, with the edge of his frosty smile inviting Matt's reply.

"I ought to take the profit," Matt mused.

Taggert's smile grew into an ugly, humorous assurance. "I thought you would," he said. "Maybe I ought to let you pay over your cash first. You've got it, haven't you?"

"Suppose I haven't?" Matt asked curiously.

"I don't like to be bluffed," Lon Taggert

118

said coldly. "But even if you can't take up your bid, I'll give you five hundred profit, instead of asking Dagley to start the bidding over again."

Matt nodded. "I'd take the five hundred, if I was short on cash. You think too fast, mister . . . or maybe too slow. Try me some other time. I've bought half a ranch. I'll think it over."

Taggert put the cigar back in his mouth. His look, ranging over Matt's figure, was remote, suddenly unsmiling. "I always keep thinking," he said vaguely, "I might try you again, stranger."

Matt watched the man go out of the courthouse with leisurely steps. A vein in Matt's temple was pounding. He noticed it and slowly smiled. For an instant that cold look of hatred had glinted in Taggert's eyes, and now they knew how they stood to each other.

The sheriff was glum when Matt walked into the office. "Name?" he asked, pen inked and ready over paper.

"Matt Landis."

"Address?"

"My half of the Block and Star."

"I thought so," the sheriff mumbled, writing. He added without looking up: "You sure fooled everyone. That poker

119

game last night did it, I reckon."

"Did what?"

"Just my fool mouth making noise," Dagley muttered. "Always did talk too much. I guess you know what you're doing."

When the signing was done, Matt said: "You'll have to come over to the bank with me for part of the money. And while I think of it, who's that Ab Tanner?"

Dagley's quick look might have meant anything. "Tanner's got a little shoo-fly spread next to the Block an' Star."

The crowd was gone when they walked out of the courthouse. Ab Tanner and the girl were gone. "Was that girl Tanner's daughter?" Matt asked.

"Well, mister, what do you think?" Dagley asked with a knowing grin.

"I don't think. I'm asking," Matt said shortly.

For a moment Dagley looked uncertain; he shrugged. "I'll answer, mister. Maybe you don't know her and maybe you do. It ain't none of my business, anyway. Her name is Miss Shannon Williams."

"Live here in Tecalone?"

"She's your pardner in the Block an' Star," the sheriff said, and, when Matt made no comment, Dagley looked at him, then looked again, and finally shrugged.

The big black gelding that had carried Matt out of Mexico took him out of Tecalone at a skimming run until the livery barn freshness was unwound.

Matt twisted in the saddle and looked back at the trees and low buildings receding in the vast sweep of range. Shannon Williams and Ab Tanner had ridden out of Tecalone. Matt had made sure of that before leaving. At the livery barn he had learned that the Block and Star was north of the Black Spring road, and the location suited his decision.

He had bid at the auction to see what would happen, hardly thinking about the land. Property anchored a man, pulled the hazy horizons close, the eyes down to dirt and slow growing grass. Land, like a girl's pretty face, should be admired and left behind while a man was free.

2

"WHIPSAWED BY FATE"

The second stream of water out of Tecalone hurried over yellow sand, and the Block and Star ruts cut north through rolling range broken by rock ridges. Matt judged the land with approval. Bunch grass was not over-grazed. Cactus, bear grass, greasewood did not grow in quantity. High hills in the dis-tance were steps to timber-cloaked moun-tains and bald peaks piling skyward beyond the curve of the world. Lush grass was there in the high mountains, and there was water in the deep and cool cañons.

"Not bad," Matt grunted aloud. "Not bad at all . . . if a man were fool enough to want to stop and watch the grass grow."

He chuckled at the idea, and the dusty road wove him back and forth across the water a time or two, bringing him past a tangled mesquite *bosque* and by the foot of a rocky ridge, to the left with the curve of the stream. There adobe ranch buildings were sheltered from the northern winter by the ridge, and cooled from the southern heat by old and stately cottonwoods. Not a big ranch, but the careful hand of ownership had long been present. Adobe walls had been built massively and with care. Corral posts and bars were stout and true. The long, low ranch house was built with a wing at each end. A broad portal in front held splinted chairs to the tree shade and the soothing haze of distance south across the range.

The faint smile of approval went off Matt's face as he gave attention to the gathering on the portal. Seven men and Shannon Williams waited his coming. Most of the men looked like ranch hands, along in years. But memory reached quickly to the big, heavily built young fellow with a puffed cheek and purplish eye who scowled behind the chair that Shannon Williams left when she walked off the portal. Matt's knuckles still had the feel of the blow that had darkened that eye.

The small and meek-looking Ab Tanner was not present, and, when Matt dismounted, his greeting had veiled caution and wry humor. "Howdy, partner," he said.

The girl's hostility was not covered. "No," Shannon Williams said coldly, "you bought half this ranch, not a partnership.

Let's get that settled now."

Their quiet talk could hardly reach the portal where the men watched them. Not a gun was in sight, Matt noted. Not even the young fellow with the puffed cheek was armed.

"Have it your way," Matt agreed. "Who's the one I met at the poker game last night?"

Angry color came with his answer. "Didn't Lon Taggert tell you he was my brother, Art?"

Matt considered the question and shook his head. "Didn't know who he was. I had no hard feelings, ma'am. Art got hotheaded. He'd have pulled a gun in another minute. Now he's in shape to stay out of the next poker game after he's been drinking."

"Lon Taggert won't need to start Art drinking again," Shannon said with suppressed anger. "Taggert got exactly what he wanted after Art lost the best part of our cash in that card game. Do you or Lon Taggert intend to live here?"

"Does it matter?"

"You own half the land and half the cattle we have left," Shannon said. "That includes the half of the house Uncle Ben Quinn lived in before he died. We'll have to share the big room. While either of you use it, Art and I will stay out. You can hire your own cook and have him use the cook house. Our men will stay on our payroll. We'll settle which grass you use and which we use."

"Sounds like a freeze-out," Matt decided gravely.

Shannon had looked taller beside Ab Tanner. Without the hat her hair was thick and dark against her fair skin. Strength was in her rounded chin. Matt caught himself admiring the bitter loveliness of her dislike for him. All the dislike was in the shrug she gave for answer.

"I couldn't help the poker game," Matt suggested. His smile flashed through. "Poker's like love . . . you take the luck as it falls."

"I've told you what we'll do," Shannon said coldly. "Make the best of it, mister. You and Lon Taggert."

Matt considered again. "I'll think it over," he decided. "Might be I'll sell my half of the cattle and let my grass grow. Would that suit?"

"Whatever you and Lon Taggert decide," Shannon replied indifferently.

Matt opened his mouth to question her, then he changed his mind and let the mystery of Lon Taggert rest a while longer. "I'll see you about it again, ma'am," he said politely, and left.

Matt was smiling ruefully as he rode away. He had the feeling that his back was a perfect and tempting target. On the ride to the Black Spring road he heard a shot and looked quickly back. A swell of the land cut off vision that way. But the shot had been in the distance and plainly was not intended for him.

Chris Fraser had a baby girl. His wife, Donna, was smiling and pretty, with gold glints in her hair and a way of looking at Chris that was rich in contentment. They welcomed him as one of the family, long overdue.

Chris had the same wiry, quick-grinning manner. But the old hard and restless core of Chris had softened. Chris was like the wild stallion that had taken the rope and would race no more with the wild mares into blue distance.

Matt said so, chuckling, and Chris laughed, and Donna pretended indignation at the idea, while her eyes adored Chris. Matt had to hold the baby and pretend he liked it. He made a face and groaned loudly when tiny fingers pulled his hair.

In the last hour of daylight Chris took Matt for a short circle on the lower end of the small ranch. They filled in the time since they had parted, and Matt told about the breaking of Padre Peso's rich faro bank at Laguna Madre, and the fighting ride against Padre Peso's gunmen to get the gold across the border.

Chris sighed with pleasure. "Wish I'd been along, Matt. Sounds like a ride."

Matt smiled. "You don't really, Chris. You struck richer pay dirt here with Donna, didn't you?"

Chris nodded, smiling. "Gets richer all the time. Why don't you stop with us? Donna would like it."

"There's a hill I have to ride around," Matt chuckled. "Places to go, Chris. I never was much for stopping."

"What you need is a hill waiting for you to ride back to at night," Chris decided with new-built wisdom. "A place of your own, Matt, with a girl in it."

Matt laughed. "I've already got that, Chris. Pretty a girl as you ever saw . . . next to Donna. And she'd like to sight a rifle on me and cut loose."

"You married?" Chris asked incredulously.

"No such luck. I'm partners with a wild-cat who wants to claw me," Matt chuckled.

"I don't know what it's all about. I thought I'd ride over here and think some on it before I cut loose from her."

Chris listened to the facts of the poker game, the auction, and the exchange with Shannon Williams at the Block and Star. Chris was grinning broadly, but he was serious, too.

"I know that set-up," Chris said. "Donna's folks live north of Tecalone. We were over there last week. Lon Taggert is pure poison."

"I gathered that."

"He owns the SX brand," Chris said. "He owns more every year. Talk says he likes the looks of your Shannon Williams, and she didn't cotton to the idea."

"She's not mine," Matt disclaimed, flushing slightly.

"You bid her in," Chris insisted, grinning. "And a wagonload of grief with her. I'm laughing, Matt . . . but it's real trouble if you stay in the way. Shannon Williams put that quirt lash on Lon Taggert's face."

Matt whistled softly. "And Taggert still wanted to buy in with her?"

"Why not? He'd be setting pretty under her roof for any move he cared to make."

"That where this Ben Quinn lived whose half I bought?"

"Exactly. We were talking about all that at Donna's folks. Quinn and Shannon's father came out partners from Kentucky, or around there, when they were young men. They stayed together. When Dan Williams married, Ben Quinn stayed on in his own end of the house. Never married. He was one of the family. But he forgot to make a will, or it got lost. And when old Ben went on one of his yearly snorters and met an argument and got shot. . . ."

"Who shot him?" Matt interrupted.

"Stranger. He got across the border without leaving his name behind. And Quinn's kin back East inherited half the Block and Star. They didn't want a ranch and tried to sell, but buyers were scarce. Word got around some way that Lon Taggert didn't invite any buyers but himself. And nobody wanted trouble with Taggert."

"Why didn't Taggert buy before the auction?"

"Price was high. Shannon Williams and her brother would have bought, but they didn't have the cash. Quinn's kinfolks finally ordered an auction. You getting an idea of what you bought into?"

"I'm reading sign," Matt said. "Let's see . . . Miss Williams quirted Taggert. That meant trouble. Meanwhile, she and her brother, Art, had some money to bid with at the auction. But brother Art went to Tecalone and opened a bottle, helped by friends of Lon Taggert. Then Art landed in a big poker game, in no shape to play."

"Lon Taggert leaks ideas like that," Chris commented. "The more Art Williams lost at poker, the less cash his sister would have to bid with next morning at the auction."

"I won the money," Matt reminded him.

"Same result. Probably suited Lon Taggert. He's got money. He just wanted a clear track at the sale. Ab Tanner must have scraped some together and tried to help Shannon Williams bid, even though Tanner knew it wasn't healthy to buck Lon Taggert that way." Chris shook his head. "You won Art's money. It was bound to look like you bid at the auction, too, on orders from Lon Taggert."

"Taggert knew I didn't."

"Taggert couldn't figure you," Chris replied. "The kinfolks back East could have sent you to push the bids up. Maybe you didn't really have the cash. Taggert dropped out and let you have it, and then tested you with an offer of quick profit."

"He didn't get anywhere."

"He found out a little more," said Chris dryly. "From what Taggert said to you, and what the sheriff said, I figure Lon Taggert's side must have decided you might be working for Art Williams and his sister. Each side thinks you're playing with the other side."

"And no one has got any use for me," Matt said ruefully.

"Your Shannon Williams and her friends won't put a bullet in your back, which is more than I can say for Taggert and his cronies," Chris said.

Matt reined to one side and shot a coiled rattler, and, when they rode on into a scarlet sunset, Matt decided. "It's clear enough now. Tomorrow I'll ride back and sell to Miss Williams and her brother on their own terms. You can keep an eye on the deal. Bank the money as they pay it, or buy some cows and run them on shares. I'll drop back someday, and we'll settle up."

"Best thing you can do," Chris agreed. "Lon Taggert isn't forgetting that quirt mark on his face. You're in his way. He'll be at your throat like a wolf when you're not looking."

"I'll keep looking until I'm on the other side of that hill," Matt chuckled.

"You'd better," Chris replied mildly.

3

" 'YOU MURDERED HIM!' "

The second stream of water on the way from
Tecalone looked just a little different when
Matt saw it again. He had cut off the Black
Spring road and across the range through
the clear hot sunlight, thinking of Chris and
Donna, the angry dislike in Shannon Wil-
liams's eyes, the look in Lon Taggert's pale
cold eyes.

His horse nuzzled the shallow current
and drank. Matt looked at the running
water and out over the range. This was his
own land, however briefly he would own it
— his own water, out of the green hills and
the deep cañons to the north.

Matt smiled at the way his thoughts were
running. This stream of his had seen the
young partners from Kentucky plant cottonwoods and build the first adobe walls at
the Block and Star. It had watched a little
girl named Shannon Williams; it had seen
her toddle, had watched her grow, had wit-
nessed her tears, her anger, and her
laughter. It would probably see Shannon's

children wade its hurrying current. The current came from nowhere, and it went nowhere that mattered, but for a little while this current on the yellow sand touched things that did matter.

Still smiling at such thoughts, Matt looked up to see dust coming on the ranch road. He made out a light buggy drawn by a pair of fast horses. He rode to the dusty ruts on the chance that Shannon or her brother was in the buggy.

The driver was a man with a great gray beard. He brought the matched bays to a hard stop in a drift of dust.

"Howdy," Matt greeted.

He was puzzled by the look he got. This big old man was broad-shouldered behind the majestic sweep of gray beard. There was an eagle-like hook to the large sun-burned nose. The voice came deep and clear, without friendliness.

"I'm Doctor Sanderson. Are you the one who bid in Quinn's half of this ranch yesterday?"

"I'm the one."

The doctor quieted the blowing team with one big hand. His deep voice was icy out of the beard. "Take my advice and turn back. This ranch is no place for you today."

"Or any day, it seems," Matt replied.

Humor had no place under the glare of those fierce old eyes. Matt met the glare with a questioning look. "Someone sick?"

"Art Williams may live, and he may die, mister. I've done all I can for him so far. I'll be back later today."

"What's wrong?"

"He was shot."

"Who did it?"

"He was shot yesterday and wasn't found until after dark. He'd followed you from the ranch house!"

Matt sat motionless and then shook his head. "I didn't shoot him, Doc, if that's what you're thinking."

A vigorous snort disposed of the statement. "Art says you're the one, mister. If he dies, it will be cold-blooded murder. I'm only a doctor. I don't carry a gun. The law will do what is needed."

"I didn't shoot him," Matt said again, slowly.

The doctor reached for the long buggy whip. "I brought that boy and his sister into the world," the deep voice stated. "I know what is in Shannon's mind now about you. I don't want her marked for years to come with the memory of killing you. Turn back."

The doctor was glaring as the whip came

down. The matched bays broke into a run. Matt swung his black horse and looked after the rising dust and receding buggy. Swearing softly, he reined around and touched a spur.

The gelding stretched into a smooth gallop. Matt stopped swearing and looked over at the running stream. He thought of Shannon Williams at the auction and facing him at the ranch. He wondered if the spirit that had made her quirt one man would break dangerously against him now. He thought not, despite the doctor's warning.

Far over to the left two riders sighted him as he neared the mesquite *bosque*. They seemed to recognize him and bore toward him at a gallop. Matt used the spur again.

He passed the *bosque* in a drumming rush. The two riders were well behind him, rifles in hands, as he skirted the ridge and swung to the ranch buildings. The place had a hushed and waiting look. A man stepped out of a shed near the corrals and shaded his eyes better to see. He called something back into the shed, then broke into a run toward the house.

Like rousing a hornet's nest, Matt thought. He pointed the black gelding toward the long and empty portal, where windows looked out from cool, dim rooms.

He was pulling up, swinging down, when Shannon came quickly out of the house. With relief, Matt saw that she had no gun. The doctor had almost convinced him. Matt saw how Shannon pushed back a strand of hair, how pallor, weariness made her look thinner. He spoke honestly.

"I'm here to tell you I had nothing to do with your brother being shot. Didn't know about it until I met the doctor down the road."

Her quiet voice had weariness, but was so tight, so intense, it seemed to shake her slim figure. "I thought I'd want to shoot you," she said. "But I don't. I only want to see you hang."

She came a farther step, to meet his final step. They were close. The eyes he looked down into were bright with aversion.

"How is he?" Matt inquired soberly.

"Still alive," Shannon replied. She swallowed. The misting of her eyes was a quick and moving sight, seen close this way.

"If I deserved a rope, I'd not be here," Matt said quietly.

He could hear the two riders coming fast. A man ran around the end of the house. A second man followed him. Matt threw a glance toward them. Each man had a rifle. They dropped to a walk and closed in.

Matt said: "I never saw Lon Taggert or heard his name before I watched that auction."

The riders were at the first cottonwoods. One of the men on foot called: "Miz Shannon, git back in the house. We'll talk with him."

She said: "Stay where you are, Ike."

"But . . . ?"

"I'll handle this." She met Matt's look again, her glance beating at him with all her grief. "Art didn't have a chance. He was shot out of the saddle before he knew what was happening."

"Why does he think I did it?"

"Think?" said Shannon. She choked up on the word as she answered him with shaking anger. "Art saw you from the dirt where he fell. He saw you ride out in the open and look to make sure he was down before you rode on."

"He couldn't have seen me," Matt protested. While he was speaking, he sensed the futility of denying the word of a dying man. He remembered the solitary gunshot that had made him turn. That close he had been when Art had been shot.

"He saw your black horse," Shannon said.

"My face? My hat? These clothes?" Matt pressed her.

"Oh, why talk?" Shannon burst out angrily. "Art saw you."

"Can Art talk to me?" Matt asked carefully. He saw the refusal hardening in her look. "It's my neck," Matt reminded. "Your brother didn't have a chance when he was shot. Is it any better not to give me a chance?"

Shannon swallowed.

Matt pressed her. "Hating a stranger can't justify refusing me a chance."

"This way," Shannon said, turning. She added over her shoulder as they entered the house: "This won't do you any good."

"Why did Art follow me?" Matt questioned.

"To see where you went, who you met." Still speaking over her shoulder, Shannon went on: "We were born here. We don't intend to be crowded off." Her voice trembled. "Not even shooting will do it."

In a bedroom at the end of the house sunlight came through a window in the thick adobe wall. The smell of medicine was in the air. On the pillow Art Williams's face was waxy under dark beard stubble.

The bruised cheek and eye showed starkly in the pallor. Art's eyes opened slowly. He stared dully.

"Got him, did they?" Art mumbled. He stirred slightly. "Good." The bit of effort made him breathe harder.

Shannon's face was soft and calm as she looked down at her brother. "He says he didn't do it, Art. He asked to speak to you."

Added luster came into the dull eyes as they studied Matt. Art's look stopped on the belt gun, and he remained quiet, without desire to speak. Matt felt again the helpless sense of futility.

"Did the man who shot you ride close enough to show his face?" Matt asked the waxen face on the pillow.

Art's sigh was a breath, a whisper. "It was you, mister."

"You see," said Shannon stonily.

Matt did not look at her. "I had the excuse to shoot at the poker game," he said mildly to the face on the pillow. "It would have been self-defense when you touched your gun. I wouldn't have missed. Can you remember?"

He might have been mistaken about the faint interest in Art's look.

"I had no quarrel with you," Matt said

139

softly. "I kept the game peaceful. There was no shooting. Nothing's happened since to change my feelings, I've had everything my way, haven't I? Why should I have shot you yesterday? You could have ridden with me, if you'd liked. I was headed over to Black Spring."

Art struggled with all that, frowning a little. He seemed to dread new thoughts boring into his weakness. "Saw your black horse," he mumbled. "Saw it come out in the open beyond those rocks near the crossing. Saw you look toward me an' then ride on."

"I heard a shot," Matt said. "It was behind me, and the gun was out of sight. It didn't mean anything. I rode on. Am I riding the only black horse?"

Art's eyes were dull, weary. "Why should anyone else be there?" Art's whisper asked. He turned his head on the pillow.

"Enough," said Shannon in a stifled voice.

Inside the front door they faced each other. Matt fumbled for words. "I was passing through Tecalone," he said. "Half a ranch didn't mean anything to me. It doesn't now."

"You bought it," Shannon said.

There was little he could say. Not after

140

that quiet bedroom. Not to her stifled grief, to the certainty of his guilt in her misting eyes. "Is the sheriff looking for me?" Matt asked.

"Probably not," Shannon said bitterly. "Lon Taggert got him elected. He'll do what Taggert says. We haven't bothered to send word about Art. I don't know what Doctor Sanderson will do."

"All he can to hang me," Matt guessed. His smile was brief and meaningless. "You won't believe this, but Taggert went into the courthouse with me yesterday to offer a two thousand dollar profit on my buy. I didn't take his offer."

"No," Shannon declared, "I don't believe you."

"Watch what the sheriff does about me," Matt suggested. "That is, if I'm allowed to leave here."

"You'll not be stopped. The ranch is half yours, to come and go."

"I'd almost forgotten," Matt said. A thought touched him and became urgent. He fished for a stub of pencil and took an envelope of papers from inside his coat. He used the whitewashed adobe wall for a backing while he wrote on the envelope.

"I'll guess this will hold in court," Matt said, handing her the envelope. "The auction papers are inside. If I'm hung or shot, there's my will written on the outside, giving title to you and your brother."

Shannon hesitated, staring at the envelope she held. "I . . . I don't understand."

"Perhaps I don't, either," Matt said. He tried, looking inward at himself reflectively. "This isn't home . . . my home. I didn't crawl, and walk, and grow here. I came riding through, and I mean to keep riding on." Matt smiled. "Like the creek," he said. "Like the water passing by. If anything happens to me, my buy at the auction will do you more good than anyone else." Matt laughed softly. "And I'll not need it if I'm hung or shot. Better not tell your men about it until I'm gone. They might get an idea."

Shannon choked. "I don't want this."

"Keep it," Matt said humorously. "I guess this is my home, after all, for this little while anyway."

There were six men outside when Matt stepped out into the sunlight. He mounted and rode away. He heard Shannon call something, to him or to her men, but he did not look back, and they did not stop him. Beyond the mesquite *bosque* Matt looked back and saw no sign that he was being trailed.

He had the feeling of a big load being lifted from his mind. He grinned at what Lon Taggert would say about that penciled will. He wished Taggert knew. Then a new thought came, and Matt swore under his breath. He'd forgotten that his half of the Block and Star might carry danger to the owner. Now he had thrust that danger — Lon Taggert — at Shannon Williams.

4

"CLUE TO A KILLER"

The road twisted across a shallow water crossing and mounted to higher ground beyond. Here were a few scrub trees spaced out. The thin, whip-like lift of ocotillo cactus reached higher than the horse's head from scattered clumps. Along here Art Williams had come riding cautiously, well back from the man he was trailing. Ahead, the rough ranch road curved around the end of a rocky dike that wandered along the landscape.

Matt estimated distance and studied the road sign closely. Presently he gave a grunt of satisfaction and dismounted. Here a horse had churned up the earth. Boot marks were in the dust, and dark spots on the dry earth were blood. Matt rode on to the rocky dike and past it, stopping where the black horse must have walked into view.

Cattle had made a trail along this side of the dike. On foot, Matt searched patiently along the trail. Shod hoofs had been here, and passing cattle had all but eradicated them. But, being careful, Matt found the one spot, the only spot that had to be a measurable distance off the ranch road.

Here a gully in the side of the high dike was like a rocksided stall. The horse that had been left here had been well hidden from most points out on the range. By the sign, the horse had been here for some time.

The rider had stepped on a bit of rock, had scuffed dirt above in his climb to the top. On top of the dike he had moved a small rock closer to a larger rock. Here was space to sit and stretch in fair comfort. A turn of the head here on the dike crest could take in the broken, rolling sweep of range in all directions.

Cigarette ends were here. Sighting through the gap between large and small rocks Matt could see the ranch road to the stream crossing. He could see beyond the stream where the road's twisting, undulating thrust bore toward the Block and Star buildings, hazy in the distance.

A rider and the man who trailed him could both be seen far off from here. The first man could be well past the dike while the second man was still approaching. Matt searched without success for an empty cartridge. Only the cigarette ends had been left with the dead matches that had lighted them.

The man had smoked again and again while he waited. Indian-style, Matt hunkered there, looking slowly around the horizons, bringing his lowered glance to an inch-by-inch contemplation of the space about him. He was the gunman himself now, waiting, thinking, reasoning among impulses which might have brought him here, exploring the thought behind the bullet that had dropped Art Williams while he, Matt Landis, rode on safely to Black Spring.

Thoughtfully Matt rolled a cigarette and lighted it. He flipped the dead match to the ground. His eyes came back to the match and to the other matches. Those used by the stranger had been put out almost before the heads had ceased flaring. Each match had been neatly broken in the middle and dropped with a right-angle bend at the break.

Every match had that same unconscious, habitual treatment. Matt put his own discarded match and a broken match inside the stained sweatband of his hat. He was smiling thinly as he went down to his horse. There was little enough of the stranger's trail sign to follow, but Matt rode confidently toward the Black Spring road, retracing his ride of yesterday.

This meant a return to Tecalone, where

Dr. Sanderson had surely gone, and where Dagley, the sheriff, could make his lawful arrests on sight. But if that was in Tecalone, it had to be met. Matt ran his thoughts back to Shannon Williams. She had faltered before the promise his penciled will had opened to her. She had been unbelieving, but hadn't she doubted, slightly, her own unbelief? Matt chuckled softly and looked out over the range.

"Like the water passing by," he had told her. He himself was passing like the current that hurried to promise beyond each bend. But alive or dead, he was leaving, like the current, his mark on the fortunes of the Block and Star and also his mark on the life of Shannon Williams. He held that thought in his mind with a strange pleasure.

The Block and Star would go on. One had only to know a little of Shannon Williams to know she would keep fiercely strong those roots her father and his partner had put down. Shannon would have her man like Donna had Chris. The cottonwoods and the hurrying stream would see children again in the sunlight, see Shannon Williams untouched by anger, grief, or fear. She would have that look Donna wore like an inner beauty, that look for Chris and for the baby, rich as gold, serene, assured, deeply happy.

Matt wondered if Shannon would disclose the memory of him in those years to come. He thought not, and he smiled slowly, without wondering why he smiled.

But when Tecalone trees were green before him in the heat shimmer of mid-afternoon, Matt rode on unsmiling. He was a solitary and impassive figure as the black gelding paced easily on the dusty street that was the heart of Tecalone range. He drew up to ask only one question from a man mounting the seat of an unpainted wagon.

The man pointed ahead. "Doc Sanderson's got an office around the corner from the Square Dance. You'll see it. Sign on the window."

This return to Tecalone was a thing of notice. Eyes watched the gelding and rider from both sides of the street. Matt guessed some interest must linger from the auction sale. The rest must be because Art Williams was near death at the Block and Star.

On the side street, behind the Square Dance Saloon, white-painted, weathered was a small frame building and peeling black letters were on the window glass: **Bartholomew Sanderson, M.D.**

Humor crinkled briefly at Matt's eyes.

The resounding, mouth-filling name belonged with the majestic gray beard, the big nose, and fierce eyes. The dusty buggy was there behind a span of fresh black horses. Matt looked at the black horses. Then, carrying his rifle, he went into the doctor's office.

"Be with you in a minute," the doctor's deep voice boomed from the back room. His black bag in one big hand, the doctor entered. He stopped, grunting with displeasure.

"She didn't shoot," Matt said gravely.

"So you went there."

"I talked with Art," Matt said, watching anger grow on the doctor's flushed face.

"My patient should have been left quiet!"

Matt nodded and asked the question. "I guess you went to Dagley, the sheriff?"

"Certainly."

"I'd do the same," Matt agreed without animosity. "What's Dagley meaning to do?"

"I'm not the law, young man. And I'm in a hurry. Fifteen mile drive ahead of me before I can start to the Williams Ranch."

Matt was rolling a cigarette. He lighted it, blew the match quickly, broke the match, bent it. "Ever see a man break his matches this way?"

"What foolishness is this?"

"I'm not making foolish moves this afternoon . . . I hope," Matt said reasonably. "You know 'most everyone in these parts, I'd guess. Your duty's done about the sheriff. Can't hurt to be neighborly about matches."

"Neighborly?" Dr. Sanderson repeated. Veins filled in his temples. He said: "Duty? It was a pleasure to inform the sheriff. And broken matches mean nothing to me, young man."

"I thought it might be worth asking," Matt murmured. "The man who shot Art Williams left broken matches like this around where he hid. Every match broken the same way. Bound to be a habit."

The doctor snorted. "It makes a good story."

Matt nodded again and let the charge stand. "I wanted Art to take a good look at my face," he explained. "Seems that Art is sure I shot him, because he saw the dry-gulcher riding a black horse like mine."

The doctor shifted impatiently. "A black horse is a black horse."

"Seems so," Matt smiled slightly. "You've got a nice pair of blacks to your buggy. Doc, is the sheriff trying to find me?

I didn't see him as I rode in."

Doc Sanderson clapped on his black hat. "How do I know?" he snapped. "I've got to go now. Hurry call."

The doctor held the door. Matt walked out ahead of him. He was in the saddle when Doc Sanderson turned, one foot on the buggy step. "Dagley rode out of town alone, mister. And I still don't know anything about broken matches."

"Thanks, Doc."

The doctor's reply sounded like an angry snort. The black span wheeled away fast from the rack. Matt rode to the livery barn and left his horse. He placed the rifle in the livery barn office and sallied leisurely into the late afternoon heat.

Tecalone had not changed. Along the same dusty street, doors invited trade. Saddle horses and wagon teams were waiting. Men and women moved about their business. Matt Landis was only one more figure in the open — tall, sun-scorched, gun sedately under his coat. His thoughtful glance more often was on the ground than on those he passed.

Yet ahead of him and behind him drew out a vague and hushed expectancy. Matt was aware of talk that died away, of faces that went carefully blank and uninterested when he passed. His back bore the feel of watching eyes.

They knew about Art Williams. They waited, watched without friendliness, certain that more was to come. Matt paused at the edge of the walk and slowly started a cigarette. He dropped the tobacco sack and stooped easily after it.

With the sack, he brought from the dust at the end of a hitch rack where he stood a bent and broken match. It was a dirty bit of wood, stepped on, days old perhaps. Matt smiled faintly, dropped the match in his pocket, and carefully shaped the cigarette before he moved leisurely on.

He stopped in two saloons for the brief moments it took to glance about the floors. A little later he crossed the dusty street and turned back on that side. So far there was no sign of the sheriff.

A man did not realize how many matches were used and dropped until his glance searched them out. Another broken match lay in some litter swept off the walk in front of Abe Goldman's General Merchandise Emporium. Matt rolled another smoke, idly contemplating the litter. At least once each morning that walk probably was swept. The match looked like part of the last sweeping. Matt left it there and moved on.

Three broken matches were in front of the Sunfish Bar. These matches were close in against the building, where a man had loitered to the left of the swinging doors, smoking, talking. Matt put his back to the building on the spot and gazed thoughtfully up and down the street. He finished his smoke and walked inside to order whisky.

He was one of eight inside, three sitting at a table. After a breath of silence he was left to himself near the back of the bar. He chose that spot to drink because under the foot rail, among cigarette ends and cigar stubs, a freshly broken match had been dropped.

The whisky spread a relaxing contentment in him. The only sign that his presence was acutely felt seemed to be an occasional quick and furtive glance. The man he wanted might be here, close by him. Matt considered that fact, and what he might do, and how long remained now to do it.

Two men departed. Then another. The three men at the table ordered bottled beer again. A customer drifted in. Two more walked out. There would be questions on the street as to what Matt Landis was doing in the Sunfish.

Along that part of the bar where the men had been standing there were no broken matches. Nor were there any broken matches around the table where the three men drank beer.

The bartender was a lean and mournful man behind the drooping ends of his brown mustache. He caught Matt's lifted brow and brought the bottle again.

"How long," Matt asked idly, "would it take to ride to Taggert's SX Ranch and back?"

"There an' back?"

"Yes."

"Three, four hours," the barman considered. "Not pushing along."

Matt struck a match and blew it out, and the wood snapped softly in his fingers. The bartender stared at him blankly. Matt struck and broke another match, watching the half doors at the front.

"Wouldn't happen in a long time, I guess," the bartender observed with a stir of interest. "Fellow stood right where you're standin' a coupla hours ago and broke a match like that. Seein' you do it makes me think of him."

Matt looked at the match and dropped it. "Habit, I guess," he said, smiling. "Who's the other man?"

"Well, now, I don't rightly know. Ain't been in here more'n a time or two." The bartender called across the table. "Nevada! Who's the man who was in here a coupla hours ago with Sam Gorley?"

Nevada had tight, sun-black features and a big hat pushed back on his head, with black curly hair showing along his forehead line. "Name's Chick Topping," Nevada said over his beer bottle.

"Ain't he with the SX?"

"Uhn-huh. Why?"

"Just curious," said the bartender. He reached for a damp towel and wiped the bar. He left the towel there and picked up the whisky bottle and shook his head. "Funny," he said. "Both of you in the same spot, breaking matches the same way."

"What's this Topping look like?" Matt inquired idly.

"Kind of flattish face. Round. Ear-high to you, I reckon. Got a tooth missing when he laughs."

Matt nodded. He did not turn as a chair scraped at the table. In the bar mirror the sun-blackened Nevada moved outside, not looking toward the bar. When the swinging doors were still again, Matt paid and left.

He paused on the walk in the sun glare slanting across the street. His eyes shook off the barroom dimness, and he saw Nevada riding out of town with a sense of urgency and purpose. But the sheriff had left Tecalone much earlier.

Matt stood, considering a round flattish face. He remembered clearly the broken tooth when Chick Topping had smiled at the auction. Topping had been one of the four gunmen at the heels of the auction crowd. The furtive seep of humor on Topping's flat face, Matt recalled, had seemed to drift out from a callused unpleasantness inside.

There was time, depending on how long the sheriff took to find Lon Taggert and make up his mind. Matt walked again, not looking at the ground now. He was judging how they might come at him, and if Dagley would try for an arrest. In Dagley's place, which meant Lon Taggert's place, it was wasted time to have him locked up. What had been done was definite and enough. Alive or dead, Art Williams had served his purpose. It was not Lon Taggert, now, against the stranger who had outbid him at the auction. It was the law and the opinion of Tecalone, and the answer seemed clear enough.

A rhythm of galloping hoofs came along the street. Matt did not turn until the sound came up behind him and swerved toward him. His move then was smoothly quick, thumb hooking lightly on his gun belt where the coat hung loosely open.

Chris Fraser came stiffly off a dusty, froth-dappled horse.

"Sure is hot today," Chris complained, pushing back his hat as they joined, "I could drink a barrel of beer."

Chris had been a two-gun man, dangerous with either hand. Yesterday Chris's guns had hung on pegs in the big room of his ranch home, with dust on the leather-looped brass cartridges. The guns now were tied low on Chris's legs.

"You rode a long circle to find beer," Matt observed judiciously.

"Sure did," Chris agreed. White teeth showed in Chris's quick grin. "Special beer here in Tecalone. I sneak over now an' then."

Matt sighed. "You plumb durn fool. Get back to Donna and the baby and hang up those guns."

Chris brightened. "Now that's an idea. I told Donna we might drift in. Where's your horse?"

"I hate a liar," Matt said accusingly. "A low-down, poor-mouth liar who never told his wife anything when he sneaked off."

Chris said cheerfully: "Got dust in my ears. Can't hear just what you're saying. Do we have a beer and ride home?"

"I'm staying."

"You always were jackass stubborn," Chris said philosophically. "I figured you might do something like this when I met a friend in Black Spring who had news that young Art Williams had been shot off his horse by the feller who bought the other half of the Block an' Star." Chris grinned. "Maybe this'll teach you to stay away from auction sales."

Between them was the understanding of men who had fought and hungered, elbow to elbow. "Running won't help it," Matt said. "Chris, don't bring Donna into this. Get back to her."

Chris let that pass. "I told you Lon Taggert was pure poison," he said.

"I climbed up to where the gun was fired," Matt said, watching the street. "Art Williams was following me away from the Block and Star. I didn't know it. The gunsights waited for Art. Couldn't have been any doubt the man knew Art from me. Why wasn't I shot?"

"You were," Chris said dryly. "Where's your brains? When you're hung for killing Art Williams, Shannon Williams will hold her half of the ranch again. And Lon Taggert will be sitting sweet to make his move."

"It stacked up that way to me, too. But killing Art Williams couldn't have been planned ahead. Art probably didn't know himself he'd follow me until he took off."

"Something was planned," Chris said without hesitation. "You were followed out of Tecalone. Anyway, we know what happened. I thought I'd find you shot up or locked up. Don't the sheriff know?"

"Doc Sanderson told him. Doc says the sheriff rode out of town quick."

"Dagley went for orders," Chris guessed. Suddenly he was brisk again. "Let's get going while your fool luck holds."

"I'm staying," Matt said once more. He told Chris about the broken matches and the man named Chick Topping, and how Nevada had quickly ridden out.

Chris said: "Dagley won't come back alone. And Nevada Miller is a friend of Lon Taggert's. You'll see this Chick Topping quick as Nevada takes word you were asking about him. Hiding Topping from you ain't the way to clear it up quickly." Chris looked slantwise, face sober. "Shooting is."

"I think so, too," Matt agreed.

159

"Then don't hang around Tecalone like a fool."

"I made a will," Matt said, watching the street. "She's got it with the papers. If I don't come out of this, look to it, will you?"

"Fool stunt, wasn't it?" Chris said. "Why?"

"Just in case," Matt smiled. "A little surprise for Lon Taggert. But I mean to move on when this is settled. She can buy my half. It's home to her."

"You're crazy. Move on and sell to her. No need to stand here and ask for trouble."

"No need," Matt agreed. "I'll walk around a little."

"Crazy," Chris grumbled, falling into step with him. A little later Chris said: "I'll stay off by myself and keep an eye peeled. No telling who's around town."

Matt nodded. They had done this before, in other towns, but it might be Chris would stray far enough to keep out of trouble. Thought of Donna and the baby troubled Matt. He toyed with the thought of leaving Tecalone with Chris, for Donna's sake. But that would mean leaving unfinished the thing he meant to do. That would leave Lon Taggert untouched, more dangerous to the Block and Star than ever. Matt Landis would be a wanted man, who had tried to kill from a hiding place.

Donna would not ask that — or would she? Donna would, Matt guessed heavily, because of the way she looked at Chris, the way Donna held her baby. And if this day brought Chris's body back to Donna, who would be to blame for Donna's grief — for the wrecking of all that Donna and Chris were living for?

"Damn Chris for coming here," Matt groaned under his breath. He had not thought before what a preacher and a girl could do to a man's way of living. Right and wrong were twisted before that look on Donna's face. It suddenly seemed more important than anything else to get Chris safely to Donna and the baby.

Matt turned back to find Chris, who was out of sight. He was scanning the street when he saw the fine fast span of blacks bring the doctor's buggy to the court-house. A saddle horse was following lead reins behind the buggy, and, while Matt looked, he saw big, bearded Dr. Sanderson help a slender girl from the buggy seat. They hurried into the courthouse together.

5

"LAST BID — IN POWDER SMOKE"

Matt started toward the courthouse, regretful that Art Williams had died. Nothing else could have brought Shannon so quickly into Tecalone with the doctor. They were coming out of the courthouse as he neared. Shannon saw him and waited. She had a look of tiredness and strain in her eyes.

"You haven't seen the sheriff?" Shannon asked.

"Why, no, not yet," Matt answered, hat in hand. "Your brother, ma'am . . . ?"

"Art's better," Shannon said. "I met Doctor Sanderson, and he'll go back with me. Your friend, Chris Fraser, stopped at the ranch, and talked to me and to Art."

"Chris did?" Matt shook his head. "That Chris," he said. "Close-mouthed. I'll bet he thinks he's tricky. Did you tell him about the will, ma'am?"

"Yes," said Shannon. Matt smiled fleetingly at how Chris had pretended surprise about the will. Shannon spoke, and Matt watched her intently, "I . . . we were mis-

162

taken about you. Unjust. Art agrees, after listening to Chris Fraser."

"I was riding a black horse," Matt reminded her.

"Not only the black horse," Dr. Sanderson said brusquely. "Young man, Miss Williams is trying to tell you she started at once to make amends. After hearing her reasons, I agreed we should tell the sheriff my report was wrong." Brusqueness hardened in the bushy gray beard. "That seems to be the sheriff now, with Lon Taggert," Dr. Sanderson observed. "He'd better know quickly."

"I'll tell him!" Shannon said.

"Wait here!" the doctor ordered so forcibly that Shannon had no reply.

Matt had turned, following the doctor's look. He saw the sheriff and Lon Taggert riding in the dusty street with five other men. He understood the doctor's harsh order and the hurried strides taking Dr. Sanderson toward the approaching riders.

Shannon started to follow, but Matt stepped in her way. "You'd do better to sit in the courthouse, ma'am."

Now he sensed the change in her. Dislike was not crying out at him with every look. "I was afraid of this," Shannon said.

"Lon Taggert will not listen to Doctor Sanderson."

"Taggert is not the law," Matt said, watching her.

"You don't know Lon Taggert."

"I think I do," Matt said. He smiled. "Or at least, I will."

"Before witnesses they'll have to listen to me!" Shannon caught her breath. "I brought this about. I'll stop it."

Matt still blocked her way. "You should stay here, ma'am." His smile lingered. "It's too late to hide behind your skirts. You didn't ask me to bid against Lon Taggert. I'll trade with him on his own terms, so he'll be satisfied." Matt gestured down the street. "It's expected," he said. "It can't be any other way."

While she was still looking, he left her. It was to be expected. This was the hour for which Tecalone had waited. The feel was in the air, from the men and even women hurrying into the open to watch. They came from all doorways on both sides of the street, watching the little group of riders, peering toward the courthouse and the tall, bearded figure of Dr. Sanderson, stepping out now into the street dust.

Matt lengthened his stride. The smile was gone from him, and with it the idle

164

saunter of a man with time to waste. Chris had not appeared. Nevada was riding at the left of Lon Taggert, big hat once more pushed back so the black curly hair showed above his forehead.

Lon Taggert had the same clean, hard look he had shown yesterday. He was almost handsome. The whip mark was still there on his cheek, and, long after it was gone outwardly, Matt knew that quirt cut would be festering in the man inwardly.

Dr. Sanderson held up his hand and spoke earnestly as the riders stopped. It was a thing that had to be done, and the doctor expected little enough from it, Matt guessed. He let them talk as he approached, out in the street himself now. Matt was watching the flat-faced man named Chick Topping on Lon Taggert's right.

Topping was off by himself, a stride ahead of the others, so that he had stopped abreast of the doctor. His horse was a big, rangy roan, nervous, throwing its head as Topping looked down at the doctor and rolled a cigarette. Topping smiled at what he heard. The same inner unpleasantness was in the smile as he looked toward Matt.

Both sides of the street could hear Dr.

Sanderson's vigorous words. Matt heard only the last of it.

"There's no doubt Art Williams was mistaken about this stranger. Art and his sister are both certain of the mistake. I want you to know that, Dagley, before you do anything hasty."

The sheriff's rust-colored mustache seemed to droop in mournful uncertainty. "I ain't hasty," Dagley said. "But if a man's been shot, there's more to it than guess work. If the Block and Star folks were mistaken once, they can be now. The man rode a black horse, didn't he?"

Lon Taggert said something, and Dagley nodded. His louder agreement carried. "I'll lock this stranger up," he said, "an' we'll look into it."

Chuck Topping was grinning as he thumb-scratched a match. A cupped hand brought the flame to the cigarette. He drew deeply and blew out the match. Then thumb and fore finger snapped the match into a right-angle break, and he tossed the bit of wood carelessly, casually in front of the doctor.

Matt saw Chris Fraser come out into the street near the livery barn and bear hurriedly toward them. Chris had been caught slow and was half a block away, with the sheriff and his companions between himself and Matt.

There was no way to stop Chris now. Matt thought of Donna, waiting at the Black Spring ranch, and he knew fear. Nothing else but fear of facing Donna's tragic eyes could ball the nerves and muscles in his middle so tightly. Seven armed men were on their horses, and only Chris and himself against them.

Two years ago they would have taken it together without hesitation, laughing. Now Matt had a flash of the long, empty trails ahead, with the memory of Donna and the baby riding accusingly with him.

He took the last two steps at a saunter and stopped, suddenly at peace. This would work out, some way. "I heard that last, Sheriff," Matt said. "Lock me up and stop arguing about it."

The sheriff looked uncertainly at Lon Taggert. This had not been expected. Taggert's sneer was quick. A man this easy was past being afraid. The change was there on Chick Topping's face, too, and in his quick, thin grin of derision.

Dr. Sanderson straightened to full height with the broken match he had picked up. The doctor looked around. His great, gray beard had the look of bristling. "Mister," the doctor said to Topping, "where's that black horse you were riding?"

"Me?" said Topping. The thin grin of derision stayed on his face. "I don't ride him every day. What's it to you?"

Dr. Sanderson's deep, clear voice rang out along the street. The doctor's big hand pointed accusingly at Topping. "Sheriff, I think you'll find this man is the one who shot Art Williams. Arrest him and we'll prove it."

"Him?" said Dagley, jaw sagging.

"I'll take the responsibility for his arrest. I demand it, Dagley, while you have him here."

Topping's vicious anger spread redly over his flat, unpleasant face. The roan horse half wheeled, crowding near the doctor. "Trying to put a rope around my neck, you loose-tongued fool?" Topping demanded with shaking anger.

Lon Taggert stepped his horse forward, too. "Made a mistake, haven't you, Doc?" Taggert questioned calmly.

Matt had some of the feeling Dagley must have had — sheer astonishment. Nothing like this had been expected. The warmth and glow of it ran through him. He had been the stranger, Matt Landis, suspected, disliked on every side after the auction and the shooting of Art Williams. Dr. Sanderson was evidently admired, liked, and trusted by most of the people on Tecalone range. The same words they would have ignored from Matt Landis carried weight when hurled from that majestic gray beard. The very feel of the hot and quiet street changed instantly. Men shifted in surprise, spoke quickly to one another. The grim, unfriendly waiting for justice to the stranger was gone.

Dr. Sanderson answered Lon Taggert in the same booming challenge. "I've made no mistake, Taggert. You're the one . . . you and this gunman on your payroll. He's shaved off his mustache. He's not dressed like a gambler now. But after he's arrested for shooting Art Williams, I want him questioned about the killing of old Ben Quinn." The doctor's booming voice carried far along the street. "Perhaps, Taggert, this man will tell who paid him to pick a quarrel with Ben Quinn so he could shoot the old man."

It was happening fast. Chris Fraser was still coming forward beyond the riders. Matt, with the feeling that all this was out of hand now, saw the quick, furious look Chick Topping threw at Lon Taggert. He saw Taggert's nod, barely perceptible, and he called: "Topping, don't do that!"

He had not thought Lon Taggert would make the move. Matt's hand was near his gun. He was watching the flat, vicious look on Topping's round face when he caught the flirt of Lon Taggert's belt gun whipping out.

Matt made the fast draw he had too long delayed. He meant to help the doctor, and he saw too late that Lon Taggert thought of everything, thought fast and with deadly certainty. Taggert's belt gun whipped up roaring in the afternoon quiet. The bullet shock knocked Matt back a step. The shuddering numbness that struck him was like a bad dream. He was staggering. He had been too late, too intent on Dr. Sanderson. He could see his gun and the hand that held it dropping helplessly to his side. He heard the crash of Taggert's second shot, saw the muzzle spurt and the jump of the heavy revolver.

Taggert missed. His horse was swerving. He reined with one hand. His cold, intent look was on the job he was doing, and the man would do it, Matt thought, as his good hand caught the gun from his useless hand. This was Taggert's day, and tomorrow, and on beyond, Shannon Williams would have to deal with this man.

Matt planted his wobbly feet doggedly and, fighting the growing numbness in him, brought the gun up in his left hand. He was vaguely aware that Doc Sanderson had moved fast for an older man. The doctor had caught the reins of Chick Topping's roan horse, crowding in close. Swinging all his weight, the doctor had thrown the horse to one side, coming in close under the head and neck where he was hard to see from the saddle.

Topping's gun crashed out, and crashed again. The last echoes were ringing in Matt's ears as he faced the third shot from Lon Taggert's gun. He saw the disbelief on Lon Taggert's face, the first fleeting uncertainty at what was going to happen. It came to Matt then, as from beyond his own perception, that Taggert had believed one shot would do it, and now fear was in Taggert's mind. The man was cowardly inside.

Matt had time to smile as he fired with his left hand, and Lon Taggert fired the third shot. Matt would have gambled Taggert was going to miss, and Taggert did miss. For a second there seemed no harm in the small blot at the bottom of Taggert's open shirt collar. Taggert sat there, gun in hand, head forward as Matt stepped back, the better to see Chick Topping.

So fast had it happened that Dagley and the other riders were still reining to the sides away from the gunfire. Topping's horse was rearing. Dr. Sanderson still had the bit chains, and Topping was leaning out and reaching down past the horse's neck with his gun, furiously determined not to miss with the next shot.

Matt shot him in that position. Topping kept on leaning over until the weight of his own body slid him out the saddle, and he pitched to the ground on top of his gun.

Dr. Sanderson stepped back, shouting: "Sheriff! Stop this!"

But it was not Dagley who answered. It was the wild yell of Chris Fraser, running in close now, both guns out and blasting warning shots above the riders. It was men to right and left who had dodged and, then witnessing what was happening, had drawn guns. One shout spoke the mind of many.

"We're with you, Doc!"

There was no more fight in the armed riders. Matt looked at Lon Taggert, face down in the dust, the back of his neck blown out. The numbness was still all over him. He sat down, rather foolishly, in the warm dust and looked at red blood crawling over his right wrist and hand. Taggert's bullet had hit well in from the shoulder.

He tried for the chest, and he was too quick, Matt thought. And then he might have been another man present there and listening to Dr. Sanderson harshly ordering men to help. Almost with surprise, Matt noticed they were picking him up and carrying him.

Chris was there, helping, lamenting: "Just my luck not to be with you when it happened."

"Tell Donna that," Matt mumbled.

Dr. Sanderson had hurried ahead. He was in the white-painted back room of his little office building when they carried Matt in and others tramped in after, until the place was crowded, full of murmurs.

In shirt sleeves, a little blood showing on the side of his shirt, Doc Sanderson was throwing shiny instruments into a white pan. "I'm all right!" Doc Sanderson said with loud impatience. "He sort of scraped my ribs with one of his bullets, but I'm all right! Get out of here, the lot of you! How can I operate with the place crowded like a cattle chute? Get out, boys! Two of you keep him there on the table until I get ready!"

They understood Doc Sanderson and quietly began to shuffle out.

Pulling a big white sack over his beard and tying it behind his head, the doctor called: "Isn't that Shannon Williams out there? Send her in. She can help me."

The hurt was running through Matt's side now. He grinned at Chris and got a grin back as Chris stood beside the long, oilcloth-covered table.

"Next time," said Chris, "listen to what I say, you fathead. Or stay close to me."

"Ask him," said Matt, indicating the doctor, "how he was so sure that Topping fellow shot Ben Quinn."

Dr. Sanderson heard and looked around, speaking gruffly. "Ben Quinn talked a little to me before he died. Said the man who shot him had a missing tooth on the right side of the mouth. I've kept quiet about it and watched for a man with a tooth missing there. When I saw this man break his match like you said, and then show a missing tooth, I guessed he'd shot Art Williams and Ben Quinn, too, and that his pay had come from Taggert. He didn't have sense enough to make me prove it." And then to Shannon Williams, touching his elbow, speaking in agitation, Doc Sanderson roared: "Of course, he'll not die! Quit acting like a fool woman and get busy there like you've done before. Going to put him to sleep while I cut into him a little and patch him up. Get his shirt off. Get some hot water there and wash his shoulder."

From the table Shannon looked calm and strangely at peace. She was quick and deft and gentle. Matt followed her movements, watched her face. Their eyes met, and Shannon smiled.

"Hurt?" Shannon asked, not flinching as she cleaned the shoulder.

Matt shook his head.

"How soon can I take him home . . . over near Black Spring?" Chris asked the doctor.

"Tomorrow, I guess. Here, hold this while I open the chloroform. And if you start getting sick, get out of here."

Matt looked straight up at the ceiling. "I've got a home, haven't I?" he asked.

"As long as I've got a roof, you have," Chris answered.

But Shannon's voice, beside the table, said: "I don't think that's what he means. The doctor will be coming out to see Art, anyway. And I'll be there to take care of him."

"Hold his arms," the doctor ordered. "Can't tell what a patient will do when he gets a whiff of this. Afterward, he can go wherever he wants."

"Home," Matt murmured. "To the Block and Star." Matt turned his head. A white gauze cone came over his face, between his eyes, and between the look Shannon Williams had for him. He breathed deeply, and he was smiling. His last thought was that he must be grinning foolishly, like a man hunting up a preacher. Shannon had that look he'd often seen before, pretty as spring over a stream meadow, not at all afraid of what lay ahead.

Then Matt felt like he was floating and the light was like the current of the stream hurrying past the ranch house. But this was different. The current of the stream never came back to the house and the corrals. The current had no home. Still smiling, Matt went to sleep, not at all afraid of what lay ahead.

The Gun Wolf

The year 1949 was one of the most inspired for T. T. Flynn, and in the first five months of it he wrote some of his finest Western stories. "Bullet Bounty" was enthusiastically accepted by Jack Burr, editor of Street & Smith's *Western Story*, the first Western story Flynn had submitted to Burr since 1943. In the interim Flynn's agent, Marguerite E. Harper, had been sending his stories primarily to Popular Publications, although she had also been selling Western fiction by Flynn to slick-paper magazines like *The American* and Popular Publications' *Argosy*. "Back Trail" was completed on April 5th and sold at once to Mike Tilden, editor of *Dime Western*. This splendid story is now collected and available in Edition 4 of *The Bold West* from DH Audio. "The Gun Wolf" came next, written in a white heat in the early days of May. Mike Tilden bought it the same day it arrived at Popular Publications' editorial offices in New York City. It appeared in *Dime Western* in the issue dated December, 1949.

1

"BAD TROUBLE AT ORO GRANDE"

There had been trouble. Bob Denton knew it when he saw the Kingsville-bound stage had turned back to Oro Grande. Denton rode back to Oro Grande on the Sun Dance road. He hit the bench to the southeast of Oro Grande, off which the Sun Dance road pitched in six easy zigs to the lower flats, and across them to the town itself.

The piñons and stunted cedars on the bench cut off his view of the country below until he reached the drop line. There, because he was in no hurry, Denton pulled up his bay and reached for tobacco. He eased in the saddle, long and flat-waisted.

His capable hands shaped the smoke while Denton looked over the lower flats to the town with its trees and orderly rows of houses. It was just another town, and Denton had seen many. Yet in a few months Oro Grande had become the focus of his life, his hopes and future.

He was twisting the end of the cigarette when his eye caught the gray dust drifting in swirls along the Kingsville road. It was a four-horse stage outfit, rolling at full gallop — and no stage was due from the south in the middle of the morning.

Denton shook the bay into a run. That stage had headed south out of Oro Grande hours ago, and should still be traveling south. Here, Denton thought, was trouble.

He came into town by a different way than the stagecoach. The fury of his gallop drew stares from townspeople he passed. They hadn't seen the stage returning.

Oro Grande had the usual main street of ruts, dust, and comfortable width. It had plenty of stores, saloons, and dance halls — especially saloons. It was a junction point and the only way out to the railroad for a great sweep of ranching and mining country north and east. A man could find better towns, but this was Denton's now, for better or worse.

The stage was entering town from the south at full gallop. Denton spurred toward the adobe stage station, with its benches under the wide sun canopy over the walk. But Tim Calhoun, the stage driver, made a locked-wheel, span-rearing stop in front of Dr. Job Reynolds's little white frame office, next to Hoffstettor's Mercantile Store, on down the street.

Tim rode the driver's seat alone. Denton closed the distance, spurring again. Men were bolting out of doorways, pounding along the walks, and running across the street toward the stage. Dust churned up as Calhoun scrambled down. Passengers were emerging and speaking excitedly to the men who ran up. Denton dropped off his horse and left it rein-tied as he made for the stage.

The story was bad. Road agents had taken the bank's money shipment and valuables the seven passengers had owned. Gray-haired Henry Jackson, who owned the stage line, had been riding the shotgun seat. Jackson was brave — and foolish. He'd tried to get the first masked man who showed. A hidden gun had drilled him before he pulled the trigger.

Denton helped lift Jackson out of the stage. Blood was stiff on the old man's brown coat and gray shirt. It was drying in smears on his gnarled hands and lined face as they carried him into Reynolds's office. Doc was out on a call. Denton heard men yelling they'd find the doctor.

Christina Jackson, Henry's daughter, was there suddenly in the little building with them, men letting her slip almost at Denton's heels into Doc's back office. Her voice was clear as they put her father on the narrow oilcloth-covered table where Doc did his work with knives, needles, and probes.

Christy said: "Dad! Can you hear me?"

That was all, but no answer came from the figure on the table.

Denton took her elbow. "He'll be all right . . . soon as Doc gets here," he said gently.

Christy had a brown-dusted, usually gay, and friendly face. She had the bloom of twenty, with honest eyes under a soft sweep of tawny hair. She came to Denton's shoulder, and her laughter had often been at his shoulder of late. But in this crowded, smelly back room office grief touched her face.

"He shouldn't have been riding that stage," the girl said slowly.

A strange look was on Christy's face. Denton had been expecting that look to appear there for at least three weeks now. It was three weeks since the Meyer girl had come to sing and dance at Bull Weather's Palace. But Denton had never expected Christy's doubt and suspicion to be linked with the possible death of her father. He thought Fred Breckenridge, the deputy sheriff, would be the man to put doubt in Christy's eyes. Breckenridge disliked Denton. He probably would have even if Christy had not been an unmentioned bar between them.

Breckenridge had stumbled on just enough truth to bring out all Christy's angry pride, if he chose to mention it. And he would, one day. But now, as Christy spoke, Breckenridge was outside on the plank walk, shouting orders to a gathering posse. "He shouldn't have been riding that stage," she said again.

Denton knew what she was thinking. So did other men who heard her words. Denton himself should have been riding gun guard today. Jackson had more to do as owner than hold down the shotgun seat while relay teams whirled the stage to Kingsville, on the railroad.

"I shouldn't have taken the day off," Denton agreed mildly. "Christy, you can't help in here. It'll do you no good to stay." But he knew she would anyhow. Then: "I wish I could stay with you," Denton said.

"You can't help here," said Christy. She swallowed hard. "You can help make sure they never shoot another man!"

"I can do that," Denton agreed. He groped for her hand and pressed it and quickly left the building, not liking all this in front of curious eyes. There had been enough covert smiles about him and Christy. Talk, too, you could be sure, although not within Denton's earshot.

Fred Breckenridge was still out front, where most of the town seemed gathered. Mounted men were ranging the street, ready to ride with Breckenridge.

Oscar Deland, the bank cashier, was talking excitedly to the deputy as Denton stepped out. "Fifty-two hundred dollars in the shipment, Fred! I counted it myself. All gold twenties! It's too much to lose!"

Denton stopped beside them. "All double eagles?"

Deland nodded. He was a balding man in his middle thirties, unmarried, and something of a sport, as far as a banker could be. He liked his drink, was seen at many of the dances, and was liked by most people. Oscar Deland got around.

Denton asked: "Anyone know the money was being sent out on this stage?"

"No one."

But Denton persisted. "It hadn't been spoken of outside the bank? No one in the bank said a word to anyone?"

Oscar Deland said: "Of course not!" And a flush that could have been anger came to his face.

Breckenridge was a powerful young man. He liked hand-embossed boots, and silver about his belt and side gun and spurs and bridle. But he backed the deputy's badge well despite his touch of bull-headed vanity. Another man than Denton might not have brought the curt remark from Breckenridge. "You trying to take charge of all this, Denton? And while we're on it . . . how did Henry Jackson happen to be holding down your job today?"

Denton had known this would come from Breckenridge, sooner or later. Christy Jackson had asked it with her own eyes as she stood beside her father.

"I took the day off," Denton said shortly.

"What for?"

"My business."

"Been in town all morning?"

"You stepped out of the saddle shop as I came in off the Sun Dance road," Denton reminded. "Wasting time, aren't you?"

Breckenridge flushed. "The Sun Dance road runs southeast," he said.

"And the stage was robbed south where a man could cut over to the Sun Dance road," said Denton. "Why don't you say it, mister, instead of hinting around?"

Dr. Job Reynolds's single horse rig came rushing up. Breckenridge shouted to the mounted men in the street: "We'll start soon as Doc tells us how Jackson is!"

Deland stepped away, and, after waiting a moment and seeing Breckenridge was breaking off the talk by ignoring him, Denton swung off along the walk. He had no illusions. Breckenridge had put it into words, and the big, curly-haired deputy would hold to the idea, worry it, and follow it out. He didn't like Denton.

The bleak irony of it stayed with Denton as he went about his business. A man never out-ran his past. It was not what Breckenridge knew or suspected now that counted. It was what he might find out. And if the deputy worried at the matter of Bob Denton long and hard enough, he might find out more than he expected.

Denton turned into Bull Weather's Palace, as elaborate a place as you'd find in a town the size of Oro Grande. The place was deserted. Not even Weather's massive, shiny, bald head was in sight. There was too much excitement down the street. But Shorty Conroy, one of the bartenders, was watching the stock and cash drawer from the doorway, where he could watch the street, also.

"Ain't one thing, it's another," greeted Shorty. "How bad's Jackson hurt?"

"Bad." Denton looked along the deserted bar. "The Meyer girl around?"

"She don't work mornings."

"I know. But I didn't see her down the street. Thought she might have stopped by."

"She went riding early," Shorty said. "Seen her pass."

"Going where?"

"Hell! How do I know? I ain't nursemaid to Bull's gals."

"I want a rye," Denton said, and took his time with the drink and rolling a cigarette. Shorty could be too curious. More than ever the business ahead needed thinking out.

Behind the thinking was anger, feeding on itself and all he suspected. Those who knew Denton, Christy Jackson included, would be expecting him to ride with the posse. Or follow it.

Denton said — "I'd better get a fresh horse." — and walked out of the Palace, back to the bay horse he'd left at the doctor's office.

Someone had wrapped the reins around Hoffstettor's hitch bar. The straggle end of the posse was on down the street, trotting in dust the leaders had raised.

Christy was inside. People were massed

on the walk and in the street. "Heard how he is?" Denton asked.

"Word come out Doc says it'll be touch an' go," a man said.

That was as good as Denton had expected. Better even, if Doc Reynolds had sent out the truth. Denton let it stand that way as he rode to Cooly's Livery. Most of the stalls were empty. Men in the posse had hired Cooly's horses. The hostler sat on a greasy box inside the wide doorway and shook his head.

"Ain't a good one left. I saddled so many so fast I got a lame arm."

"Did one of Bull Weather's girls hire a horse here?" Denton asked.

"Nope."

"You sure?"

"Been here since dawn. I seen her pass, though. That purty, new one. She was on one of Trimble's hosses."

Ed Trimble's barn was up at the other end of the street. Denton rode first to the horse sheds behind the stage station. Henry Jackson had only the best for his stage teams and saddle stock. The place was deserted. Denton was glad of it. The horse he wanted and meant to buy from Jackson was in one of the end stalls. It was deep-chested, powerful, fast. Denton shifted saddles, found a canteen in the supply shed, and filled it at the pump.

He never rode out these days without his saddle carbine and belt gun. He considered riding to Trimble's barn and asking questions about the girl. Then he decided it would be time wasted. She had started from Trimble's at the north end of town and passed the Palace, heading south, and made the turn off Main Street, past Cooly's Livery. This headed her out of town west, where one could ride a mile or a hundred miles and not get anywhere. And that was about as much as Denton needed to know.

He rode south out of town, the way the posse had gone, running the horse easily until it got its wind. Denton's anger was cold rage now.

Miles out, with the posse still out of sight ahead, Denton turned off the Kingsville road, heading west by south. He headed toward the south sweep of the Yamapaís badlands, and before long the horse was lathered.

Denton had little use for a man who punished a horse. But in any lifetime there was a day when the rules were broken. This was Denton's day. If the pony suffered from this ride, it had to be.

Two hours later he was in the badlands. Rock dikes and deep gullies criss-crossed the lonely miles. Lava, too, brownish-red, writhed in frozen streams. There was nothing to bring a man this way.

Equally dry and desolate, the Yamapaís range thrust its fluted spires to the sky ahead. Beyond the western slopes of those low mountains were the Salt Horse Flats, where the sun shimmered and blazed on miles of salt and alkali beds. Breckenridge's posse had gone the other way, east of the Kingsville road. Denton wasn't too sure he wasn't making a fool of himself. But he had reasons for this ride and had to run them out.

The girl must have sighted him from some higher vantage point. She rode out suddenly from the cover of a lava dike that ended just ahead. Denton's carbine was out of the scabbard, cocked, at the first sign of another rider. Then he saw who it was and slowed to a trot, then a walk. The woman rode like a man, in saddle pants and jacket, with rifle and canteen, cream sombrero, and gauntlet gloves of soft leather. Denton knew those hands. They had a tender touch.

She was a lush and lovely girl. Her face had the slightest olive tint, and her eyes were soft and wise. Long lashes, ripe mouth, in her middle twenties, she was slender and always graceful. She was Rita Meyer, and Denton had known her before he came to this country.

He had been dismayed to see her arrive in Oro Grande three weeks ago. He had guessed she meant trouble. Rita had a leather-cased spyglass thonged to her saddle horn. She lifted it and called: "I saw your dust, Bob. Then I saw you in the glass. I was surprised."

"Who's with you, Rita?"

"No one."

Denton scanned the terrain. Lava blocks, big enough to hide a horse and man, had tumbled off the main lava flow. Rita watched him in amusement.

"What brings you so far from town, Rita?"

"Riding." She shrugged. "For fun."

"Rough country to ride in for fun."

"I ride where I like, Bob." The woman's smile showed perfect teeth. "Were you following me?" And then Rita laughed at him. "You could have found me any night in town."

"Stop that," said Denton impatiently. He reined over beside her. With a quick reach he caught out her saddle gun. The action turned her face white with anger. "Bob, what are you doing?"

Rita had come out without a side gun. Denton was mindful of the Derringer she had always carried somewhere out of sight in the old days. He considered searching her for the small gun, then decided to risk ignoring it.

"Let's ride, Rita."

"Where?"

"What difference?" Denton countered. "You're riding for fun."

Rita's dark eyes were narrower, and her voice became sharper. "You're out here for trouble."

"No trouble with you, Rita. Who else?"

"Stop it!" said Rita angrily. "You must have found out Dick Wilson and his friends are around. You wouldn't be out this way if you didn't know."

"So," Denton said. He'd been right, then. "Did you know the Oro Grande stage was going to be held up today?"

Rita's wide-eyed astonishment was instant. Fear shadowed her look. A quick tightness was in her reply. "I haven't heard anything about it."

"I didn't ride gun guard today," Denton said evenly. "Henry Jackson took my place. He was shot. Probably going to die."

Denton's voice was harsh. "Would have been me if I'd made the trip."

"Dick had nothing to do with it," the woman said.

Denton stared at her silently.

Rita swallowed. "Dick was your best friend," she reminded him. The strain was greater in her voice.

"And you're still Dick's girl!" Denton snapped. "You drifted into Oro Grande and tried to tell me different when we talked. Ride with me." Denton squinted at the sun. Heat waves shimmered over the badlands. Noon was two hours past. The full strike of the afternoon heat was about them.

For a long moment Rita's calculation held her, stiff in the saddle. Then silently she rode with him.

"There's one good water hole out this way," Denton observed. "Bear Butte Pool. The stage passengers said four men were in the hold-up bunch. They headed east, like they meant to swing down through Squaw Creek Flats and take the old rustler way to the border. Any sensible gunnies who'd lifted six thousand off the stage and passengers would take it on the run that way."

"If you say so," Rita agreed. "I don't

know this country very well." She was friendly again. Too friendly. Denton knew her. "So what's the use of riding on like this and talking about Dick and a stage hold-up?" she protested.

"I was one of the old bunch," Denton reminded. "That's the way they liked to lay out a job. Every sign pointing to where they'd head if they had any sense. They'd start that way, split up and cover tracks, and make a long roundy, and come right back, through the back door, you might say. They'd bury the money and lay low for a time, smooth as sheep-killing dogs."

Denton said it matter-of-factly, with an undertone of harshness. That had been part of his past. Rita knew it. She was watching him, thinking hard, fast. Rita was cleverer than she looked, more dangerous than a stranger would guess.

"All that was four years ago," Rita reminded.

2

"The Parson's Stolen fortune"

"Dick Wilson is fast with his guns and slow on new ideas," Denton said. "If a thing works, he keeps trying it. Also, he's not ready to leave these parts."

"How do you know?"

Denton's thin smile was frosty. "You're still around. Dick won't be far away. When you showed up in Oro Grande, I began expecting Dick. Didn't pay much attention to your story of breaking off with him. You wouldn't have made the ride out this way today if you knew Dick's bunch was working," he decided. "Has he been afraid to show up in town and see you?"

Denton let her ride in silence. They were bearing southwest now, toward Bear Butte. The butte wasn't impressive, rising as it did from a lower trough of the landscape, with the greater mass of the mountains on beyond. Only the small seep spring at the always shadowy and cool north side gave reason for travelers to approach the place.

Denton didn't head directly for the butte, badly as his horse needed water. He turned south, keeping to the lower washes. A man could ride all day this way through the badlands and not be seen.

"Where's their camp?" he asked Rita suddenly.

She shook her head.

Denton said: "Whatever you're thinking, honey, don't try it. We both know Dick. Try to warn him and you'll start him shooting. Dick and I were friends. Had the same bedroll many a cold night. I don't want to kill him before we talk."

Rita's lip curled. "Dick's hard to kill."

"Every wolf has his bullet," Denton said. "Risk it, if you want to."

The woman bit her lip gently but said nothing.

He kept her riding a little ahead. She could shoot too well with a Derringer. They worked south of Bear Butte, still bearing to the east of it. Denton finally pulled up a notch that cut through the higher ledges siding the trough running north and south, from which the butte's sides soared. He had been calculating time all the hours of his ride.

"If Dick makes a roundy this way from the hold-up, he won't get there much before dark," Denton said slowly. "He'll come in from the south. If he's expecting trouble, he'll be looking for it at the butte water. We'll wait for him here. You be comfortable . . . might be a damned long wait."

Rita was white again with anger. "I don't know why I'm letting you give orders like this!" she snapped.

Denton grinned. "You aren't sure where Dick is. I won't let you look for him. What else is there to do?"

An angle in the notch's south wall gave some shade. Advancing, one could see out over the rough lower ground, north to Bear Butte and south two miles, where the head of the trough pinched in.

Denton took Rita's glass, studied the butte and the trough. Each was barren. The dry horses were on his mind. But the butte water was where Dick Wilson's bunch would have a look-out. There was where most riders would stop first.

Denton could be a patient man, but sometimes things got real tough. Patience was needed now. The brassy sun crawled down toward the Yamapaís spires. His water was almost gone. Rita was smoking cigarettes constantly. Buzzards soared lazily.

Rita said suddenly: "You're a fool!"

Denton looked at her for a moment. Then: "If I'm right, Dick's bunch will slip in from the south for water. Probably one at a time."

Another girl might have tried to get away. Rita knew Denton. Knew the bloody, dangerous business around which all this revolved. She was used to taking orders from a man who meant them — Wilson. Rita was part of the bunch. She worked in towns, picking up any information Wilson might use, while the gang hid out. It was dirty business for a girl. It had started almost a year before Denton left that way of life. He hadn't thought too much about it then. She was Dick's girl.

She could have been Bob Denton's girl. In those days he'd suspected for a time Rita had never forgiven him for not wanting her. But all that had been almost forgotten until Rita appeared in Oro Grande. Now it was part of his life again, and dangerous.

He was rolling a cigarette before using the glass when movement in the south caught his eye. He dropped the cigarette and adjusted the spyglass. A moment later he was looking closely at Wilson himself.

"What is it?" Rita asked sharply.

He turned his head. "It's Dick's life. Take a chance if you want to."

"Are you going to shoot him?"

"Want to talk to him."

Denton hunkered behind a large boulder. He laid the carbine on the ground and rolled another cigarette. The rage that had stayed down deep began to feed again on the memory of Henry Jackson and the grief on Christy Jackson's face. And yet Dick Wilson had been a close friend.

Wilson pulled up, leisurely built a smoke, and scrutinized the ledge rim and on toward Bear Butte. Then he came on toward the notch itself. He meant to come through the notch and use the cover of the higher ledges to get abreast of Bear Butte, unseen, using the same way Denton had come.

Denton came to one knee behind the sheltering boulder and pulled the Colt gun and checked it. He motioned Rita to keep back in the notch out of sight, and watched her from the corner of his eye. A rough natural trail angled down from the notch. Wilson put his horse steadily to the climb. Denton waited until he heard the hard-breathing horse top the trail, a few yards beyond the boulder. Then he came up suddenly, gun cocked.

"Climb down, Dick! Easy!"

The started horse swerved. Dick swore, and a quick grin of relief hit him. "You near jumped me into a gun play, Bob. Howdy, boy!"

"Been too bad if you'd tried it," Denton said briefly. "Step down, Dick. On this side of your horse."

Wilson's mouth got ugly-looking. "What's the idea, Bob? This a joke?"

The past was with them, strong with memories. These men had bunked together, drank together, ridden, fought, yarned around far campfires. But the rage Denton had brought across the Yamapaís badlands had not abated.

"Same kind of joke you and your men played on the stage," Denton said. "Same kind of fun Henry Jackson had when he was shot off the stage seat. Get down, Dick. Keep your back to me while you unbuckle that gun belt and step away from it."

Dick said: "Hell, you ain't the law! Nobody hurt you! Put up that gun, Bob. We got a lot of talk to catch up with. I been meaning to get in touch with you since Rita said you were in these parts."

"That's all I wanted to know," Denton said. "She told you. And you went ahead, even when you knew I'd settled peacefully in Oro Grande and was working for Jackson's stage line. Get down, Dick, damn you!"

Rita moved forward into view.

Suspicion darkened Dick's gaunt face. "So you hooked up with Bob! You double-crossing. . . ."

"You fool! Keep quiet!" Rita blazed. "I told you Bob's calf-eyed over Jackson's daughter. I was riding out here to talk to you when Bob came along. He made me ride along here with him." Rita's sarcasm thinned her voice. "Bob's all worked up because you shot her dad! No telling what he'll do! Let him have his way!"

Wilson stepped slowly off the sorrel. Silently, his back to Denton, he unbuckled the gun belt with an angry yank and dropped it.

"Why'd you move in on this range?" Denton demanded.

"Didn't know you were here," Wilson said. He stepped away from the gun belt and wheeled carefully, palms open and away from his thighs. "I didn't know where you'd faded to." A sour grin touched his face. "Things got warm up north. We drifted this way where we weren't known." Dick pursed his lips. "Hell, Bob, if you're working for wages, you ain't doing so well. Look! Whitey's still with me. Got a couple more men just as good. Big Tex went to San Antone to see a girl. He ain't staying long. Throw in with us again. Easy pickin's. We'll be fat as feeder steers without half tryin'."

"Had all that out once before," said Denton. "We were younger then, hotheaded . . . with not too much sense. Made our first play for easy money without thinking too much about it. Dick, it never was easy. It got harder. We were shaping into a bunch of hardcases when I added the tally and quit. Remember?"

Dick's smile had little meaning. It could have been friendly or just short of a sneer. Dick's voice was the same way. "Bob, when you pulled out, Lefty Dane offered to bet the boys his share of the next haul you'd gone faint-hearted."

"I read in a Denver paper Lefty was killed by a sheriff's posse out of Cheyenne," Denton said without emotion. "What happened to Sam Foote and Cal Whitehead?"

"Sam pulled a gun on the wrong man over in Utah. Cal got careless in Arizona and didn't make it away from a stage job he was trying alone. One of the passengers was a deputy who didn't have any more sense than to start shootin'."

"Lefty and Cal weren't faint-hearted," Denton said. "They were plain damned fools to keep on at it."

"I'm still at it," Dick reminded, grinning. "An' I'm here, Bob. Not much of a damned fool. Listen, the ones I travel with now use their heads."

The past was close about them. Too close. For they were older now, and the smiling youth Dick Wilson had been was gone somewhere in the quick passing years.

Denton made one more try to reach back to the past. "Dick, you used to talk of your own brand and a piece of land with good water. And settling down when you had a stake. Remember that night at Indian Spring when you got to talking about how Rita wanted a house and kids? And deserved them?"

Dick spat his disgust. "Talkin' through my hat. Can you see Rita nursing brats an' washing dirty dishes? She's a loud-music girl. She wants crowds and plenty of men thinkin' she's the prettiest sight that's stood in front of them for a long time."

"One time I could see her as the prettiest girl who ever bossed her own kitchen," Denton said slowly. "It was a good sight.

Better than tramping the dance halls, doing your dirty work for you, Dick."

Rita flared. "Don't worry about what I do! Dick and I get along all right!"

"It's your business," Denton agreed. "The stage hold-up is my business. Dick, those saddlebags look heavy. Get 'em on the ground beside your gun."

Dick grunted with effort as he heaved the heavy leather bags down. They landed hard. One reason, Denton guessed, why the sorrel horse was so jaded. It had carried a heavy burden far and fast.

Dick looked past his horse into the south. Looking for more of the bunch. They'd be coming.

"You and Rita," Denton said, "walk on down the trail and wait for the others. I'll drift your horses a couple of miles. You can get them by dark."

"You ain't taking me in?" Dick asked.

"No."

"Why not?"

"Call it old times. All I want is to see the last of you, Dick. Move on with your bunch."

"Wouldn't be planning to make a haul of that bank money yourself, Bob?"

"I don't work that way now, Dick. How much is there?"

"All of it." Wilson grinned. "Bob, you don't dare take me in. Won't help to shoot me. Rita would still be around to talk. The town wouldn't like it, would they, to hear what you used to be? Or get the idea you been working with us all along. Rita could tell 'em. They'd believe her."

"Kind of thought that would get in your mind," said Denton. "That's why I'm not taking you in. You're in the clear on this hold-up as long as you keep quiet and move on. Start talking, and no matter what happens to me, the sheriff will be after you. Won't be worth it, Dick. Now get going, you and your woman."

Rita began to laugh. It had a hysterical pitch. "He's got you, Dick! Neither one of us can make a move. Let's go before Bob decides to shoot me, too. He's on a trigger edge about that girl and her father."

Wilson's profanity was loud as he swung to the trail and kept going without looking back.

"Is it worth it, Bob?" Rita asked, and she followed her man.

Denton didn't bother to look in the saddlebags. He heaved them on his horse and led the other two horses back through the notch, and turned them loose a good two miles away. He rode openly now back to the seep spring at Bear Butte, watered his pony, drank deeply himself, filled the canteen, and headed back toward Oro Grande.

Twilight came down as he covered the long miles home. Denton rode, glumly conscious he'd done the wrong thing. Wilson was a hardcase now, killer and outlaw by choice. He'd never change.

Christy Jackson wouldn't understand this day's business. Nor would anyone else. Denton faced it squarely. He was a prisoner of his own past, and what he'd hoped to build for the future.

Lights glinted along Main Street and in a few houses. Denton rode into town quietly from the north, not using the stage road. He cut through a rutted alleyway and stopped behind the plank shed where the Reverend Amos Clegg kept his buggy horse.

The Clegg house was dark. Denton heaved the heavy saddlebags over the whitewashed back fence, and retraced his way out of town, hoping he hadn't been seen.

He rode a wide swing around town and came in from the south on the Kingsville road, openly, leisurely, and rode to the stage stables with no more than a brief greeting to several men along Main Street.

He had hoped the stage station would still be deserted. But old Shack Mason, night hostler and watchman, came out the back door with a lighted lantern when Denton had almost finished rubbing down his horse with a grain sack, after watering and feeding him liberally.

Old Shack had been dozing in the station. He was still yawning. "Fred Breckenridge bring the rest of the boys in?" Shack asked.

"Didn't catch up with his party."

"Some of the boys come in couple of hours ago," Shack said. "The trail split, an' they lost the tracks they were follerin'."

Denton stepped out of the open front of the shed and paused to roll a smoke. Shack's dim lantern light fell on a white smear along Denton's pants leg.

In the dark Denton hadn't noticed how hard he'd brushed Amos Clegg's whitewashed fence when he'd heaved the saddlebags over. He turned so that the leg was away from the light.

"How's Jackson?"

"Holdin' his own, which ain't much," Shack said. "Folks are riled. There's talk of a rope party if Breckenridge brings back any prisoners."

"I'll go by Jackson's house," Denton said.

He stopped first at his hotel room, washed quickly, and hauled on clean clothes. Brushing with his palm had failed to remove all trace of whitewash. And old Shack was shrewd. He noticed things. Tonight the white smear had meant nothing. Not worth a comment. Tomorrow Shack might recall it. He was a talkative man. He was also fiercely loyal to Jackson and Christy.

Lamps were still burning in Jackson's clapboarded cottage. Several men were talking on the front steps; women were in rocking chairs on the porch. Christy would have help tonight.

They told him Christy was in the kitchen. Denton stepped in the back door, and Christy let him in.

His brief — "No luck." — disposed of the long day's ride, and he asked: "What can I do tonight?"

Shadows had gathered under Christy's eyes. But the first shock had passed. She was calm. "I have all the help here I need, Bob. But I won't be able to leave the house much. Doctor Job doesn't know himself what will happen." Christy hesitated. "If you see that the stages run . . . take charge of everything else for us. . . ."

"Don't worry about that, Christy." Denton was silent a moment, looking down at her. "I'd give my right arm if I hadn't taken today off."

"You couldn't suspect there'd be trouble, Bob."

Denton took that thought back with him to his hotel room. But his last thoughts, as he dropped off to sleep, were ominous. This wasn't the end of trouble; this was the beginning.

In the morning he felt no better about it. But there was work to do. Stages had to run. Jackson's business went on. Fred Breckenridge and the rest of his posse returned toward noon, hungry, tired, empty-handed.

Breckenridge had taken his posse ahead on a fast night ride, hoping to come up with the outlaws somewhere around Mc-Closky's Well. It had been a bad guess. They'd found nothing at the well. Their horses had been in bad shape. By morning it had been too late to follow any trail toward the border.

Late in the afternoon Denton was at Henry Jackson's scarred old desk in the back room of the stage station. In the next hour or so stages were due in from the north, from Sun Dance, and from Kingsville on the railroad. Denton was thinking about his first meeting with Christy. He'd been heading toward Oro Grande for the first time, cutting through the mountains to the east. His horse had floundered on a bad spot in the trail. Saddle cinch had broken. Denton had brought up fifty feet down the steep boulder-choked slope below the trail, his ankle broken. The horse had bolted on down the trail, stranding him.

A man could have stayed there a long time before any other rider came along the little-used trail. Hours later Denton had crawled and hopped three miles down toward the lower country. Christy had found him there. She had been riding out in the foothills, had sighted Denton's bridled, saddleless horse, and guessed something was wrong. She had caught his horse and back-trailed the animal.

Denton had ended up in Christy's house in Oro Grande, given hospitality and care by the kind-hearted Jacksons. When he could walk, he had gone to work for Jackson, and he had known how he wanted the future to be shaped.

Now here he was at Jackson's desk, bossing Jackson's affairs. Voices suddenly lifted in excitement in the front room of the station, and out front where more people were gathering to meet the stages.

Denton swung out of the desk chair. Old Shack Mason came in from the waiting room and closed the connecting door again. Shack was excited, too.

"Preacher Clegg jes' found all the stuff that was took off the stage!" Shack exclaimed. "Found it in saddlebags left in his back yard!"

3

"THE LAW LOOKS FOR SIGN"

Denton hoped he looked startled and surprised. "The hell! That doesn't make sense! Left in the open right here in town?"

Old Shack was a wispy-built, stooped-shouldered old-timer. He had been a wild horse hunter and top hand in his better days, until age and stiff joints made him useless for most work. But Shack's mind was still sharp enough. "It's one to figger out," Shack said. He shifted his chewing tobacco to the other cheek. Bloodshot eyes were guileless as they looked at Denton. "Bound to have happened last night. Some feller dropped them saddlebags over the whitewashed fence at the back o' Clegg's lot, an' then eased off."

Denton sat on the desk edge, frowning. "Not much sense to that, Shack. Why hold up the stage, then bring the money back here to town and leave it in the open?"

"Can't figger it a joke," said Shack. "Tryin' to kill a man like Henry ain't a joke. It'll make sense when the truth comes out. Some gent here in town shore knows who shot Henry." Shack stepped over and spat in the sand box beside the desk. He was not looking at Denton. "Some feller in town here looked them killers right in the eye yes'day an' don't aim to admit it."

"The posse scattered out, Shack. Half of them got back after dark."

Shack nodded. "There's gonna be the durndest watchin' of one another you ever seen. Everybody wonderin' if the other feller done it, an' why."

"Fred Breckenridge will find out what happened," said Denton, and wondered if he were speaking more truth than he intended.

"He'll try," Shack agreed grimly. "An' the whole town'll be helpin' him." Shack's glance rested ever so briefly on Denton as Shack turned back to the door. "I'm goin' down the street an' watch Breckenridge bust a gut tryin' to figger it out."

Denton drew a long breath when he was alone again. Shack hadn't mentioned the smear on Denton's pants leg. It was possible he hadn't noticed. It would be Breckenridge's business now.

Stages came and went. At supper, in Chow Loon's Fan Tan Café, there was more interest at counter and tables in the finding of the saddlebags than in the food. Denton sat near the middle of the counter and listened, saying little. He was there when Breckenridge stalked in, showing the strain of his long ride, lack of sleep, and rising temper. Questions were fired at the big deputy.

Breckenridge answered the men nearest him loudly enough to be heard by all. "Don't know any more than the rest of you. But I damned well mean to find out." Breckenridge hadn't come in to eat. He was checking on who was in the place. Thumb hooked in cartridge belt, he let his half scowl rove around the room. "Got my ideas?" he asked. "Take a little time to prove them. Meanwhile, some man in town is guilty as hell. Keep looking for him. He'll break in time."

Breckenridge swung on his heel and walked out. He hadn't singled out Denton by so much as a look, but Denton was thoughtful as he paid for his meal and walked to Jackson's house.

Nothing much had changed there. Christy looked more tired. "At least, Father isn't worse," she said. "It gives some hope." They were out back where Christy had flowers growing, and two shade trees spread leafy masses above. "What do you make of this queer business of the money being returned?" Christy inquired.

Denton wanted to say that he had brought it back, and tell her why, but that, he guessed, would finish everything. He was glad of the first night shadows as he took his time about answering. A man could keep just so much off his face and out of his voice. "Different ideas about it, Christy. But I'd hold to one thing. Whoever dropped that money over Clegg's fence can't be the one who shot your father."

"Why not?"

"That man was trying to right a wrong. The man who fired at Henry wouldn't try to right any wrong. That shot was cold-blooded."

Christy agreed doubtfully. "Someone else in the gang must have had a change of heart." Her emotion came hotly. "I can't forgive any of it. They are all guilty as far as I'm concerned."

Denton had that on his mind a little later when he entered Bull Weather's Palace. The place was noisy as usual in the evenings. There was some dancing. Rita Meyer was at a table with an expansive drummer who had come in on the Kingsville stage.

Denton drank a whisky, then another while they danced once. The drummer joined a man at the bar. Denton went to Rita. "Sit down," he said.

"Don't give me orders now," Rita said coldly, but she sat at an empty table.

Prettier than ever, Denton thought, as he sat across from her. "Leaving town?" he asked.

Rita said deliberately: "No."

"Dick pulling out?"

"Ask Dick." Rita put elbows on the table and bent fingers under her chin. "You fool, Bob. The others won't like losing that money. Dick might not shoot you . . . I don't know. The others . . ." — Rita shook her head — "you don't know who they are, but they'll know you."

He left the Palace with the answers he wanted. Dick and his bunch weren't pulling out. They counted on Denton's keeping quiet because he had to. They'd have him out of the way with a bullet at the first chance. That was the way they worked. Meanwhile, Henry Jackson's business went on.

The town was watching itself, wondering who had dropped the saddlebags over Clegg's fence. Any man was apt to find other men regarding him speculatively.

There was open joshing of one another. But back of it all loomed a gallows.

Denton had his share of it. He agreed good-naturedly he might be the man. Next time he'd keep the money and buy a stage line of his own. He was managing Jackson's business. It was common knowledge Christy liked him as well as she did any man. Perhaps better. How could he have had a hand in shooting her father?

All that could change quickly. Wilson's bunch, Denton finally decided, was his danger. Dick had always been restless, impatient, and eager to get on with the business at hand.

Walt Seymour, the sheriff, had come in on the Kingsville stage, stayed overnight, and returned to the Kingsville courthouse. A veteran lawman, Seymour had a reputation for taking an outlaw trail and hanging onto it. The law must believe at least one man of the hold-up bunch was in Oro Grande. It seemed to be turning into a cat and mouse wait. Something had to happen. It did.

Denton ate breakfast as usual at the Fan Tan Café. The usual morning crowd filled counter and tables with the usual hum of talk and mild clatter of service and eating and men entering and leaving. Denton sat at the front end of the counter. He was putting down the cup of hot black coffee when he glanced out the door and saw a rider with a lead horse slowly entering town from the south.

This was not an unusual sight in Oro Grande. Strangers were constantly passing through. But that short-bearded profile, burly chest, broad shoulders, feet turned out in the stirrups, and lounging, insolent ease in the saddle — that was Big Tex Mallory, back from his girl in San Antone. Big Tex of the booming laugh, wide-set, hard-smiling eyes, club-like fists that could brawl or shoot with equal facility.

Denton had barely started eating. If he left the food and stepped outside now, men eating near him would quickly wonder why. Denton finished breakfast while his foreboding grew. There was no sign of Big Tex or his two horses when Denton walked to the stage station.

Rita was there on one of the benches, in a dark, severely tailored traveling suit, black gloves, and small modest hat. A leather bag rested near her feet. In the severe clothes, Rita could have been one of the most respectable of the younger married women. She was alone in the room, save for old Shack Mason behind the counter, until Tom Colter, the clerk, came to work. Any other early passengers were probably out behind the station watching the stages being readied.

Rita nodded, and Denton said: "Leaving town?"

He saw Mason's morose stare on them, not missing anything. Shack's interest might be the reason Rita acted like a stranger.

"I'm taking the Kingsville stage," Rita said briefly.

Big Tex was on Denton's mind. Shack Mason or not, he had to speak with Rita. "We can sit in my office until the stage is ready," he said, and he saw Shack's mouth open as if to protest, and then close silently.

Rita shrugged, left the leather bag there, and walked in the back room when Denton held the door open. She stopped as Denton followed her in and closed the door.

Denton stopped, too. Christy Jackson was standing by the desk chair, where she had been sitting, waiting. Shack had been about to warn of this and hadn't, and it was not good.

Christy's manner left no doubt that she

knew Rita was one of the Palace girls. Rita turned a glance on Denton, obviously not liking it, either.

"Christy, I didn't know you were in here. How's your father this morning?" That was all Denton could think of to say. He was struck by Christy's pallor, then aware of Christy's sudden flush as she looked at them.

"Father's a little better," Christy said.

Rita might have had a trace of mockery, of satisfaction in her remark. "I'll wait in the other room, Bob."

"Stay here," Christy said, and now Denton knew it was bad.

Bull Weather's girls weren't introduced to girls like Christy, but this was Christy's choosing.

"Miss Jackson . . . Rita Meyer, who's been working at the Palace," Denton said, and felt like he was perspiring.

"I know," Christy said. Her flush was deepening. Rita was looking her over coolly, and Christy didn't like it.

The back door was open to the sun-baked yard where the Kingsville stage was being readied. They heard Tim Calhoun's loud demand that his matched spans be better curried before they went into the oiled, brass-studded harness. Half an hour later the Sun Dance stage would leave, then the northbound stage. Yard and station would be busy until all that was out of the way.

"I came to ask you a question, Bob," Christy said. "Where did you ride the other day when you missed Fred's posse?"

That was the moment Denton laid the future aside, as he had guessed for days he would have to. "I didn't try to find the posse, Christy. For reasons of my own, I rode over into the badlands."

"Alone?"

"I met Miss Meyer out there and rode with her part of the afternoon."

Christy said huskily: "That's what a woman friend suggested last night. You asked about her here in town and followed her and spent the rest of the day with her."

"He could have done worse," Rita said. "Bob, you left a trail, and the gossips sniffed it out. Serves you right."

Christy's voice showed a growing strain. "So it *is* true?" she snapped. "Don't misunderstand me, either of you! I don't care whom Bob Denton rides out with. I don't care what girls he knows. But my father took over Bob's job that day, and may yet die from what happened." Christy was close to stammering. "Any decent man would have tried to hunt the outlaws who shot Father. Bob pretended he was, and rode off to spend the afternoon . . . *that* afternoon . . . with a dance-hall girl!"

Denton broke in harshly: "Stop it, Christy! There's. . . ."

Christy's rushing words cut him off. "I'm stopping everything, Bob. A man who would do that isn't one I want at Father's desk, trusted with his affairs. Pay yourself what money is due you. I'll take charge now."

Denton said: "All right, if that's what you want."

"Why, you fool, Bob," Rita said in a choked voice. "After all the preaching you did to me, you're walking out like this in the end." Rita stepped to Christy. "Bob wouldn't wipe his feet on me," she said. "He knows I've loved another man for years. He used to be that man's friend. What do you know about men, or trust, or what you want? Work the dance halls like I have because your man wants you to. Lie in bed at night and think about the home you'll never have because he doesn't want it. You won't worry then about what the gossips are saying. Why didn't you ask Bob what he was doing out in the badlands the other day? He didn't have to make that ride to see *me*. I've been at the Palace every day."

"Never mind," Denton said, and he doubted that either girl heard him.

That was the moment Fred Breckenridge came in from the waiting room, old Shack Mason at his heels. Somehow Denton wasn't surprised. This all went together.

"Did you have Breckenridge waiting?" Denton asked Christy, and hard, bitter lines at his mouth went in deeply as Breckenridge pulled his gun.

"Shack will take your gun, Denton. Hold easy."

Christy protested. "Fred, what are you doing?" She moved to come between them.

Shack Mason had jerked Denton's gun from its holster and stepped aside. "Kept my mouth shet tight, 'long as I figgered he was a Jackson man," Shack said. "I heerd through the door when you fired him, Miz Christy, an' I stepped out fer the law. Denton's the one dumped them saddlebags over Clegg's fence!"

"Shack! Are you sure?"

"Dern sure, ma'am! I been watchin' him to see what he'd try next. But didn't aim to talk, 'long as he was runnin' things fer you."

"So that's why?" Christy said to Rita, and Rita nodded.

Breckenridge's satisfaction showed dourly on his solid face. It roughened his voice. "Like I thought, Denton. You're one of them. Knew what the stage was carryin' and missed the trip on purpose. Lost your nerve after Henry was shot. Or maybe you got another idea quick. You'd bring the money back and hope folks would forget it, while you got your hands on a lot more, if Henry died. Like that, wasn't it? Had your eye on Christy?"

Thinly out of the rage building again in him Denton said: "Put up the gun and step outside and say it!"

Breckenridge sneered. "Had your chance to tell the law what you knew, Denton, and you didn't. We're stepping out back to the Kingsville stage, before the town gets together for a hanging. Not that I hate a hanging, mister. But Walt Seymour ordered it handled this way."

Denton bit out: "Don't you go to Kingsville. Got reasons not to. Stay in town today . . . trouble's coming . . . probably the bank."

He saw Rita's startled look. Christy had a strange, intent expression.

Breckenridge snapped: "It won't work,

Denton. We're takin' the stage."

"We're not running the Kingsville stage today," Christy said slowly.

The deputy snapped: "Calhoun's out there getting ready to leave!"

"Tim hasn't heard, either," Christy said. "I'll tell him."

"It will run. You're trying to interfere with the law, Christy." Breckenridge exploded. "I won't have that! Not even from you. I'm the law, Christy."

"*I'm* the stage line," Christy said.

"Then I'll take him handcuffed on the bed of a buckboard," Breckenridge said thickly. "Christy, you've been blind ever since you hauled this stranger home. Why, a day after this Meyer girl came to the Palace, Denton had his head close to hers in a booth."

Breckenridge had handcuffs ready. His gun muzzle had stayed steady on Denton's middle. He was sweating with anger as he ordered: "Damn you, Denton, turn around! We're going to Kingsville."

"Watch him, Fred . . . he's dangerous," Christy said sharply.

"All right!" Breckenridge said, and Denton's gun barrel, in old Shack Mason's hand, buffaloed the deputy behind the ear.

Even Bob Denton hadn't noticed how

old Shack had sidled casually into position. Some look must have passed between Shack and Christy, some order to the old man whose loyalty to the Jacksons was known to everyone.

Denton's jump caught the deputy as he sagged down. Denton wanted gun and handcuffs. Breckenridge was out cold. While he let the heavy figure down and snapped handcuffs on one wrist, Denton heard Rita speak to Christy.

"Well, since there's no stage today, I'll go back to my room." She was leaving when Denton clamped compelling fingers on her wrist.

"Stay with us, Rita. What's Wilson planning today?"

Rita tried to break away. "I don't know!"

"Rita, it can't be," Denton said. "You can't warn Dick."

Rita gasped. "I've got to, if he's hitting trouble!"

"Not this time," Denton said. "It's Dick's choosing. I warned him." Denton dragged up the deputy's handcuffed wrist and snapped the steel loop around Rita's wrist. "Sit down beside him, Rita." He caught her other hand as it dipped quickly inside her tailored jacket. "Not the Derringer, either," said Denton, and grabbed the weapon.

Old Shack had closed and bolted the back door. He shuffled over and slid the bolt on the door into the waiting room.

"We've clumb out on a limb an' cut it through," Shack said. "Now where we gonna light?"

Denton asked again: "Rita, you don't know what's planned?"

She shook her head.

"I'm not sure, either," Denton said. "Big Tex is in town with a spare horse." He had his gun back from Shack, and he stripped off the deputy's gun belt and held it and Breckenridge's gun while he looked at Shack. "Can you hold Breckenridge quiet?"

"Fer a little . . . but this is the stage station," Shack reminded. "Whyn't you get some help, mister?"

"Stir up the town and maybe nothing happens," said Denton. "Be all to do over some other time. I may be locked up by then. You, too, and Christy. Breckenridge won't feel kindly after this."

His carbine was leaning in the corner. He caught it up and let himself out the back door. He heard Shack bar the door behind him. Tim Calhoun, shaved, brushed, and elegant as usual, was watching the harnessing of his stage span.

Denton walked to him. "No stage to Kingsville this morning, Tim."

"No stage?" Tim repeated. "Why the hell not?"

"Orders," Denton said, "and none of your damned business, you loud-mouthed Irishman." Denton lowered his voice. Hostlers were near. "If you had a gun on your hip and were standing around on Main Street with your mouth shut, you might get a shot at one of the men who put that lead in Henry Jackson."

"You don't say? Well, I got the shuttest mouth and the standingest feet this side of Kingsville for a chance like that. Where do I stand?"

"Anywhere. Watch any stranger with a lead horse. There's one in town. Might be more by now. Might not all have an extra horse. If you hear trouble, you'll know what it is."

4

"UNDERCOVER MAN"

Denton skirted the stage station, nodding to men already on the benches under the walk canopy. He crossed the dusty street and turned right on the plank walk, six-gun unobtrusively under his coat and the carbine carelessly held by the barrel.

He looked across at the bank on the street corner. The window shades were still pulled down. He looked at his watch. Nine minutes before Oscar Deland would run up the green shades and unlock the front door.

At the end of Main Street, Denton turned around and started back. He was winding tighter inside as his gamble ran thinner. He might have been wrong. He wondered what was happening in the stage station office, wondered if Breckenridge had managed a shout for help. That would be the end. Breckenridge was the law. The town would back him.

Stumpy Giddings, a gnome of a man with pointed chin, red-veined, pointed

229

nose, and a hand-whittled wooden leg, probably the most liked of the town idlers, came stumping along the walk planks.

"What's wrong with the Kingsville stage? It ain't runnin' today," Stumpy demanded, blinking.

"Little change in the schedule," Denton said. Then, to stop more questions: "Seen a bearded stranger with a lead horse?"

"Sure," assented Stump. "He was gittin' a loose shoe on his lead hoss fixed at Stovell's shop. Said he was ridin' to Sun Dance today. Come from Kingsville. I asked. Sure had two fine hosses."

"He might trade for that lead horse, if the dicker was right," Denton speculated, and passed Stumpy the price of two drinks.

Denton crossed the street. Stumpy would string the drinks out for the next hour, not interested in anything else. The blacksmith shop — he should have thought of it! On the side street, a hitch lot on the far side littered with old wagon gear, a stranger at Stovell's would be well out of sight of everyone looking for him.

Big Tex was not at Stovell's. The smith was working his big leather forge bellows in the smoky open-front shed. He had a wagon tie rod in the heat.

"Said he was heading on to Sun Dance," Joe Stovell said. "Had me look at the shoes on both his horses. Said he hated to lose a shoe when he was traveling. Know him?"

"Wanted to look at his lead horse," Denton said.

"A man with horses like that ain't likely to trade when he's travelin'," Stovell said.

"Every man's got a price," Denton judged, turning back to Main Street. It looked like the gamble was lost.

And yet, Sun Dance. What was at Sun Dance to draw that bunch? Nothing that Denton knew of. And Big Tex had had all shoes of his two horses checked. It meant nothing to Stovell. To Denton it suggested Big Tex was carefully making ready for a hard, fast ride. A harder ride, and faster, than he would ever make on a trip to Sun Dance. It didn't sound right, not when you knew Wilson's habits.

Denton crossed Main Street again and passed Hoffstettor's store. Henry Murchison, who owned the hotel, came across the street.

"I was just asking Tim Calhoun why he's not taking the stage out to Kingsville," Henry said. "Had two at my hotel meant to take it. Tim said he was waiting for orders."

"That's right, Henry," Denton said, and left Henry standing there thinking it over.

Denton had the feeling his time was running out. Calhoun had been loitering across the street, and now was moving on the opposite walk as Denton moved back toward the stage station. Their glances met. Tim shook his head. Denton shrugged, and then he reached the bank corner. The green, fly-specked window shades had been run up, the door was open, and several customers were already inside. Denton leaned the carbine against the corner of the bank and rolled a cigarette, unwilling to move on to the stage station, where irritated passengers waited, and Christy and Shack Mason held all the worst of the gamble now.

Standing there, the anger began to eat at Denton again. His cold rage built against Dick Wilson, who had brought all this to Oro Grande. It was then Denton looked up the side street and saw a rider coming toward Main Street with a lead horse. He looked along Main Street beyond the stage station and saw another rider with a lead horse.

He dropped the cigarette and looked across the street where Tim Calhoun had stopped on that corner. He caught Tim's eye and nodded and reached for the carbine and walked into the bank.

This was the pattern Wilson had often talked out. Everything timed to the minute. Come in town from different directions. Get the money and get out before the town knew what was happening.

Oscar Deland, the cashier, was alone behind one of the two wickets in the iron grillwork. Hornsby, the bookkeeper, was either late to work or had stepped out. Miss Finch, the milliner and dressmaker to the best of the town ladies, and the best dance-hall girls too, if truth were admitted, was talking through the wicket. Cal Anderson, the saddle-shop man, waited with some impatience behind her. Dr. Job Reynolds and a rancher were making out deposit slips or checks at the wall desks.

Denton went to Miss Finch's elbow and spoke evenly through the grillwork. "Deland, your bank will be held up in about two minutes. Lock your safe and run before they have guns on you."

Miss Finch gasped. Cal Anderson stood as if uncertain he'd heard right. Oscar Deland's balding head ducked a little.

"Whose going to hold up the bank?" Deland asked loudly.

"The same men who shot Henry Jackson," Denton warned. "Lock up."

Miss Finch squeaked. She was beyond screaming as she snatched up her open bank book and fled.

Cal Anderson blurted: "Damn it, Deland, I got all my savings in this bank! Don't take a chance!"

"Now, now," Oscar Deland soothed.

The front door slammed shut. Miss Finch's cry choked off into a strangled gasp, and the sound was inside the closed door, still in the bank. Denton wheeled around. Miss Finch was fainting as the gunman who had shut the door barred her way with a drawn gun. Denton had never seen the stocky, sandy-mustached fellow before, but Dick Wilson was running with new men now.

Miss Finch and her elaborate hat seemed to sink slowly down out of the way. Actually Miss Finch crumpled fast, but Denton was moving faster. His hand slapped to the hickory handle of his belt gun. No need to think, to plan. He saw what was at the door and knew what had to be done.

Miss Finch and her hat were still going down. The stranger had already pulled his gun. He'd heard Denton's name and knew what to do. He dodged a step over to the right, crouching a little as he saw Denton facing him.

The saddle-shop man and Doc Reynolds were out of it. Denton had forgotten they existed. His target was there at the door. But he heard the saddle-shop owner cry: *"Watch Deland!"*

Denton lunged to the right, also ducking. He heard the roaring report of Deland's revolver behind him. The smash of Deland's bullet in his left shoulder drove him down to a knee. Deland had tried cold-blooded murder from behind. It made many things clear. Denton felt no pain, but he'd never known the great, wild, searing anger that caught at him now. The fury steadied him on one knee. It held him on the target there beside the front door. Deland's second bullet would smash his back. Denton left his back an open target while he drove shots at the man who had stopped Miss Finch. Two shots — one long crash of sound, so fast did the hammer fall.

The fellow must have thought Deland had settled it. He had hesitated. Lead tore through his chest, the second bullet ripping his midsection above the gun belt buckle. It drove him reeling against the doorframe, a dying man — a dead man.

Deland must have thought the shoulder hit was enough. Perhaps Denton's speed in dealing death had shocked the cashier into slowness. Denton was coming around on his knee before Deland fired again. The shot missed and smashed one of the front windows into a cascade of clattering glass.

Through the muzzle vapor of the shot, Denton saw why Deland had missed. Cal Anderson had hurled his bankbook and soiled canvas sack of deposit money squarely into the wicket as Deland had fired.

Oscar Deland's face, still livid behind the grillwork, reflected an awful knowledge as he missed and looked squarely into Denton's face and gun. His record now was clear. He must have known Rita well at the Palace, and told her when the bank was shipping money. When the money was stolen and returned, Deland had worked with Dick Wilson's bunch to clean out the bank this time. When Denton had stepped up with his warning, Deland had made his gamble to help the bunch and leave town with them. He would have broken the bank, the town, the men and women who had trusted him. He was only a cheap sport, greedy for easy money. He'd made his try at a man's back. Now he was through. Oscar Deland must have known it in that instant when his nerve broke and he ducked down behind the counter out of sight. Denton drove the big .45 slugs through the thin, dry wood. One bullet reached the safe front and howled up into the white plaster overhead.

It was only then Denton noticed his left hand had dropped the carbine. Cal Anderson had snatched it up. Levering a shell into place, Anderson kicked open the gate at the end of the counter. His finger on the carbine trigger, Anderson looked and relaxed. He stepped in fast, bent over, and came out with Oscar Deland's revolver.

"Right in the face!" Anderson said loudly.

Denton's left arm was numb and dripping blood as he made the fingers grip his big revolver while he flipped empty shells out and thumbed in more. "More coming!" Denton warned.

He faced the door and saw Dr. Job Reynolds stooping for the big Colt that had landed on the floor beside Miss Finch's hat. The black-coated, pink-cheeked little doctor seemed in no hurry. He had saved lives in the same calm way as he would now methodically take life. But the rush of horses and dust to the front of

the bank was not methodical. It material-
ized outside the broken window in a flurry
of savage action, horses yanked up, men
launching from saddles. One man was Big
Tex, gun in each hand as he lunged across
the walk to the bank door.

There was a back door to the bank.
Denton had forgotten that back door. He
heard gunfire out front. Saw one of the
bunch go down at the edge of the walk.
Saw Big Tex shooting through the door
glass at Doc Reynolds. Saw Anderson
sighting the carbine at the front door.

But Dick Wilson wasn't in sight out
front. Denton's rage was centered on
Wilson who had had his warning. Calhoun
was in action out on the street. Anderson
was triggering the carbine. Reynolds was
staggering away from Miss Finch as
Denton jumped for the gate leading behind the grillwork. He knew as a man
knows destiny that he'd meet Wilson there
by the big safe with its door left open invit-
ingly.

Denton had his instant of regret that
he'd probably never again see Christy. It
had been a great warm, hopeful experi-
ence, knowing her and planning. The ride
Denton had made toward Sun Dance, the
day the stage had been held up, had been

to see about a small brand and a piece of land he'd heard was for sale.

Deland was sprawled in front of the safe — and Dick Wilson was coming through the room at the back. Wilson came in a snake-like dart, a gun in each hand blasting lead across the front of the safe before Dick's body showed fully. Any man standing there would have been cut down. Deland would have, and that would have suited Wilson, too. Wilson could see beyond the grillwork as he jumped to the front of the safe. His storm of lead was for any man standing where Denton had stood.

There was one thing Wilson couldn't see. The big safe door was open, and Denton had stepped behind it. Wilson stopped shooting. Denton stepped out fast.

Wilson hadn't expected it. His wide mouth was slightly parted in the gaunt, dark-tanned face. His gun hammers were down. The base of his high-bridged nose flared out, and Wilson's wide mouth went ugly. Neither spoke a word. They knew. Wilson's thumbs violently hooked the gun hammers back, but Denton's gun was already cocked. Dick Wilson died standing, heart shattered as he bent back, back, his guns slanting up and discharging high in his last movement on earth. There was a man behind Wilson, who saw Dick falling back past the corner of the safe. That one had enough right there and bolted back out the rear of the bank.

Denton let him go. The great rage was fading. He saw, without much interest now, that Big Tex never had gotten inside the bank. The street was in an uproar, shots still pounding out there. Tim Calhoun's gun had roused the town. Oro Grande would take care of the rest of it. Denton dropped his bloody left arm on the counter, above Oscar Deland's money drawer, and leaned wearily there, looking down at Dick Wilson. In the old days Dick would have stayed with him. He stayed with Dick now for a little, until Doc Reynolds ordered him to his office.

Reynolds had been creased hard in the side and was loudly profane that a little blood and a cracked rib were all in the day's work. But if Denton didn't get to the doc's office and get the bleeding stopped, no telling what. Denton went.

Christy, with Rita Meyer at her side, found him in the doctor's smelly office, shirt off, while Doc worked on the shoulder.

Rita said: "I knew it would happen. I've known for a long time it was going to happen. You convinced me, Bob. I was walking out on Dick today . . . for good."

"I wondered," Denton said.

"But you can't ever walk out on it, can you?" Rita said in a leaden voice. "You walk away and it walks with you." Rita bit her lip hard. "Good luck, Bob."

"Why, yes," Denton said. Rita was walking out. Christy stayed. Denton looked up at her, and gritted his teeth against Doc's probing, then Denton smiled. "You never did ask me what I was doing the day I took off and the stage was held up," he reminded.

Christy said: "I'm never going to, Bob. That's your business."

"Our business," Denton said. "You see, I wanted to settle here for good. . . ." Denton paused, thinking about it, and, when he looked up, he saw that Christy knew and had probably guessed the rest. He grinned and reached for Christy's hand.

Ride to Glory

The first Western story T. T. Flynn wrote in 1935 was completed on March 5th and sent off to his agent. It was written in the Chrysler Airstream trailer in which he and his wife Helen now traveled. His title for it was "Ride and Fight". It was quickly bought by editor Rogers Terrill of Popular Publications, Inc., for $500.00, and it appeared as the lead story in the July, 1935 issue of *Star Western* under the title "Three Outlaws Ride to Glory". For its first appearance in book form this title has been somewhat modified.

1

"AFTER THE TRIAL"

The dim, shabby courtroom in old Santa Fé was crowded when the jury went out at fifteen minutes past four. Judge Strong did not adjourn court. He remained seated in the high-backed, leather-padded chair behind the desk, as if expecting a quick verdict.

Dan McNeil, handcuffed, with the armed Mexican-American deputy, Gomez, standing beside him, remained seated in the plain wooden chair he had occupied all day during the trial.

The slow minutes dragged past. The oil ceiling lamps were lighted. Some of the crowd left; others came in and took their places. Old friends of the judge drifted up and visited with him. The prosecuting attorney and Lewis, Dan's fat lawyer, argued amiably.

Now that the trial was over, calm had settled over the courtroom, but it was an assured, expectant calm, Dan thought bitterly. You could feel the certainty that kept the spectators from leaving to eat, and held

Judge Strong there at the bench. They all knew — the judge, the crowd, the lawyers, and Dan McNeil himself — that the result was a foregone conclusion. Life paused here for a bit in this grimy courtroom while everyone waited.

It happened as Dan knew it would happen. The bailiff hurried in, whispered something to the judge, who abruptly terminated his conversation with some friends and rapped for order. The jury filed in.

Eight of those jurors were Mexican-Americans. Not that it mattered. Twelve good Anglos would probably have reasoned the same way. When the jury was seated, Judge Strong looked at them sternly over his spectacles and pursed large lips under his ragged gray mustache. He cleared his throat.

"Gentlemen, have you reached a verdict?" he questioned gruffly.

Which, thought Dan wryly, was funny, considering that half the jury couldn't understand English. Every word spoken during the trial had been translated into Spanish and English so that all the jury could understand it.

The jury foreman was a rancher named Dougherty. He drawled his answer complacently: "Yep, I reckon we have, Your Honor."

"What is it?"

"He's guilty, an' we hope you hang him quick."

The courtroom echoed with laughter as Dougherty sat down with a grin of satisfaction. Judge Strong testily rapped for order.

"The court," he informed Dougherty severely, "will decide what sentence is to be passed. All the jury had to do was to find him guilty."

"Well, we done it," Dougherty said, grinning.

Judge Strong motioned to the deputy, Gomez, at Dan's side, and reached for a glass of water with his other hand.

"Stand up," Gomez said. He was lumpy and stolid and filled with a sense of his own importance here in the public eye.

Dan was already getting to his feet. He stepped over before the judge's bench and smiled crookedly. "Let's have it, so you can get out to that rye whisky you've been itchin' for," he said. "That water'll rust your innards." He spoke without bitterness, but he hadn't liked the man since he first saw him.

Judge Strong was a bit too red in the nose, flabby in the cheeks, thick about the loose mouth. His little eyes, peering over gold-rimmed spectacles, had no friendliness and little understanding. It was common knowledge in New Mexico Territory that Strong liked his liquor. But Dan was suddenly tired of the crowd. He wanted to get out of the courtroom and be alone.

Several hoarse snickers sounded. Judge Strong glared over the room, and then glared at Dan. "That'll be enough from you, McNeil! Stand up and get your sentence!"

"I'm standin' up. I've got my sentence already, I reckon. If it'll make you feel any better to put it into words, go ahead."

Dan was twenty-three. Gomez, the deputy, was not a tall man, yet he stood half an inch higher than Dan. The resemblance ended there. Gomez was dark-skinned and inclined to fat. Dan was beef and whipcord. The hot southwest sun had not been able to tan his blondness away. Dan's face was weather-beaten, but there were freckles where another man would have tanned deeper. He had managed to get himself shaved and buy a new shirt before the day in court. But ten days in jail had not made the rest of his clothes look any better.

Judge Strong leaned forward. "Daniel McNeil, the jury having found you guilty, as charged, the sentence of the court is that you shall be taken out into the jail yard some time between noon and sunset tomorrow and hanged by the neck until you are dead!" *Bang!* went the judge's gavel. "Court's adjourned!"

Judge Strong left the bench hurriedly. A babble of talk filled the courtroom. Strong had delivered one of the surprises for which he was notorious. No condemned man for years had been sentenced to be hanged so quickly.

Gomez clapped a hand on Dan's shoulder. His black mustache looked fierce, his voice was truculent, warning. "You come now, McNeil, an' don' make no trouble. Onderstan'?"

Smiling, Dan faced the deputy with a look of wintry aversion. "I'm comin', but take your hand off my shoulder. I don't like you pawin' me. *Savvy?*"

Gomez hastily jerked the hand away, then realized what he had done and was angry. He caught Dan's elbow gingerly. "W'at you theenk you do now, McNeil . . . run thees courtroom an' ev'thing?"

He got no reply. Dan ignored his hand on his elbow. Quarreling with a cheap *po-*

litico like Gomez wouldn't do any good.

They walked through the quick coolness of evening to the jail. Gomez got the keys from the jailer and slammed the barred cell door and locked it. He lingered outside the bars, showing bad teeth in a grin of derision.

"Well, *pendejo*, thees time they get you plenty, huh? That neck . . . she stretch long way when they hang you, no?"

Dan grinned also, which was the last thing Gomez wanted him to do. "Lookin' at it thataway, mebbe so," Dan agreed amicably. "It's been a good neck. It oughta have lots of stretch. But a Mex chili picker like you oughtn't to strain what little brain he's got about such things. Run along, *cabrón*, an' tell that lazy jailer I'm hungry . . . an' don't forget an' grab an apron an' start cleaning dishes in the kitchen. It must be mighty hard to keep pretendin' you're a deputy instead of a dishwasher."

Gomez left, swearing under his breath in Spanish. A dishwasher before a turn of politics and the right relatives had outfitted him with a deputy's badge and a gun, Gomez didn't like to be reminded of his past.

Dan chuckled, rolled a cigarette, stretched out on the bare hard cot until the jailer brought supper on a tin plate. The bread, *frijoles,* and meat were no better or worse than they had been the last ten days.

Handcuffs off, Dan finished the food, rolled another cigarette, and fell to pacing the cramped cell. It was three steps forward — three back — with thoughts turning over and over.

At first it hadn't seemed possible — but here it was, a fact. A queer, twisted, painful fact that Dan might have known lurked in the dim future. A man might be resigned to its happening — someday, but when it actually happened, it was different.

He was young yet. The world had been pretty nice. Perhaps he hadn't been everything he should have been. The West was big. There had been a lot of ground to cover, a lot of things to do. Some men were hard, some soft — but most of them were hard. You had to take them as you found them. Too often it was a problem of getting a gun out first, shooting fastest — straightest. The law usually was far away, nebulous. When it caught up with you, the things you had done sounded different in a courtroom.

So thinking, Dan paced the cell. There was so much to think about, and so little time to do it in. There'd be no reprieve, of course. No use thinking about that. Tomorrow the scaffold — and the end.

A door slammed. Steps approached. Gomez appeared outside the bars once more. Dan regarded the deputy with disgust.

"You back again, Gomez? Thought I was through with you for tonight. They must be turning this jail into a hog pen."

Once more Gomez cursed him in Spanish and drew a revolver. Dan eyed him narrowly, not knowing what would happen. Gomez would be glad to shoot him. But the Mexican-American jailer came up behind Gomez, carrying a pair of handcuffs. He unlocked the door, and Gomez growled: "Come out with your wrists ready, McNeil. The governor . . . he want you. I must waste my time taking you to the palace." And as the handcuffs clicked on Dan's wrists, Gomez spat and grumbled: "I don' see why the governor bother with you. Tomorrow they hang you. That ees enough. Come on!" Gomez yanked on the handcuffs.

2

"DOUBLE-CROSS PROPOSITION"

Gomez was surly as they walked through the night. But he was careful, too. Not for an instant did he take the muzzle of his big Colt out of Dan's back. Rather at every excuse he pushed it in, gouging roughly.

"Go easy with that gun, Gomez!" Dan finally snapped. "I ain't aimin' to run out on you. Ain't you got sense enough to see I'm handcuffed?"

Gomez gouged with the gun again, keeping hold of Dan's arm with the other hand.

"How do I know w'at you do, *gringo?* You escape queeck, if you have one chance. I know."

"Not until I see the governor," Dan said. "Maybe he's got an idea or two about this hangin' tomorrow. I've heard he's all puffed up with his own idea of how big a man he is . . . but he's still got a chance to do something about that rope tomorrow."

The idea seemed to infuriate Gomez. He muttered to himself, swore under his breath, and finally delivered his judgment with a growl. "The governor don't give one damn about you, *gringo*. Tomorrow the governor . . . he drives to Taos. He only wants a look at you now before he goes."

And that, Dan thought, might be nearer the truth than Gomez really knew. The governor had no interest in Dan McNeil, outlaw. There wasn't a chance that the governor had any idea of interfering with the hanging. But still — what did the governor want?

Around the old plaza, saloons were lighted and doing brisk business. Horses were tied at hitch racks and wagons waited for owners who lingered among the lights and entertainment of Santa Fé as long as possible before hitting the trail for the wild country from which they might not return for weeks and months.

Long, low, massive, the governor's palace filled the north side of the plaza. Two hundred and fifty years it had stood there. About the old building clung a sense of permanence one could feel even in the darkness.

The territorial governor occupying the palace now had been appointed from Washington — but his predecessors for centuries had been appointed by the kings of Spain. From that massive-walled adobe building captain-generals of the Spanish crown had ruled from the *Llano Estacado* to the Pacific mountains.

Every time Dan had ever passed the palace he had thought of those haughty, fearless soldiers of old Spain who, never numbering more than a handful, had conquered a great wilderness. Mighty deeds, great decisions had been made and done in that old building to which the deputy now took him. And it was hard to believe that the Yankee successor of those old dons could be concerning himself with a mere hanging that had been ordered by a legal court of the territory.

Gomez and his prisoner evidently were expected. A tall, sour-faced secretary with a red mustache led them back to one of the rear rooms of the palace.

"Here's the man you wanted to see, governor," he announced. "Shall I . . . er . . . wait?"

The governor got up from an easy chair, closing a book he had been reading. "Yes, you'd better wait, Cummins," he said in a rasping voice.

Dan understood he was regarded as a desperate prisoner. The governor did not feel any too comfortable at being alone

with him. The idea made him smile crookedly.

The governor was a big man, inclined to
be paunchy, running to loose jowls on
which Eastern pallor lingered despite two
years of the Western sun. Frowning, the
governor looked Dan over.

"You're McNeil, I understand," he said.
"I believe Judge Strong sentenced you to
hang tomorrow?"

"If I heard him right, he did," Dan
agreed.

The governor's frown deepened. He
seemed to feel levity was out of place.
"Your case has been brought to my attention, McNeil," he said with a trace of pom-
posity. "It is my opinion that you deserve
to hang."

"Did you bring me over here to tell me
that?" Dan asked disagreeably. "It don't
matter a damn to me what your opinion is,
Governor. You run your job . . . an' I'll
hang."

The governor's lifted hand looked soft
and puffy. "Just a minute, McNeil," he said
quietly. "I want to help you, if you'll let
me."

"Go ahead and help me," Dan invited.

"I expect your help in return, McNeil."

"Huh . . . I figured there was a catch.

What kind of help?"

"Just this, McNeil. You have run with the Rigby-Costillo gang for the past two years, helping to terrorize the entire southern part of the territory. I have had trouble with the lot of you ever since I have been in office here."

Dan laughed. "I'll bet you have. If you had men instead of rabbits like Gomez, here, you might have gotten somewhere. But there ain't a man with Costillo and Rigby who can't lick half a dozen like Gomez."

Gomez glowered and jammed his gun in Dan's back. The governor frowned, also.

"I didn't bring you here for talk like that, McNeil. You were caught on your way here to Santa Fé and I . . . *umph* . . . have no doubt the court gave you exactly what you deserve. But I can use your assistance, so I'm going to make you an offer."

"Let's have it," Dan invited shortly.

"Help me to round up the Rigby-Costillo band and I'll give you a pardon on your promise to leave the territory and stay out of it, McNeil."

Dan laughed. "I wondered if you weren't sneakin' up to somethin' like that. You've been a *politico* too long, Governor. You're talkin' to a man now. I'll hang half a dozen times before you get any help like that outta me."

The governor reddened. "They are outlaws, McNeil. You'll be doing the territory a service."

"And what'll the territory be doing for me?" Dan snapped. "I started to Santa Fé a man, an' I'll stay one, if I have to take a noose around my neck to do it. What if Costillo an' Rigby are outlaws? Who made 'em that way?" His voice was rising in cold anger. "I'll tell you! *Politicos* and so-called law-abidin' citizens," Dan went on. "Rigby and Costillo were crooked every way they turned. I was a top hand for 'em while it was goin' on, an' I know what I'm talkin' about. I got the edge shot out of my left ear one night while I was still herdin' cows for 'em. We all throwed in together after that . . . and we've done pretty well, I reckon you know."

The governor controlled his temper with a visible effort. "I'm not interested in Rigby's and Costillo's background. The territory has courts to which they could have applied for relief, instead of taking the law into their own hands. They have been outlaws ever since I was appointed governor . . . and, as far as I'm concerned, that is all they are. It is my duty to round them up . . . and I'm going to do it before I leave office."

"Not with my help, Governor."

The red-mustached secretary sidled over and said something in a low tone to the governor, who nodded and pursed his lips as he turned to Dan. "I wonder, McNeil, if you are aware that Rigby and Costillo sent word to Santa Fé that you were coming here? Those men are not your friends. They want you out of the way . . . and the easiest and most plausible manner was to turn you over to the law. Do you know that?"

Dan eyed the governor narrowly. All that was too close to the truth to have been made up on the spur of the moment. None of it had even been put into words among the men who followed Jake Rigby and Juan Costillo. It couldn't have been known here at Santa Fé. But it *was* known. How did the governor, Dan asked himself, know of the friction that had been slowly growing between Costillo, Rigby, and himself? Rigby had been drinking heavily the past year. Costillo was a jealous man — and a poor shot. Too often Dan himself had put in the right word, done the right thing. It had been getting so the men looked to Dan, instead of Rigby or Costillo, when decisions were to be made.

More than once Rigby had growled sur-
lily when he noticed it. Costillo had never
said anything — while his eyes missed
nothing. But all that had been under the
surface, never out in the open. Too many
hands were against them all. The various
rewards offered, dead or alive, were growing
too large. They *had* to trust one another.
Neither Rigby nor Costillo would have
dared to send one of their men into a trap.

Or — would they? Dan began to wonder.
The sheriff and his deputies had appeared
too suddenly at that ranch house near
Galisteo for it to have been an accident.
Until this moment Dan had thought old
Gonzalez at the ranch had decided the re-
ward money was worth more than the
friendship of the Rigby-Costillo men. Evidently it hadn't been that way. The surprise Gonzalez had shown when the
sheriff's men had appeared had not been
pretense.

But Dan's answer to the governor's offer
was a shrug. "You missed fire on that one,
Governor. Nobody tipped the sheriff off.
He was just lucky. If you're aimin' to make
me mad enough to double-cross the boys,
you ain't gettin' anywhere. I'll take the
hangin'."

The governor lost his temper then. "You're a fool, McNeil!" he exploded.

"Maybe, but I'll stay a fool."

"This is the last chance you'll get. I'm leaving town early in the morning. I won't be here if you change your mind."

"Drive right on out tonight," Dan invited. "I'm ready to hang."

"You'll hang then!" the governor said angrily. "I've done all I can for you." He turned to his men. "Take him back to jail."

The governor swung to his chair and his book, breathing hard with righteous indignation. The secretary shrugged, stepped to the door.

Gomez caught Dan's arm and swung him around. "Come along," Gomez ordered, grinning with satisfaction. "Back to the jail weeth you, *hombre*."

"Back to jail?" said Dan McNeil. "Sure. Take me . . . if you can."

With a quick jerk he freed his arm and crashed the steel handcuffs squarely across Gomez's eyes.

3

"ESCAPE TO TREACHERY"

The deputy's howl of pain filled the room. The gun blasted an instant later. But Gomez shot at the spot where Dan had been — and Dan was not there. The bullet just missed the red-mustached secretary and buried itself harmlessly in the adobe wall. Blood was running into Gomez's eyes. He was staggering blindly when Dan leaped back at him and grabbed the gun with handcuffed hands and tore it away.

The secretary bolted out the door to safety, shouting in alarm. The governor dashed toward the other end of the room, dropping his book and knocking over a chair.

Gomez backed off, swiping at the blood in his eyes, bawling: "Don't shoot! *Jesús, María* . . . I am blind!"

But Dan fired a shot into the floor and ran out into the hall, holding the gun between his hands. The secretary vanished into the nearest doorway as he appeared.

Two men had paused outside the front

hall door, which opened on the plaza. The secretary had reached the plaza by some other door and was shouting for help. Dan fired at the two men who were peering in. They vanished. Escape by the plaza was cut off. At the back of the hall was another door. He lifted the latch and stepped through, finding himself in a rear patio.

Overhead the moon was bright. The patio was deserted. Over the low palace drifted shouts from the plaza. Everyone within hearing was running to the front of the palace. But here in the patio, which ran the full length of the palace, quiet lingered.

Along the back of the patio was a row of rooms. A Mexican servant woman looked out of one door, saw him standing there in the moonlight with a gun, and screamed and slammed the door.

The ends of the patio were enclosed by high adobe walls, pierced by solid wooden gates. Dan ran to the east gate. It was fastened by a heavy wooden bar on the inside. He lifted the bar, slid it back, waited a moment as someone ran past outside toward the front of the palace, then opened the gate cautiously, and stepped out.

All the excitement was still at the front of the palace. He could see men running across the end of the plaza toward the scene of the trouble. Turning his back on all that, Dan shoved Gomez's revolver down inside his belt and walked briskly north, away from it.

In the next block he was lucky enough to find a saddle horse standing before a house. It looked like a good horse. No one saw him swing clumsily into the saddle. But he had not ridden two hundred yards north before a shout behind him, and light streaming from an open house door, warned that the loss of the horse had been discovered. Yet he still had a chance, for no other horses had been at the spot. Some minutes would pass before pursuit could be started. By that time he would be out of sight.

Riding hard, Dan turned to the east among the first low hills north of town, fol- lowing up the dry sandy bed of an arroyo. They would pick up his tracks, of course, but they wouldn't be sure where he was heading, and even in the moonlight he could make faster time than those who would be trailing him.

Keeping to the arroyos, showing himself only briefly on the juniper-cloaked ridges as he crossed them, he circled the eastern edge of town, crossed the narrow, brawling width of the Santa Fé River, left its shallow cañon behind, and rode hard up a narrow valley that cut into the south. He passed a few adobe houses on the outskirts of town, rode past walking men, but they did not know what had happened — and they did not molest him.

Miles south of Santa Fé Dan rode out of the heavily wooded foothills and struck across rolling land covered with patches of piñon trees interspersed with stretches of grass. As yet there had been no sign of pursuit. He crossed the Santa Fé railroad below Lamey Junction some time before midnight.

Not long after that he topped a ridge and looked down to the adobe ranch buildings of old Diego Gonzalez, an uncle of Juan Costillo's. Juan Costillo's uncle! Dan hadn't thought of it that way until the governor spoke of treachery. Blood was thicker than water. It would have been mighty simple for Costillo to send word ahead that Dan McNeil was coming that way and stopping at the ranch house — and easy enough for old Gonzalez to get word to the sheriff.

The horse had traveled fast from Santa Fé. It was about ridden out for the night and wanted water badly. Dan had to spur it through the shallow stream running beside the cottonwoods. Half a dozen dogs burst into full cry as he rode to the door of the ranch house, and, when he dismounted, the door opened. Old Gonzalez stood there against the lamplight inside, peering to see who it was.

The old man's surprise was very near dismay, as Dan loomed up before him. Gonzalez spoke in Spanish, for he knew no English.

"*¡Dios!* How do you come here, *Señor* McNeil?"

Gonzalez stammered it. His hands suddenly began to shake as Dan whipped out the gun. Gonzalez looked guilty and afraid in that moment when he was caught off guard.

Dan smiled thinly at him. "Surprised, aren't you?" he said in Spanish. "Get back in there, you old wolf. I'm coming inside. Keep your hands out where I can see them. We won't have any more surprises around here."

In the low-ceilinged room lighted by a single oil lamp clustered eight or nine of the Gonzalez tribe. The old grandmother, the wife who looked almost as old, children, boys and girls, and a young woman who was the wife of Gonzalez's oldest son. The old grandmother crossed herself at sight of the gun and began to mumble prayers under her breath. All the older ones looked guilty and frightened. Dan knew, as he kicked the door shut with a heel and surveyed them, that the governor had been right. Costillo had betrayed him — and undoubtedly Rigby knew all about it.

"Where's your oldest son?" Dan asked curtly.

Gonzalez stammered again in answering, while his eyes watched the gun in fascination. "He is in Galisteo, *señor*. What has happened? I do not understand. Why do you come into my house with a gun in your hand?"

"Did you figure I'd come here without one after getting caught once?" Dan rasped.

Old Gonzalez raised his hands and turned pious eyes up to the grimy logs supporting the low ceiling.

"You are wrong, *señor!*" he swore. "As the good God is my witness, I know nothing of that. I sent word to my nephew at once, telling him what had happened. I have been waiting for him to come himself. Have you not heard from him in Santa Fé?"

Dan spat on the floor in disgust. "If I'd

stayed in Santa Fé until I was as old and ugly as you are, *pelado*, I wouldn't have heard from that double-crossing nephew of yours. I know what happened. Don't try to lie out of it. I want a fresh horse and saddle, and this handcuff chain busted in two. Jump quick, damn you! An' don't start wondering what you can do about it. If any of this brood of yours tries to slip over to Galisteo and get help, I'll put a bullet in *you!* Savvy?"

Gonzalez crossed himself hastily. "*Sí, señor.*"

The old man turned on his family and spoke to them fiercely. "All of you stay in this room."

While Dan stood watchfully with the gun, Gonzalez picked up an oil lantern from the corner and scratched a match. His hand shook as he lighted the wick.

"This way, *señor*," he said meekly, moving to the door.

From a woodpile back of the house Gonzalez picked up an axe. In a little shed at one side he got a small sledge. A wagon stood nearby.

"Use the wagon tire," Dan ordered.

Gonzalez understood exactly what was to be done. He put the lantern on the wagon seat. Dan stretched the handcuff chain across the iron wagon tire. Gonzalez laid the axe blade across one of the links, gripped the sledge near the heavy head with the other hand, and swung carefully.

Before the little link parted, the axe blade was ruined and Gonzalez was almost in a state of collapse. With the broken links swinging against his hand, Dan prodded the old man with the gun.

"Now the horse," he ordered.

"In the corral, *señor*. But my horses are poor. They are not fit for a long ride. Your own horse is much better."

"My horse is damned near foundered. Jump fast, you old wolf, and get your saddle on the best horse you've got."

Gonzalez argued no more. While Dan held the lantern, the old man lugged a saddle out of the shed, took a rope, entered the corral, and a few moments later led forth a long-legged, rangy black that looked as if it had plenty of endurance.

Dan held the lantern high and inspected the horse. "Good enough," he decided. "Slap the saddle on him."

When Gonzalez had done that, Dan tested the cinches. The back one was too loose.

"Tighten this one up," he ordered.

While Gonzalez was hastily obeying, the

horse suddenly lifted its head and looked into the north. It had detected something of which they were not aware. But from the north could only be coming riders from Santa Fé at this time of the night.

"Hurry up with that cinch!" Dan snapped.

A moment later a shift in the wind brought the fast roll of hoofs. The riders were nearer than he had supposed, riding hard as if certain he had headed here for his first stop. Dan shoved Gonzalez's fumbling hands away from the cinch, finished the job himself, caught the reins, and swung into the saddle.

"Tell them to return the horse I borrowed in Santa Fé!" he called.

Leaving Gonzalez standing there beside the lantern, Dan slashed hard with the reins and raced past the ranch house into the south once more.

He was galloping up the long grassy slope beyond the ranch house when the first riders reached Gonzalez. Looking back, Dan saw them milling around the faint spot of lantern light, and a moment later he heard them yelling. A rifle cracked thinly back there. A bullet whined viciously through the night nearby. Leaning forward in the saddle, Dan rode hard for the top of the slope.

The posse followed, firing from the saddle, but even if visible in the moonlight, Dan made a poor target at that distance. Lead whined close, some of it too close for comfort, but he was still unhit as he passed over the slope and out of sight.

A last look behind gave him a glimpse of the posse stringing out along the slope as each man rode hard to get within gunshot. But their horses were tired, and Dan was freshly mounted. He drew steadily away until only two of the pursuers, mounted better than the rest, hung on tenaciously. Lead from their guns shrilled close more than once — but presently piñon and juniper became thicker and the posse's shots stopped.

Miles farther on, when Dan McNeil stopped and looked back, he found himself alone in the night.

4

"BACK WITH THE WILD BUNCH"

Four days later a different horse, a claybank roan mare, threaded its way through the pine-blanketed high country south of the Ruidoso. To the east, far down in the lowlands, was the smiling valley of the Pecos. To the south lay the unmapped depths of the Guadalupes.

Few men ever ventured into the heart of the Guadalupes. An occasional prowling Apache, a bolder prospector than the ordinary, men who had taken the Outlaw Trail were all one would find in that country to the south into which Dan McNeil boldly rode. The long miles behind him to Santa Fé had been hard and dangerous. Twice Dan had engaged in running gunfights. The governor evidently had stirred himself and aroused the various sheriffs. Posses had been scouring the country through which he had been forced to pass. But all that lay behind. Ahead was a familiar wilderness where posses did not ride and friends waited.

Where Jake Rigby and Juan Costillo waited.

The pines were thinning out. Cactus and Spanish bayonet were beginning to dot the gravelly slopes and cling to the sides of deep, frowning cañons as the sun touched the horizon and quickly dropped from sight. Dan struck a narrow trail and angled off to the west. Fresh hoof marks and signs showed that the trail had been only recently used. He rode along it, lounging at an angle in the saddle and smoking contentedly. This was home ground. He was almost there.

Black night, before the rise of the moon, lay thick about him when the trail dropped precipitously and tortuously down the almost vertical slope of a deep, narrow cañon and twisted up the other side. This was the only crossing of the cañon for many miles each way, and, as Dan expected, he was gruffly hailed before he reached the crest on the other side.

"Hold up there! Who is it?"

"Dan McNeil!"

"Pull yore hoss back! You ain't Dan McNeil!" the voice hailed him from some invisible spot in the rocks above.

Dan laughed. "Don't go tellin' me who I am, Pete Canfield!" he called. "I reckon I oughta know."

The man above him whooped with delight. Small rocks cascaded down the steep slope as he rushed recklessly to the head of the trail. "I'm a ory-eyed sidewinder! We heered yuh was hung, Dan!" Pete Canfield found Dan's hand in the darkness and wrung it enthusiastically. "Costillo come back from Carlsbad with thet news. They had yuh in jail in Santa Fé an' was fixin' to hang yuh the next day. It caught us with our britches off, an' there wasn't nothin' we could do about it. Jake Rigby cussed fer half an hour straight an' was all fer takin' the boys up to Santa Fé an' cleanin' the place out."

"Rigby an' Costillo took it hard, did they?" Dan asked.

Canfield spat in the darkness and sobered somewhat. His voice was guarded as he answered. "You might say they sounded thataway. Was there any especial reason yuh asked that, Dan?"

"Nothin' to talk about right now. Everybody up to camp?"

"Everybody. There's visitors." Canfield spat again. "Leacock and Colby."

Dan had swung down from the saddle and was stretching himself. He turned quickly to Canfield. His voice was sharp with unbelief. "Leacock and Colby? From the Running-J and the Rafter-L?"

"Bull's eye," said Canfield.

"What in the devil are Rigby and Costillo cooking up?" Dan exploded. "A year ago Leacock was going to have us run out of this country if it took every dollar he had."

Pete Canfield grunted. "I ain't sure what they're doin' here . . . but Rigby give out word to let 'em by if they showed up. An' a couple hours ago they came by, an' I let 'em pass. I reckon you'll get the straight of it when you get to camp. How in tarnation'd you get away from that noose?"

Dan swung up into the saddle. "Tell you about it later, Pete. I want to get into camp and see what Leacock and Colby have got in mind."

"An' I'll rest easier fer you doin' it," Canfield confessed. "I been powerful uneasy ever since I let 'em pass. 'Tain't right them two jaspers bein' here so friendly. No, sir, 'tain't right a-tall." As Dan started on along the trail, Pete Canfield called after him: "Anything yuh makes up yore mind about, goes double with me, Dan! An' there's more of the boys'll say the same thing!"

"Thanks, Pete. I'll bear that in mind."

The day had been long and hard, the days and nights before it harder, but Dan felt no weariness as he urged the roan along the narrow trail at a faster pace. He had come looking for trouble, but he had not expected it to take the turn it had. His way led a full mile farther, and then the trail made an abrupt turn and the glow of a leaping campfire pushed back the darkness some hundreds of yards ahead of him.

As he came closer, the bulk of low adobe huts became visible. The huts were clustered haphazardly about a two-acre space surrounding the campfire. Set together in a hollow square they would have made a small fort that would have been formidable against any posse which came against it. But on the other hand a fort could be surrounded and starved out. Here on the high, windswept, open space, the Rigby-Costillo men rested but ready at any moment of the day or night to take saddle and ride. That was the way they lived. Ride and fight — never get cornered — keep on the move. The few possible ways to get to this isolated spot were all covered when they were in camp. A distant warning gunshot was enough to send them into the saddle ready for action. By such methods they had kept safe and prosperous.

Tonight every man seemed to be gathered outside around the fire. There were between fifteen and twenty of them, all men Dan had eaten with, ridden with, fought beside. All but two — and, as he rode up, he picked them out in the firelight. Leacock and Colby were standing with Jake Rigby and Juan Costillo.

They heard him coming. Heads turned, staring. Men who had been squatting came to their feet. But there was no alarm. One lone horseman riding at a trot could not be bringing danger.

Shorty Pyle was the first to recognize him. Shorty's startled shout rang out. "My Gawd . . . it's Dan McNeil!"

Shorty jerked out one of his six-guns and emptied it into the air. Pandemonium broke loose as others did the same.

Dan was grinning as he rode through them and reined in before the four men who were not joining in the vociferous welcome. The grin grew cold as Dan swung down and faced the four. Jake Rigby and Juan Costillo had been standing there with their jaws dropping. They looked like men who had suddenly been paralyzed with astonishment.

Long Tom Taylor grabbed Dan's arm, yelling: "Lemme see if he's a ghost or ain't! *He ain't!* It's the son-of-a-gun hisself! Where'd you come from, Dan? We figgered you was planted in the ground days ago!"

They packed around him, shaking his hands, slapping his back. Something went tight in Dan McNeil's throat for a minute. A hard-bitten lot, this bunch around him, they were men who had killed and would kill again. Wanted by the law, most of them had prices on their heads. But he was one of them, he understood them, and they were glad to see him. That is, most of them were glad, although here and there a man hung back silently.

Dan answered Long Tom Taylor. "The governor called me over for a talk, Tom, an' I walked out on him. The more I thought about that rope the more my feet began itchin' to travel."

Long Tom guffawed. "Was you shore enough talkin' to the governor when you busted out?"

"I was doin' that very thing, Tom."

Juan Costillo broke in softly. "What were you talking to the governor about, McNeil?"

Costillo was a slender, wiry man, dark with three-quarters Mexican in his blood, soft with Spanish courtesy, handsome with a black mustache — and his bright black eyes more than once in the past year had reminded Dan of a poised rattler

278

watching, and waiting.

Dan smiled at Costillo now. Only a man with guilt in his heart would have sensed how cold that smile was. *"Amigo,"* said Dan, "the governor sent for me to have a little powwow."

"Ahh," Costillo breathed softly. He continued to smile, too, but his eyes wandered away, and he did not press the matter.

But Jake Rigby did, in his harsh, blundering way. "What'n blue-blazes did that old coot have tuh talk about, McNeil? You was gonna hang, wasn't you? An' he damn' well wasn't givin' yuh a pardon or you wouldn't 'a' busted out."

Rigby stood a head taller than Costillo and a head and a half taller than Dan McNeil. He was a burly man, thick through the shoulders, with abnormally long and powerful arms. His habit was to stand hunched slightly forward, with his black-bearded face thrust out in a challenging manner.

The ragged black beard covered most of Rigby's face. The flat nose, the heavy eyebrows, and broad forehead were about all one had to go on in judging Rigby, and they weren't much. When he was drinking, he was mean; when he was sober, he could be polite, friendly, and a good fellow — always with that undertone of harshness. Sober he could ride and fight with the best of them. Drunk he was likely to try to.

"He'd have turned me loose if I'd been willing to bargain with him," Dan said slowly, showing his teeth as he grinned.

"Bargain with him? I don't get it," Rigby grunted.

"He had a pardon for me . . . an' a set of ropes for the rest of you, if I'd talked turkey."

Rigby swore violently. "So the dirty son-of-a-bitch tried that! And yuh wouldn't talk with him, huh?"

"Nope," said Dan, still showing his teeth in that broad grin. "What would you have done, Rigby?"

Rigby swore again. "Ain't no use askin' me that. You oughta know. We all stick together here." Then a sudden thought struck Rigby. His forehead furrowed as he scowled and stared. Involuntarily his hand moved toward one of his belt guns.

Dan's belt and gun, and the rifle and scabbard at his saddle, had been picked up with the roan horse on the long ride south from Galisteo. His own hand dropped casually to the belt, near his gun, as he watched Rigby.

5

"WHEN THREE FRIENDS RIDE"

Costillo probably was the only man there who saw the two moves and understood them. He broke in quickly. "*Sí*. We all stick together. McNeil is back, an' everything is all right now, eh? Tonight I think we can open that whisky we have been saving and celebrate a little."

"You're talkin'!" Long Tom Taylor whooped.

Lifting a hand for silence, Dan turned to the two strangers who had been standing there silently. Leacock's red, bold face had, as usual, no expression. He was a tall, powerful man, bigger, stronger than Rigby, but his face was clean-shaven. His boots were black as were his broadcloth pants and coat and broad-brimmed hat, sober and expensive apparel. Leacock was something of a dandy in his sedate way, even to the silver mountings on the gun he wore under his coat. Colby was just the opposite. He was an untidy, fattish man, whose loose mouth was partially covered by a tobacco-stained, blond mustache. He wore no guns at all, and, as he stood there, his jaws moved ceaselessly on a large quid of tobacco in one cheek.

Dan spoke loud enough for all to hear. "I been wonderin' since I got here just how much is right. What are Leacock an' Colby doin' standin' there like they joined the bunch? This couldn't have happened three weeks ago when I went north."

Colby directed a stream of tobacco juice at the edge of the fire. His loose mouth twisted in a grin under his blond mustache. "Lots of things c'n happen in three weeks, McNeil."

Leacock contented himself with speaking to Rigby curtly. "Has this man got a say in what's being done around here?"

The firelight showed Rigby getting red around the eyes. He had evidently been drinking some during the evening, and his temper was touchy. "He ain't got a damned thing to say, except as one of the men! McNeil, if yo're not lookin' for trouble, keep outta this. Colby and Leacock are throwin' good money our way. We've decided there's more fer all of us in bein' friends than in shootin' lead back an' forth."

Sarcasm edged Dan's voice. "Did I hear

you say *friends*, Rigby? Friends with two of the biggest cattlemen in the valley? Men who helped run you outta the beef game? Friends with two jaspers who've backed the rewards that've been put up for us? Are you talkin' crazy . . . or am I just hearin' it that way?"

Costillo spoke softly. "This is business, McNeil. No friendship. Oh, no. The boys all see it. Leacock and Colby have trouble . . . and they can use us. They will pay. . . ."

Rigby broke in nastily: "Stop wastin' yore breath smoothin' him over! The boys are all honin' tuh go into this. It ain't none of McNeil's damned business."

"Hell!" said Shorty Pyle, bracing his hands on his hips and looking around for approval. "I'd like to get Dan's idea, an' I reckon I ain't the only one. I ain't been too easy in my mind about this myself. Give him the lowdown, Rigby."

"Nothin' to it," Rigby growled. "Leacock, Colby, an' some of their friends are havin' more trouble'n they want tuh mess with. Old Hatch Gillian, of the Diamond A, an' some of his friends are importin' gunmen. They've busted off the reservation an' are gettin' ready tuh raise hell. Leacock and Colby figure we're squattin'

283

here behind their holdings, an' Hatch Gillian is in front. They can do better with us helpin' 'em. It's simple an' profitable."

Long Tom Taylor sobered down. He said: "How about it, Dan? How does it strike you?"

They were all watching him, as they had many times before, waiting for him to say the final, cool word. Dan spoke his mind abruptly. "It looks like a fool deal to me. Most of us are here because we couldn't get a square deal from the big cowmen. We've rustled their stock, shot it out with 'em, an' generally raised hell. But we've always been fighting the big cowmen . . . Leacock, Colby, an' their friends. Most of the ridin' and fightin' we've done went back to them some way. Now you're fixin' to do the very thing you've been fightin' against. You all know old Hatch Gillian by reputation. He bought Crazy William's outfit an' busted in among the big fellows an' stood his ground. He's in the same boat we were in, only I hear he had some influence to back him up. Leacock an' his friends are tryin' to get us to pull their hot potatoes outta the fire for 'em. What'll we have, if we do? They'll be stronger than ever . . . an' after us once more. Start killin' for them an' you won't even have the satisfaction of thinkin' you're doing right. My advice is to run Leacock an' Colby back where they come from an' forget it."

Jake Rigby had been controlling himself with an effort. Now a bawl of anger burst from him. "Yore advice ain't worth a damn an' ain't wanted! I an' Costillo are givin' orders! Any day you don't like it, mount yore hoss an' ride! Savvy? I've been gettin' damned sick lately of the way you been hornin' in!"

There were murmurs of assent and dissent. Scantling Deene, six feet and a half tall and no thicker than a pine scantling, said: "There's a heap in what Dan says."

Dan was smiling thinly again as he spoke to Rigby. "There's been a lot of hornin' in needed lately, Rigby."

"What do yuh mean, McNeil?"

"If it's plain speakin' you need, you'll get it," said Dan. "You've been drinkin' too much lately, Rigby. Your ideas get wilder. As a leader you're draggin' like the feathers in a turkey cock's tail. Costillo's smooth an' tricky . . . but he ain't half the man you are. You're a frost, Rigby, an' Costillo ain't any better."

Before Dan finished speaking, Rigby was grabbing for his gun. The men in line of fire scattered. Dan's hand slapped to his gun a fraction after Rigby's, but his gun came out more quickly. The muzzle flipped up. He shot from the hip without aiming. Rigby did the same. He was fast. No doubt of it.

The double report of their guns made one long crash of sound. But Dan's shot was first. His bullet, a lucky shot, struck the guard of Rigby's gun. The big pistol went spinning. Rigby stood there shaking a bloody, numb hand.

Costillo, who had reached for his gun a second later, swung his hand hastily away as Dan's gun covered him. Costillo's face was ashen in that moment. Stark fear glinted in his bright eyes.

"Damn you, Costillo!" Dan said thinly. "I oughta kill you! Stand still, Rigby, before I finish you! The rest of you keep outta this. It ain't your quarrel."

Other guns were out. Other men were poised for trouble. In those short, flashing seconds passion had slashed through the Rigby-Costillo men and divided them. Men glared at one another suspiciously. They were waiting for something that would show which way to jump.

Long Tom Taylor's voice rose in a shout of warning. "I'm coverin' McNeil's back! Don't nobody sneak up on him!"

Shorty Pyle said: "That goes fer me, too!"

Leacock and Colby had slipped quickly to one side. They stood there now, silently watching.

Blood was dripping from Rigby's hand as he stood motionless. The black beard hid his face. His eyes were narrowed, glowering. He was chewing his lower lip with fury. His eyes shifted, took in the line up of the men. He became surer of himself. "This is gonna cost you plenty, McNeil," he choked.

Dan spoke coldly. "I oughta kill you, Rigby. You figured you was catchin' me nappin' then. That dirty trick at Santa Fé didn't work out, so you aimed to finish it here, huh?"

"What d'you mean, McNeil?"

"I mean, Rigby, you're a rotten, low-down, double-crossin' skunk. You and Costillo . . . an' his smooth ways was behind it . . . sent word to Santa Fé I was comin' there. You sent word I'd stop with Costillo's uncle, near Galisteo. That's where the sheriff's men jumped me. You didn't dare double-cross me on the home ground here . . . so you played snake an' hooked up with the Santa Fé sheriff."

Costillo looked more than ever like a

waiting rattler as he stood there with fear written on his face. But he, too, was taking heart as he saw the men hesitating. He spoke quickly, slipping back into his Spanish accent under stress. "I don't know what you talk about, McNeil."

"I didn't look for your memory to be so good about it," Dan grunted.

Jack Bent, a slow, easy-going man, who was a terror when aroused, spoke for the first time, with an ominous restraint in his voice. "Are you tellin' us straight, McNeil? Did Rigby and Costillo tip off the Santa Fé folks you was headin' that way?"

"That's what the governor told me. I figured he was lyin' at first. When I busted away, I wasn't sure. Then when I got to Galisteo an' seen Costillo's uncle, I knew the governor was right. That old Mex looked guilty as hell. I rode south here intendin' to keep my mouth shut an' see what Rigby and Costillo'd try next. I wanted to catch 'em cold before I called their hands. But Rigby couldn't wait. He's been drinkin' again, an' he busted loose tonight. Rigby, damn you, an' Costillo, too, have either of you got any reason why I shouldn't put lead into you both?"

Costillo licked his lips. Fear sat heavier than ever on him. But his voice burst out thickly. "It's one damn' lie I tell you!"

Rigby's eyes suddenly glinted with malevolent satisfaction. "That's your story, McNeil. I got another story. A straighter story. We all know you was grabbed up there in Santa Fé an' sentenced tuh hang. I don't know how come they trapped you. I reckon Costillo don't, neither. Why should we take all that trouble when we had yuh here? Huh?"

"You were both yellow, Rigby!"

Rigby spat again. "If I had a good hand an' a gun, I'd put that back in yore throat again, McNeil! Was I yellow when I drawed on yuh a minute ago? I'd 'a' done that before if I'd been minded to."

That made a powerful impression. From the corners of his eyes Dan caught some of the men nodding sagely. One of them spoke aloud. "By thunder, Jake wasn't playin' it yellow then."

Through his black beard Rigby's teeth showed in a nasty grin. "Yuh got a gun on me, McNeil," he said softly. "But I'll still tell you what *I* think. They had yuh in Santa Fé. Had yuh cold. They'd sentenced yuh to hang. I reckon the governor did send for yuh. I reckon he did make yuh a proposition tuh come back here an' turn us all in. But I'm thinkin', McNeil, yuh didn't

289

bust away. Yuh didn't have to. The governor let you go. He traded yore neck for what he wanted. You come back here workin' for him. How was yuh aimin' tuh turn the lot of us in, McNeil?"

Juan Costillo showed his teeth also at that. Some of the fear had left his face. "Jake, you're a quick thinker," he said. "That's about what happened, ain't it?"

Rigby's story was plausible. Some of the men were swayed by it. Dan's face grew hard and bleak as he noted it. "You would figure out somethin' like that, Rigby," he said. "If you could hold a gun, I'd kill you for it."

One of the men behind Dan called out: "Don't get so hasty, McNeil! I reckon we all know how you've been. Ain't nothin' ever come up yet like this. But it does look damned funny you gettin' away so easy there at Santa Fé. You sure Rigby ain't halfway right? Maybe you told the governor you'd see things his way just to get him to turn you loose?"

"That's you, Joe McGinnis, ain't it?" said Dan. "You're talkin' soft, but you're comin' right around to Rigby's way of thinkin'. An' you're lyin' as much as Rigby is. I'll back it up with guns, if you want to draw an' shoot it out."

"I ain't lookin' to swap lead with you!" Joe McGinnis retorted angrily. "But I reckon we're all sittin' in on this."

Dan looked around quickly. "How many of you are with me on this?" he demanded.

Long Tom Taylor said promptly: "I am."

"Me, too," Shorty Pyle chimed in.

Scantling Deene said slowly: "I reckon I'll string along with you boys, too."

The other men were silent, uneasy. Some of them were scowling outright.

Dan's face remained bleak and bitter as he looked around at them. "It ain't enough," he said. "I could kill Rigby and Costillo, an' we could all have it out right here. But I won't. We've all been through a lot together. When we start shootin' each other up, it's the end for us. I told you my idea about Leacock an' Colby. A lot of you don't figure that way. You've hit the Outlaw Trail hard, an' you're ready to go through with it. That's your business . . . not mine. But I'm makin' my choice now. I think you're wrong. I'll have none of it. Hook up with Jake Rigby an' Costillo, if you want to. String along with Leacock an' Colby an' their kind, if you like the smell of their money. Me . . . I'm pullin' out now. An' I'm tellin' you all straight out where I'm going. I'm headin' for Hatch

291

Gillian's Diamond A. He's still stickin' up for the things I hit the Outlaw Trail for. From now on, if you're fightin' Hatch Gillian, you're fightin' me. Savvy?"

Jake Rigby sneered. "I reckon that's plain enough, McNeil. But I don't reckon the boys'll see you ridin' away to trip up our plans."

"If any of the boys figure they're man enough to stop me, they can call the deal!" Dan snapped.

One of the men spoke loudly: "Aw, hell! Let him go! This ain't no time to start shootin'. If McNeil don't want none of this, I reckon he's got a right to ride off."

Others echoed that sentiment.

Dan backed toward his horse, keeping an eye on Rigby and Costillo. Leacock and Colby were still standing silently in the background. But the firelight on their faces showed plainly what they thought about it. They were surly and furious.

Shorty Pyle said: "Well, boys, I've had a good time ridin' and fightin' with you-all. But I reckon I'm packin' off, too, an' wishin' you all good luck."

"That goes for me, too," Long Tom Taylor said. "You boys keep Rigby quiet until we get outta here . . . or I'll put lead in him, if it's the last thing I do. Get the horses, Shorty. I'll sorta keep an eye on things. I reckon we can get blankets an' what-all we need at Hatch Gillian's."

Dan swung up on the roan horse and faced the fire with the belt gun resting on a knee. Long Tom Taylor and Shorty Pyle rode in beside him. Scantling Deene was not with them. He had evidently changed his mind.

"All right, boys," Dan said. "Let's get going."

They galloped off between the scattered adobe huts. The last thing Dan saw over his shoulder was the men gathered about the fire talking excitedly. Jake Rigby was gesturing violently.

6

"GUNS FOR A GIRL"

They rode around the rocky escarpment beyond the sight of the fire and lined out along the narrow trail, pulling in to a walk.

Long Tom Taylor spoke. "Well, boys, we sure did it quick. Two years of ridin' an' fightin' with the boys . . . an' here we're off on our own."

"Suits me," Shorty Pyle growled. "I had a bellyful of Rigby an' Costillo long ago. I seen the way things was headin'. I didn't like this Leacock-Colby set-up when Rigby started talkin' it. Only reason I strung along was because some of the boys seemed to favor it. What d'you reckon is on the cards fer us, Dan?"

"Plenty of ridin' an' plenty of fightin'," Dan said over his shoulder. "We know what they're fixin' to do now. We'll know what Hatch Gillian is fixin' to do when we see him. But there'll be hell to pay quick, if I don't miss my guess."

Long Tom Taylor chuckled. "Suppose Gillian ain't so pleased to see us? We never treated him better'n the others."

"If Gillian ain't so pleased to see us, we better drift on over the border for a while," Dan decided. "We've crawled out on the limb an' sawed it off. Rigby'll be gunning for us. The big outfits'll be doin' the same."

Sadly Shorty Pyle said: "I don't like chili . . . but I reckon I can down it if I got to. There'll be plenty of tequila to cool it off with, anyway."

Pete Canfield's voice hailed them out of the darkness. "There's a heap of ridin' back an' forth around here tonight."

"We're pullin' out, Pete," Dan said.

"How come? Didn't I hear some shootin' back there at camp?"

Long Tom Taylor said: "McNeil an' Rigby had some words. Rigby was ugly and drawed a gun. McNeil shot his hand up. What with one thing an' another, we're quittin' the outfit. The boys have throwed in with Leacock an' Colby against Hatch Gillian an' his friends. We're ridin' down to take Gillian grub fer a while."

Pete Canfield spoke without hesitation: "I'll ride along. I've seen this comin'. I figgered when Dan went in tonight there'd be trouble."

So they rode, the four of them, down the

steep, looping cañon trail, up on the other side, and east toward the lower lands. Presently the rising moon threw light over the lonely countryside. The shrill yapping of coyotes rose to the still, bright stars. Once they heard the deeper, savage challenge of an old wolf, and in the far distance the answer of another wolf.

When the terrain allowed, they rode four abreast, leisurely, silent for the most part, lost in their thoughts. Each knew they were riding out on a gamble. For two years they had been a part of many. There had been a certain security in numbers. Now but four, they were riding down into the lowlands where all men had been against them. They were gambling on what they would find.

The moon lifted high in the night sky. The hills broke away before them. They followed a dry, winding cañon into the lower foothills. The country beyond rolled out to far horizons. Shortly after two o'clock they pulled up out of a long, space-eating lope.

Shorty Pyle said: "Thunder Creek oughta be two, three miles ahead. On the other side we'll hit that old road between Red Town an' Slick Jack. It'll take us within a mile of the draw where Hatch

Gillian's headquarters is. If we take it easy, we oughta get there about time for breakfast."

"You always was a hopeful cuss," Pete Canfield declared. "Maybe Hatch Gillian ain't feedin' any Rigby men. Yo're apt to be chewin' yore breakfast on lead an' washin' it down with alkali dust, with old Hatch Gillian fannin' yore tail to 'Who tickled Sally.' "

"You're too mournful," Shorty complained. "With flapjacks, bacon, an' hot coffee to think about, you got to go snortin' about lead an' alkali dust."

Long Tom Taylor chuckled. "Pete's one of these here *maybe* guys. Maybe it's goin' to happen . . . so get the worryin' over with before it does."

"It don't work that way with me," Shorty said. "If my belly goes empty past breakfast, I really start worryin'."

Dan chuckled, also. "Hatch Gillian'll give you plenty to worry about if he's minded to. Got plenty of holes in your belt, Shorty?"

"Always struck me I had."

"Strap your middle up tight then an' stop thinkin'."

They crossed the shallow trickle of Thunder Greek, and beyond struck the deep ruts and high center of the old road. A generation earlier the road had carried much traffic. But a newer, shorter road had thrown the old one into disuse.

They had ridden a mile or so along the road, when Dan spoke abruptly. "Ain't that a fire ahead?"

"Shore is," Pete Canfield agreed.

Shorty exclaimed: "That'll be about where Hatch Gillian's place is! Whatcha reckon's going on there?"

Long Tom Taylor broke in warningly: "Lissen! Ain't that someone ridin' this way?"

They stopped. On the sudden quiet the faint roll of fast-running hoofs sounded in the distance ahead. It grew louder as they listened.

Dan said: "Boys, he's sure punishin' that horse. Maybe we'd better wait down in that arroyo ahead there an' see what he's got on his mind."

The road pitched down steeply into the dry arroyo, and up out of it on the other side. On the dry, gleaming sands of the arroyo bed they waited, two on each side of the road. The drumming hoofs of that furiously ridden horse swiftly neared.

To the last moment horse and rider were invisible. Then suddenly they were there, racing down the steep pitch into the arroyo bed. Too late the four waiting men were sighted. Too late the stranger reined sharply in along the bank in an effort to ride up the arroyo ahead of them.

"Hold on there!" Dan shouted. He spurred in close and cut the stranger off.

The others swung in behind, trapping horse and rider against the bank.

Reining the hard-breathing horse around so they were all in sight, the stranger demanded fiercely: "What do you want?"

"God All-Mighty!" Shorty Pyle gasped. "It's a woman!"

Dan reined back a little. "Sorry, ma'am," he apologized hastily. "We . . . uh . . . we thought you were a man. What brings you riding out this way?"

She wore no hat. In the moonlight her hair could be seen caught close against her head. Her gloveless hands holding the reins were small and white in the moonlight. She was young — and anger made her almost incoherent.

"What business is it of yours?" she flared at Dan. "Who are you?"

"My name is McNeil, ma'am. Dan McNeil."

Almost in the same breath, Long Tom Taylor yelled: *Look out, Dan!*

Dan had already seen her hand coming up from the holster at her side. Even as it came, he knew there was no bluff about it. He had no time to ride away. He threw himself back out of the saddle as the gun blasted at him.

His horse shied. Long Tom and the others spurred out of the way. And the strange girl slashed hard with the romel ends and galloped on up the arroyo, firing back at them as she went.

Coming down on the sand hard, Dan hung onto the reins and quieted his horse. The girl had ridden around the next bend out of sight before the confusion was over.

Pete Canfield called anxiously: "She hit you, Dan?"

"Missed my ear by half a tickle," Dan said, climbing into the saddle again.

"Which just goes to show," said Shorty Pyle, "you ain't as popular with the ladies as I've heerd made out. Next time I meet a female in the middle of the night, I'll make smoke gettin' away from there while my hair's safe."

"Hatch Gillian's got a daughter," Pete Canfield remarked. "I'll bet that's her."

"She knows where she's going, anyway, and don't want trouble," Dan said. "Let's make tracks to that fire and see what we find. The answer'll be there."

As they rode out of the arroyo, there was no doubt that miles ahead a building was burning. The glare was bright and steady against the sky, and, as they drew near, they could see white smoke billowing high.

They topped a rise and looked down a long slope into a wide, shallow draw. The scene lay clear-cut, vivid before them. Several buildings were blazing. Roofless, gutted walls of adobe vomited fire and smoke. Door and window openings showed the licking flames inside.

Farther off beds of glowing coals showed where haystacks had burned quickly to the ground. Two empty corrals off to one side looked like the old bare bones of weathered skeletons. This was the Diamond A headquarters. The buildings old Hatch Gillian had repaired and added to when he took over the big ranch were gone now. As the four of them raced down the long slope, Dan saw men dodging into the shadows. Rifles cracked faintly. Lead screamed warningly overhead.

Reining hard, Dan waved his sombrero. The other three gathered behind him.

7

"DIAMOND A WELCOME"

Pete Canfield spoke hoarsely: "There's our reception from Hatch Gillian! The old rooster's honin' fer trouble!"

"I'd say he's expecting trouble," Dan differed. "He don't know who we are. Ride in slow behind me, boys, with your hands up. There's enough light so they can see we're peaceable."

"*Bueno,* if you say so," Shorty Pyle grumbled. "But it'll be the first time I ever rode up to guns while snatchin' for the moon. Pete, you're a danged hoodoo. You started talkin' up this lead an' alkali business."

Slowly they rode on down the slope with their hands up. Men with ready guns stepped out to meet them.

Most of the Diamond A men were only half clad. One man was still in his underwear. Old Hatch Gillian headed them, holding a rifle. He wore boots, trousers, and shirt, but his head was bare, his hair tousled, and his red beard was bristling pugnaciously. Hatch Gillian was a tall, burly man, deep through the chest. His shout had a warning rasp.

"Who are you men?" he bellowed.

The flames were still crackling loudly. In the nearest building a length of wood dropped, and a cloud of sparks wafted up. In the red glare the faces of the men around Hatch Gillian were dark, threatening.

Dan saw something else as he rode up. Off to one side two bodies lay on the ground side by side. Several of the Diamond A men were bleeding from wounds.

"We're friends, Gillian," Dan said.

There was no softening in Hatch Gillian's harshness as he replied: "That's your story, mister. We ain't expecting friends right now. What are you doing out this time of night?"

Dan rode close and looked down into the muzzles of the Diamond A guns. It was a tense moment. There was no welcome here. These men were fighting mad, darkly suspicious. At a word from Gillian they would readily open fire.

"I don't reckon you know us except from talk, Gillian," Dan said calmly. "We've been ridin' toward the Diamond A all night. We've got some news for you, an' we figured you'd be glad to see us."

"Mebbe so," said Hatch Gillian, relaxing somewhat. "Friends are always welcome. We need friends now. Who are you? What news have you got?"

"My name is Dan McNeil, mister."

Behind Gillian a man called sharply: "Dan McNeil is one of the Rigby-Costillo men! He's been with 'em ever since they went wild! It's a trick!"

Guns moved threateningly. The tension tightened. Stark, savage threat was visible on every Diamond A man.

"Hold your men, Gillian," Dan said evenly. "Don't go off half-cocked before you hear us. We're friends."

Gillian lifted a warning hand. "Hold it, boys," he ordered. "You men on the outside keep your eyes peeled. We don't want to be caught napping while we're talkin' to these fellows."

"You'll not be caught napping by anything that brought us here," Dan said. "We're only four. There's eight of you. Would we have been fools enough to ride in here with our fists in the air if we had any cards up our sleeves? We're Rigby-Costillo men, right enough, Gillian. But we pulled out tonight and rode to join you. Rigby and Costillo are throwing in with Leacock an' Colby an' the rest of the pack they run with. Hell will bust loose in these parts pretty soon. We figured you could use four men who can ride an' fight."

Another Diamond A man said harshly: "McNeil ran out on that hangin' in Santa Fé! He's a bad one! We've had enough of the Rigby-Costillo men tonight!"

Hatch Gillian's red beard was bristling pugnaciously again. His voice had a warning edge. "You came to warn us about the Rigby-Costillo men, did you, McNeil?"

"That's right."

Hatch Gillian's voice boomed like the savage roll of a war drum. "You're too late, McNeil. The Rigby-Costillo men have been here. Your eyes can tell you what they did. Came down on us while we were sleepin' peacefully. Shot us down when we ran out. Fired the buildings, not giving a damn who got caught inside. Cleaned us out, lock and barrel. Run our horses off. Left us here with a warning that more was coming if the Diamond A wasn't vacated quick." Hatch Gillian's booming voice shook with a terrible passion as he cried: "An' now you four come after it's all over, offering what we've already found out with lead and blood. Offering to help us, when it's too late for help. What trickery is this?"

Behind Dan, Long Tom Taylor said bitterly: "This is Costillo's doing. They saddled and rode hard right after we left."

"Gillian," Dan said evenly, "we didn't look for this to happen before we got here. We left the men back in the hills still arguing with Leacock an' Colby. We rode easy, thinking we had plenty of time. Taylor is right. They outrode us an' got here first. But this ain't the end. You'll need us yet."

Hatch Gillian swore a violent oath. "You're right, McNeil! There's more to this. We managed to get one horse saddled. My daughter is riding for help now. Leacock an' Colby will rue the day they set those wolves against me. While I've got breath in my body, while my hands will hold a gun, I'll make war against them from this hour on."

There was harsh, terrible threat in Hatch Gillian's statement. He looked like some avenging prophet of old as he stood there under the waning moon, with the fiery ruins of his home throwing a blood-red glow on his bearded face.

"We met your daughter," Dan told him. "I guess she thought we were part of Rigby's men. She rode away from us. We're here . . . and you've heard our say, Gillian. The law has got a rope waiting for my neck. There's a price on all our heads. We earned it all by riding against Leacock, Colby, and their crowd. We've got no more love for them than you have. You've got friends, but you'll need more. If you want us, speak out. If you don't, we'll ride on south across the border an' let you settle it any way you like."

The man who had first spoken raised his voice again. "It's smooth talk, but it don't ring true. Yuh can't cure a sheep-killin' dog."

"But you can keep him on a short leash and use him," Hatch Gillian said curtly. "There's no damage these men can do to us tonight. I think we'll use them."

Shorty Pyle muttered angrily behind Dan.

Dan spoke for himself and the three who waited on his word. "Damn you, Hatch Gillian. We didn't ride here to be called sheep-killing dogs. We're not the kind you can put a leash on. You'll not use us. I thought you were a man we wanted to help. I've changed my mind. Pack your troubles an' swing your own guns for all of us. You weren't asked to hire gunmen. You were offered help. And you've talked yourself out of it."

Hatch Gillian quickly lifted a protesting

hand, and then deliberately smoothed his beard. "I like the way you say that, McNeil. I guess I was wrong. My men and I have had too much tonight to be reasonable. I apologize for my hasty talk. If you're friends, light an' take your places with friends. Hatch Gillian never picked a quarrel when it wasn't forced on him."

"Your apology is accepted, Gillian," Dan said. He swung out of the saddle. "What comes first? Where are your horses?"

"They're all corral-broke an' can't be far away," Gillian replied. "We got some saddles over there by one of the corrals. Give us your horses for a little an' we'll bring in our own."

"Help yourself," said Dan. "We'll need fresh stock, too, if you've got it. My roan'll give out in a few more miles. I could use an hour or so's sleep, too. I been ridin' all day an' night."

"The ground is all I've got to offer you, McNeil. But such as it is, you're welcome. We'll wake you when we're ready."

Two hours later, when Hatch Gillian's big hand shook Dan out of a drugged sleep, the sun was rising. Dan lurched to his feet, stretching, yawning, rubbing his eyes open.

Horses were saddled. The Diamond A men were ready to ride. Long Tom, Shorty, and Pete Canfield had been roused, also.

"We're ready to ride," Hatch Gillian said gruffly. "We've buried our dead an' done all we can around here. It's war in the valley from now on . . . an' we'll make it a bang-up fight. Your saddles are on fresh horses. We're riding to Little Dick Powell's Saw Horse Ranch, over beyond Slick Jack. My daughter rode there last night to warn 'em. They'll get word out to the other ranches, and by noon we'll have an idea of what we're going to do." Gillian turned and shouted: "Fork your leather, boys! Let's ride!"

8

"SCORN OF A WOMAN"

Golden and warm, the sun was rising in the east as they left the empty corrals and ruins behind. The day would be smiling, fair, but not a man among them but rode grimly.

Miles north of the Diamond A, six hard-riding men met them. With them was the girl. In the sunshine she looked to Dan as she had the night before in the moonlight when her image had been branded deeply into his mind. As she pulled up now before him, he thought he would have known her anywhere in the whole wide world, day or night. She was still without a hat. Her hair still lay close against her small head, and her head was high and proud. Prouder, that head, Dan thought, than any woman's head he had ever seen. She was not pretty, but she had everything he was eager to see again, all that sureness, certainty, all that fire and flame and fierce pride he remembered.

She recognized him instantly. It was like two sparks meeting and leaping together — and clashing as they flew apart. Angry color stained her cheeks. Her voice was clear and scornful as she pointed to him and said: "That is Dan McNeil, one of the men who helped burn us out last night."

Hatch Gillian answered: "I know who that is, Lia. McNeil and the men with him weren't among them last night. McNeil told me he met you."

"He wouldn't have had a chance to tell me anything!" she said angrily.

"Peace, girl," Hatch Gillian ordered not unkindly, but firmly.

She bit her lip and was silent, but the anger, the scorn, the dislike for Rigby's men remained.

Little Dick Powell had led the new riders. He was a stocky man, barely turned thirty, with a heavily tanned face that normally was cheerful. Now under the wide brim of his dusty, black sombrero his face looked hard and bleak.

"I've sent men out to the LXO, to Tom Keenan, and east to the X Slash B," he said to Gillian. "I asked 'em to bring their men to Red Town, and to send the word out as far as it'd do any good. I used your name."

Gillian nodded approvingly.

Powell's face grew bleaker as he looked at Dan and the other Rigby men. "I don't understand what those four are doing here,

311

Gillian," he remarked bluntly.

Dan said: "I'll answer that, Powell. We've quit the Rigby outfit. They've thrown in with Leacock, Colby, an' the big cowmen. Leacock and Colby turned Rigby loose on the Diamond A last night. More than likely they added some help."

"Is that straight, Gillian?" Powell demanded.

"I'll answer that, too," Dan said curtly. "Years ago you and I were halfway friends, Powell. You never knew me to tell a lie. Now I tell you we're riding against Leacock, Colby, and the Rigby men."

Lia Gillian's lip curled. The rush of unreasoning anger Dan felt at that sight was strange to him. Her scorn was like a lash, a maddening challenge. He would have raged to think it was because he wanted her to think well of him.

Powell evidently had believed him. Dropping the argument, Powell stared at Gillian. "Then . . . it's war?" he said slowly.

Hatch Gillian nodded. "I'm afraid so, Powell. I see nothing else to do." Gillian was an honest man, for he added: "And I'm not exactly sure what to do now. They're many, and we'll be few."

For a moment silence held them. For all their grimness, all their willingness, they did not know where to start. They were men of peace, ranchers, used to riding and not to fighting. Dan saw more than one man look at him. They looked at him as the Rigby men had looked, men who were willing, but who wanted a confident leader whose judgment they could follow with certainty.

"Gillian," said Dan, "this is your show. But I'll give my advice. You can take it or leave it. You know what you're up against. All the men you can get together won't amount to much, if the big cowmen ever get a chance to throw all their men against you. Your only chance is to hit hard an' quick. They won't be lookin' for it. None of you men has ever gotten together and smashed back. They've gone a little further an' a little further, testing you out. They think you're cowed. They're set to break you up, outfit after outfit. That's why they got Jake Rigby to tackle this dirty work. Don't think . . . if they were willing to come out in the open . . . they couldn't do what they've hired Rigby to do. But there's more law in the territory than they can swing in this one county. They'd rather do it under cover, through Rigby, so their hands'll be clean for the world to see. When Rigby, with their help, has smashed you all, then they'll smash Rigby. He was too big a fool to see it. Leacock and Colby have been up all night. So have Rigby's men. They'll be taking it easy now, and my guess is Rigby's men will not be far from Leacock and Colby. They won't figure it's necessary to ride clear back into the mountains today. Colby's Rafter L is the nearest. If we can clean that out and get Colby, it'll be a big step in the right direction."

Lia Gillian was the one who answered Dan first, with a rush of anger, addressed to her father. "How can you wait there and listen to this . . . this outlaw tell you what to do? He is probably trying to trap you. Can't you see?"

"Lia," said Hatch Gillian sternly, "this is not a woman's business. You don't belong here. Powell should not have let you come."

"I couldn't stop her," Little Dick Powell said apologetically.

"I can understand that," Gillian agreed curtly. "Lia, you will keep out of this from now on. McNeil, I'm inclined to think there's a heap of sense in what you say. It will take time to ride into Red Town and wait for the others. And there'll be no lack of people there to carry word that we're gathering. If you're agreeable, Powell, we'll ride for the Rafter L from here, an' get our breakfast later, where we can. Enough guns and cartridges were saved last night for what we need at first."

Little Dick Powell's look at Dan had no greater friendliness, but he agreed: "We're with you. If this business isn't settled quick, my place may be the next to go."

"Then it's Colby first," said Hatch Gillian grimly. "Lia, ride to Red Town, rent yourself a room in the hotel, an' stay there until I call for you."

"I don't want to go to Red Town, Father."

"Do as I tell you," Hatch Gillian ordered angrily. "Haven't I enough trouble now, without your adding to it? Get where I'll know you're safe, and stay there."

She went, spurring her horse to a gallop and not looking back. Dan rode beside Hatch Gillian and Little Dick Powell back into the southwest, toward Colby's Rafter L.

The sun was higher in the sky, the day was hotter, and hunger and thirst were spreading among the men who rode hard through the low, heavily brushed hills on Rafter L land. For half a day a man could gallop south and still be on Rafter L land, but Colby had located his headquarters at the northern part, nearest Red Town, the county seat.

Through here the country was broken and rolling. There were patches of scrub oak and cactus, cholla cactus, spiny beds of prickly pear, the tall, whip-like stands of Spanish wife-beaters. But there was grass, too, and bunches of white-faced cattle stared and moved off uneasily as the line of riders swept past them.

And then — there were Colby's ranch buildings lying in a sunny twenty-acre flat, with the low, wooded hills circling round-about, and the vanes at the top of a tall windmill spinning slowly in the upper air currents. Horses were in the corrals, and more saddled horses were hitched behind the house as Dan burst out of the scrub trees and led the line of riders across the flat toward Colby's place. Men were out in the open, and by the number of horses there were more men out of sight. More men than should have been around the place during an ordinary ranch day.

The nearest man stared an instant, emptied his gun in their direction, and ran for the shelter of the house. The place came alive suddenly, and yet all sounds were drowned to Dan by the hammering sweep of racing hoofs following behind.

316

9

"NOOSE NUMBER ONE"

A rider on the outer fringe raised a shrill cowboy yell. Others took it up. More Colby men tumbled out, saw them coming, and began shooting.

One of Little Dick Powell's men, riding a big bay, drew abreast of Dan, yelling as he rode. And then suddenly he was silent, tumbling out of the saddle, rolling over and over on the ground. Throwing a look over his shoulder, Dan saw a second rider veering out of the rush as he bent limply over the horse's neck and held on with both hands.

Gillian's men had held their fire at first. Now they were shooting, also. The thin, lashing reports added a staccato beat to the thundering rush of their advance.

Hatch Gillian was well in the forefront, riding straight up, a big single-action .45 carried shoulder high, muzzle up, waiting for the moment of action.

Dan saw all that in a swift succession of vignettes — and then the Colby men were dashing for cover in the bunkhouse and in the big house. A rifle barrel poked through a pane of glass in a front window. Dan heard a sharp, spiteful report from it. From the corner of his eye he saw another man go down, and he veered sharply away from the rest of the men to the north of the big house.

There for a moment the windows were deserted. Let them once be manned with guns and it would be an all-day job to get at the men inside. Pulling his horse up hard against the wall, Dan hit the ground running, jerking his rifle from the saddle scabbard as he went. The first thing he saw was a rider at the far side of the flat just spurring into the trees. One of the Colby men had leaped in the saddle behind the cover of the house and was riding for safety.

With the rifle Dan took a snap shot at him — and seemed to miss, for the rider vanished among the scrub trees. There was no time now to try and catch him. The Colby men had been unexpectedly alert. Guns were blasting on all sides of the house but this north side. Undoubtedly they would be here, also, in a moment.

Dan tried the nearest window. It was locked inside. He smashed glass and frame with his rifle butt and hauled himself through, heedless of the sharp glass edges around the frame. He landed clumsily on the floor beside a bed, and, as he came up, a bearded man jerked the door open and jumped inside with a revolver in his hand.

"Drop it!" Dan yelled.

The man shot instead. The report in that small room smashed against the eardrums. Colby's man should have killed Dan — but Dan was coming up off the floor at an angle, and the bullet only cut through the upper part of his leg, spinning him half off balance over against the bed. He fired as he went — twice — thumbing the single-action gun so fast there was hardly a perceptible interval between the two shots.

Both bullets hit Colby's man in the middle. He bent double, dropping his gun. He opened his mouth as if to say something, but he uttered no sound as he pitched forward to the floor, still doubled up.

Dropping the rifle and catching up the gun off the floor, Dan stepped into the open doorway. A small, low-ceilinged hallway led toward the middle part of the house. At the moment it was deserted. As Dan advanced along it, a man put his head and shoulders out of a doorway ahead. He dodged back and slammed the door just as Dan's bullet fanned the spot where his head had been.

The door was shut as Dan limped warily past it. The hall was a short one, closed at the end by a door that opened inward to the next room. Guns were barking in that next room as Dan kicked the door open and jumped through.

The room was a long, low-ceilinged living room, roofed with log *vigas* in the Mexican style. Three men were in it, watching windows, front and back. One of them was Colby, handling a rifle.

The nearest man, a cowpoke wearing scarred leather batwing chaps, caught the movement at the doorway from the corner of his eye, turned his head, and then dropped the gun he was holding. "Yuh got me!" he yelled. "Hold it, mister!"

Colby swung and saw what had happened. He staggered as if he had been struck a physical blow. Under his blond, tobacco-stained mustache his loose mouth opened, then slowly closed. He made a convulsive movement with the rifle, then dropped it suddenly.

The third man, at the far end of the room, was the last to see. He threw his short gun away immediately and lifted his hands. As it struck the floor, Colby called angrily: "Why didn't you do something with that gun, Shepherd! What the devil am I paying you for?"

Shepherd was a tall, loosely built man with a clean-shaven face. His answer was curt. "You hired me to punch cows, Colby, not get myself cut down with lead. I ain't sure yet what this is all about, but if the gent was willin' to let my back alone while he gave me a chance to get my fists up, I'm willin' to meet him halfway and heist 'em. I warned you I wasn't mixin' with your feuds. I told you when you kept us all around the place this morning that, if there was trouble, you could count me out."

Colby could still swear. He did. "Thank God the rest of them aren't like you, Shepherd."

"Shut up, Colby," Dan ordered. "Trot on out ahead of me an' call your men off. You've rolled your hoop to the end. There's no use lettin' your men be slaughtered now to help your vanity."

The shave Colby had given himself sometime during the morning had not helped his fat, untidy face much. Drawn and weary, he had the look of a man who had ridden far and hard, and had not slept after it, and he was afraid now and tried to cover it up with bluster. "What's the meaning of this outrage, McNeil?"

"Save your breath," Dan told him disgustedly as he placed his back against the wall and motioned the three of them into the middle of the room with his guns. "Hatch Gillian has come for you, Colby. Rigby made the mistake of lettin' him live. Call your men off."

"I'll be damned if I will!" Colby refused.

But the man was afraid. His loose mouth was working. His eyes had a deep-seated, apprehensive look. His bravado was that of a cornered man who had everything to gain and nothing much to lose by standing his ground.

Shepherd said: "Mister, what's going to happen if the boys put down their guns?"

"Nothing to *them*," said Dan. "It's Colby we came for . . . an' I've got him. I reckon you-all better get out the front way ahead of me. Shepherd, call that man outta the room along the hall there. Got any women folks in the house? We don't want to hurt them."

"They're hid out in the bedrooms," Shepherd said as he walked toward the door through which Dan had entered the room. He stood there in the doorway and called: "Alf, come out! They've got Colby!"

After some parley, Alf came into the room with his hands up. He was a young man, and his grin was sour as he spoke to Dan.

"You almost got me when I looked out in the hall, mister. Too bad I couldn't have got a draw on you first."

"Better luck next time," Dan chuckled. "Out the front door, men, with your hands in the air."

Four of the Gillian and Powell men had gotten close to the front wall of the house where they could cover the windows. They held their fire as the men walked out with their hands in the air, and, after that, it took only a few minutes to get the prisoners around to the back and convince the men in the bunkhouse that there was no use continuing the fight. Colby cursed them as they came out. There were nine of them — not all of the Rafter L men by any means.

Standing before Colby in the open space behind the house, Hatch Gillian curtly demanded: "Where are the rest of your men, Colby?"

Colby glared at him and said nothing.

Gillian squinted at the horses behind the house and in the corrals. "You got about ten or eleven horses ready to ride, an' spares in the corral there," he decided. "Your men ain't around here. Colby, what have you got to say for yourself?"

"Plenty," Colby told him angrily. "There'll be hell to pay for this."

"But I reckon it won't worry you much," Gillian told him. "You had me burned out last night, Colby. By rights I oughta burn you out . . . but I won't. You Rafter L men, in case you don't know what's happening, I'll tell you plain. Colby had me burned out last night. He struck me in the dark, with no thought for any women around. The big cowmen have decided to clean house on this range. We little fellows know what to expect now. There's only one way to protect our homes and stop this quick. We're taking it. We're running your horses out. We're taking your guns and Colby along. Two of you men tie his hands, put him on a horse, and take him over to the edge of the trees there and wait for us."

It did not take long to do that. They were in their saddles, waiting to ride away when a woman came from the house. She was a thin-faced, not very happy-looking woman who nevertheless faced Gillian defiantly. "What are you doing to my husband?" she asked, looking up at him.

Hatch Gillian removed his hat. Through

his red beard, his voice turned sad beneath its hardness as he spoke to her. "We're protecting our homes, Missus Colby. My place was burned to the ground last night, on orders from your husband. My daughter was lucky, or she would have been killed. You couldn't have helped the kind of man you married. We're leaving one badly wounded man of ours . . . who ain't likely to live . . . for your mercy, an' one dead man for your men to bury. Good day, ma'am."

Hatch Gillian bowed to her from the saddle and rode away, leaving her there with the Rafter L men.

Colby, his guards, and two wounded men who could ride were waiting at the edge of the trees. At a curt order from Gillian they rode on a mile or so, and stopped beneath the tallest tree in sight.

"It ain't so high, but there's a limb up there you can get a rope over," Gillian said, squinting. "Put 'er up and put the noose around his neck."

Colby's face turned the color of old dough. "You wouldn't dare do a thing like that," he said thickly.

Gillian did not reply until the noose was around Colby's neck, and then he spoke evenly. "Where are the Rigby men, Colby?"

"Get this rope off my neck before I'll talk to you," Colby raged.

Hatch Gillian stroked his red beard. "Colby," he said slowly, "you're a low-down snake with the disposition of a hog. That goes for Leacock, too. Things were running all right on this range until you men decided to hog it all. You had enough, but you still wanted more. Men who were trying to build up something an' live a decent, peaceful life didn't mean anything to you. You and Leacock set the pace, and other men who thought like you followed along. You had the power, an' you used it, fair or foul. But I'm a home-loving man, Colby. When my roof is burned down over my head in the middle of the night, when my men are shot down as they roll out of their bunks, when you turn a wolf like Rigby loose on me, not caring whether he kills my daughter or not, then I've no other cheek left to turn. I know now that I can never expect mercy from you on my own land or off. And Colby, when a man like that crosses my path, I stomp him out like I would a rattler. If you have any prayers to say, get them out quick."

Colby swallowed twice in a throat that suddenly was tight. "Y-you don't mean to do this?" he stammered.

"May God have mercy on your black-ened soul," said Hatch Gillian solemnly. He leaned over, slashed Colby's horse with the end of his rope, and rode off.

Dan looked back as he galloped away. The tree branch was stout enough to hold its burden. Colby's heels were a good two feet from the ground.

10

"COYOTE TRAP"

The bullet hole in Dan's leg hurt. Most of the bleeding had stopped, but pain was there and probably fever later, and already the leg was beginning to stiffen. But there were men riding with them who were wounded more seriously than he. The first time they slowed for a breather, Powell spoke to one of his men who was white and weak.

"Cut off here, Dickson, an' make for Red Town and a doctor. You aren't in any shape to go on to Leacock's."

Dickson showed his teeth in a tight grin. "You're gonna need me," he replied painfully.

"Git on to Red Town, you idiot! If you think you can't make it, I'll send another man along with you."

"I c'n make it all right," Dickson said. He rode off into the northeast and left them standing there.

Dan looked thoughtfully after the man, and then addressed Gillian loudly enough for others to hear. "I've got a hunch he spoke truer than he knew. A man rode off from Colby's place just as we got to the house. I shot at him, but missed him. The last I saw, he was in among the trees. I didn't have time to follow then, an', when I got through in the house, it was too late. My guess is he was ridin' hell-bent to carry the news you were on the prod. Leacock's Running J is the nearest. He'd head there. An' if Leacock gets word in time that we're comin', he'll have a sweet reception for us. He'll have enough men there to do it."

Hatch Gillian waved the objection aside. "We'll hit them as hard as we did Colby. Right is on our side, and our luck is holding good."

Dan shook his head dubiously. "You may be right as hell an' the luckiest critter who ever forked a bronc', but a clever man an' a gun can even up any argument an' make his own luck. It's my idea we need some fast brainwork now."

Gillian did not take kindly to that. "We're using all the brainwork we need, McNeil. Without meaning offense for what you've already done, my orders are to get to the Running J so fast Leacock won't have time to make up his mind about anything."

Hatch Gillian's word carried, of course.

He led them into the north, riding fast and easy, with his big red beard outthrust and his head high with the same fierce pride his daughter had displayed. Dan would not have done it this way. He went dubiously, trying to decide whether to take a stronger hand.

Miles farther on, the distant report of a gunshot sounded to the left. In that direction, almost a mile away, they sighted a horseman racing down off an open hilltop to cut them off. For a moment there was confusion. It looked like an attack. But no other riders appeared. They waited while the man approached them.

In astonishment, Pete Canfield blurted out: "That's Scantlin' Deene."

"Who is he?" Little Dick Powell snapped.

"One of the Rigby men," Dan replied, "I thought he was comin' with us, but he stayed behind for some reason. Looks like he's got somethin' on his mind now."

Scantling Deene looked longer and thinner than ever as he galloped up to them. He was sweating, and chewing tobacco steadily. "Hello, boys," he said to Dan and the other Rigby men. He wiped his face, directed a stream of tobacco juice at the ground, and spoke to them all. "I snuck off from the Running J an' hightailed it out this way to try an' cut you fellows off. One of Colby's men rode in a little while ago an' said you had come down on the Rafter L like a keg of blasting powder. Leacock refused to ride to Colby's place. Said you might land on his own buildings while he was gone. He's lookin' out for himself first. He's got an idea you're comin' to him next. All the Rigby men an' his own are there, an' he's fixin' up the prettiest trap you ever saw. If you ride in there, he'll wipe you out."

Hatch Gillian fixed him with a hard glare. "Why did you ride out to tell us? You're a Rigby man. What's it to you what happens to us?"

Scantling Deene spat again and grinned. "I ain't worryin' about a red-headed old rooster like you, Gillian. But some of my friends are ridin' with you. I almost came with 'em, an' then I stayed behind, figgerin' I could do more for 'em by being around to see what devilment Rigby cooked up. He's a snake, an' he hates 'em all now. He'll get 'em first chance he can. He's waitin' there at Leacock's all primed for slaughter now."

"Thanks, Scantlin'," Dan said.

"Shore," Scantling said, grinning. "I reckon I'll have to stick with you boys now.

331

Whatcha gonna do?"

Little Dick Powell swore a round oath. "I was afraid something like this would happen," he said with visible chagrin. "I don't see anything else to do but get into Red Town and see how many friends we have there to ride with us. And if there aren't enough, it looks as if we'll have to let Leacock alone for the time being . . . until he parts company with the Rigby men, at any rate."

"Hmm," said Hatch Gillian, frowning. He was indecisive himself. His new run of luck had been jolted hard. He was willing, but uncertain again. Once more his eyes wandered to Dan. "Well, McNeil," he said abruptly. "Have you got any ideas?"

Dan nodded slowly. "Plenty, Gillian. Riding into Red Town for more men won't help you much. Start playing cat an' dog with Leacock, an' he'll beat you at it. Smash him quick, an' I think you've got this whole trouble licked. He and Colby have kept all the other cattlemen stirred up. They've been the leaders. Colby's gone. But you'll never get Leacock at his ranch now. You want to draw him out in the open. Let everyone get a look at what he's doing. There's a heap of folks that still don't believe he's as bad as he is. They wouldn't figure he'd deal with Rigby, for instance. Parade all that in front of everybody, get Leacock if you can, settle Rigby an' Costillo, an' you'll hold a winning hand."

Hatch Gillian made a quick, impatient reply to that. "Fine words, McNeil. But they don't tell us anything. How are we to get them out in the open? And if we do, what then?"

Dan grinned faintly. "Get 'em into Red Town an' settle it there for the world to see. Make Leacock start the fightin' right out in public, there in town. You'll have the rest of your friends there to help you."

"That don't make sense, McNeil. How could we get Leacock into Red Town with his men?"

"Out-fox him," Dan said, grinning faintly. "Bait him in. Take some of the men here an' ride easy for that trap he's got set, savin' your horses. Let him see you're there for business . . . only stay away from his guns. He'll come out after you, all right. Then ride like hell for Red Town. He'll be sure he's got you. All you got to do is stay ahead of him into Red Town."

"Why don't you do that for Gillian?" Powell put in suspiciously.

Dan gave him a level look. "Not because

I'm afraid of my skin, Powell. But Leacock don't want me. He wants Gillian."

With a disinterested drawl Scantling Deene broke in. "I reckon that's right. Colby's men said Gillian had come down on the Rafter L. It's Gillian that Leacock was frothin' about, an' it's Gillian he's waiting for."

Hatch Gillian tugged hard at his red beard for a moment, then abruptly came to a decision. "I'll take seven of you with the best horses. The rest of you go into Red Town and wait for us. Take the extra guns along. If they're needed at all, they'll be needed there when we get in."

When Gillian picked his seven men, no former Rigby man was among them. Dan noted it and smiled wryly to himself. Despite all that had happened, Gillian was not trusting them in this vital bit of business, and, Dan had to admit, perhaps Gillian couldn't be blamed so much at that.

11

"OUTLAW DEPUTIES"

Two thousand and an odd hundred or so was the population of Red Town. It should not have been that big, for there was small excuse for Red Town. The truth was a great county had been split into two counties, that certain men might better control the law.

Once Red Town had had an open plaza, a small, sleepy plaza, shaded by great cottonwoods. The brick courthouse for the new county had been built, two stories high, in the plaza. The cottonwoods still stood about the red brick. There was shade over the hitch rack where saddle horses and wagons and buggies waited — shade and drowsy peace for strangers to see.

But this noon, as the remnants of the Gillian men rode into the courthouse square, they found horses racked along the east side of the square. Armed men who plainly were not townsmen were gathered in little groups along the sidewalk in front of the two-story building that housed the Boston House Hotel.

More townsmen than usual had business in the square, also. Heads turned, and men and women and children stared as the men rode by. Dan recognized big, bearded Tom Keenan among the men on the sidewalk before the Boston House. Saddled horses waiting there in line carried the LXO brand. Hatch Gillian's call for help had been heeded quickly. And from the saddle he saw Lia Gillian waiting on the porch of the Boston House.

As they dismounted, they were surrounded by the waiting men. Half a dozen men at once asked where Gillian was. Tom Keenan himself asked the question of Dick Powell, but before Powell could reply, the men gave way to let Lia Gillian through. She asked the question again, of Powell, breathlessly and with a growing fear in her eyes.

No townsmen had mixed in with the armed men standing around close. Powell told her the truth. "Your father took seven men an' went on to Leacock's ranch. He'll be along."

She stared at Powell for a moment. Standing there, where he could have touched her with an outstretched arm, Dan saw the flush stealing up into her cheeks. Her voice was remote, cold as she asked: "You let my father go on to Leacock's place with only seven men?"

Powell still was not easy about it. His face showed that. He answered her uncomfortably. "McNeil here sold the idea to your dad. It's a little trick McNeil figured out. But I reckon your dad'll be along all right."

When Powell uttered his name, Dan knew what was coming, and it did. She turned on him. All that angry defiance and scorn she felt for him flared out again.

"So *you're* behind it! You thought of a trick that would send him to Leacock with only a handful of men. Send him into a trap from which he couldn't escape. You didn't even go yourself. You skulked back here where you'd be safe."

Keenan and the LXO men had not been surprised to see him. She must have told them he and the others were with Gillian, but their distrust was plain, and her words inflamed them. Dark looks were cast at them.

Dan had removed his hat. His face was even with hers. He was unshaven, dirty, gaunt with weariness and hunger and thirst. He wished it could have been otherwise. There were many things he wanted to say — and it all vanished before the same unreasoning antagonism that flamed up to meet her scorn. "I figured it out, ma'am," he said curtly. "I knew what I was doin'. Your father's in danger, all right. We all are today. But he'd have been in greater danger later on if he didn't try somethin' like I suggested. He told you plain this mornin' . . . a woman should keep out of this. He was right. Hell's due to pop around this town pretty soon. If your father was here, he'd tell you to get into the hotel an' stay out of sight until it was over. That's all I can tell you to do."

"If I were only a man," she choked, and she whirled to Tom Keenan. "Can't you do something about these . . . these outlaws mixing in this with their trickery and their deceit?"

Tom Keenan shrugged. "I could do plenty, I reckon, Miss Lia. But your daddy's sorta got charge of things today, seeing he sent out the call to us. If he's satisfied with 'em, I reckon it goes with us. Maybe you'd better wait in the hotel. If trouble's coming this way, we'll have to get ready for it."

She went unwillingly, furiously, but she went.

Powell quickly explained what Hatch Gillian was trying to do. "We've got to get a bite to eat and ourselves a round of drinks," he finished. "We brought a bunch of extra guns along, if anybody is short. We'll want more cartridges, though."

"I had all the extra cartridges in town bought up," Keenan said. "I figured, if we couldn't use 'em all, at least no one else'd be able to buy 'em and use 'em against us. Grab your food in the hotel dining room, an' we'll keep watch out here."

Dan limped in with the rest. There was a limit to what a man could do on an empty stomach. On the wide hotel porch Lia Gillian gave him an angry look as he passed.

They ate hurriedly at one long table in the hotel dining room. Others were in there eating, also. Curious looks were cast at the new tableful of weary men who wolfed their food without talking.

When they went out, there was still peace in the courthouse square. Lia Gillian left her chair when Dan limped out the door. He forgot the pain in his wounded leg as he snatched off his dusty sombrero and faced her.

The others went on, and they were alone. Her face was set, cold. She wasted no words. "I love my father," she said. "If anything happens to him through your trickery, I'll bring it home to your door-step, if it takes the rest of my life. Do you understand?"

Dan smiled at her thinly, without humor. His low voice was savage in its politeness. "Look at this leg of mine, ma'am. There's a bullet hole through it. I got that helping your father. I'll probably get another before the day is over. I quit Rigby an' come to help your father because Rigby and his men were throwin' in with Leacock an' Colby. We hung Colby on his own land this morning. We're ready to do the same to Leacock, if we can catch him. But this is man's work . . . and a man-handling woman has no place in it. I've taken insults from you today until I'm tired of it. Even an outlaw . . . even a man like Jake Rigby . . . has got the decency to thank anybody who risks his neck to help him. That seems to be more than you have. Good day, ma'am."

He limped on off the porch. He did not know that she stood there looking after him until he had mingled with the men down the walk.

Powell was frankly worried by now. As Dan came up, he heard Powell say to Tom Keenan: "I wonder if they've been trapped or run down? Their horses weren't any too fresh."

"Maybe McNeil here has got an idea," Keenan said curtly.

Dan said with equal shortness: "He had a lot more ground to cover than we did. You'll get nowhere standing around here, worryin' about him. Have you decided what you're going to do if they show up here on the run?"

"What is there to decide?" Powell replied shortly. "We'll fight it out."

"You wouldn't last long with a price on your head," Dan told him shortly. "You'll get whipped yet if you keep on this way. I thought you two'd have it all figured out by now. What are you going to do about the sheriff? I saw him walk into his office over there in the courthouse as I came down off the hotel porch."

"Damn the sheriff!" Powell said violently. "We know who put him in office an' whose orders he takes."

"He's the sheriff just the same, an' he'll be a rallying point for a lot of strength against you, if you're fightin' here at Red Town, an' Leacock gets to him. Take care of him first an' then place your men an' hold 'em ready. I'll bet you haven't even put in a complaint about what happened at the Diamond A last night."

"What's the use?" Powell retorted.

"Plenty," Dan snapped. "After this is all over, there'll still be law. Make your appeal to the law before witnesses, even if you know it won't do any good. Hell, man, are you crazy? Go on over to the sheriff's office an' get it over with before it's too late. Leave out Colby an' Leacock for the time being. An' send two or three men out to the edge of town to keep a lookout. They can see men coming several miles away." Dan turned, saw Pete Canfield nearby, and said: "Go along with 'em, Pete."

His angry eloquence swayed them. Powell dispatched men to watch, and then led the way over to the courthouse. The jail was on the ground floor, and the sheriff's office was in front. He and his deputy acted as jailers.

The sheriff was a man named Gratney. He had held office three terms, and there was yet a man to be found who could say that Gratney was a coward. This was as it should be, except that Gratney had other faults. He remembered who had put him into office and had small thought for anyone else.

Gratney and the deputy were in the office. Gratney stood up and put his back against his desk and looked from under heavy lashes as the men crowded through the door until the room was filled.

Little Dick Powell acted as spokesman. "Last night, Sheriff, the Rigby-Costillo men attacked Hatch Gillian's Diamond A Ranch," he said briefly. "They shot it up, killed two men, an' burned the buildings down."

Gratney was a big, slow-moving man. His face was angular, long, and the broad sweep of his jaw moved slowly on a quid of tobacco. A heavy black mustache shaded his mouth. His look was slow, and his manner unruffled. If he was surprised, he did not show it.

"Where's Gillian?" he asked.

"He ain't here right now," Powell answered. "He don't have to be here. What do you aim to do about it, Sheriff?"

"I'll get a posse out after them," Gratney said deliberately.

Powell hesitated.

Dan had pushed forward into the front row, over at one side. He spoke for Powell now. "Here's the posse now. Just deputize us an' we'll save you the trouble of collecting men, Sheriff."

Gratney shook his head without troubling to see who had suggested it. "Nope," he said with the flat manner of one whose mind was already made up. "I'll get my

343

own men together. I've been wondering what you men were doing in town today. Ride out to the Diamond A and I'll come along with a posse this afternoon an' pick up the trail from there. Won't take me. . . ." Gratney had turned his head as he spoke. His glance had crossed Dan's face and flashed back with a startled look as he broke off what he was saying. He ripped out an oath as his hand grabbed for his gun.

"Don't, Gratney!" Dan snapped.

Gratney didn't, for Dan's hand was already on his gun. But quick anger darkened the sheriff's face. "That's McNeil. One of the Rigby men. What's he doing here?" he asked Powell harshly. "There's a price on his head. I want him."

Long Tom Taylor drawled: "I reckon you don't know me, Sheriff, but there's a price on my head, too."

"Don't forget me," Shorty Pyle said.

"I never could get a price on mine," Scantling Deene said sadly.

The sheriff looked at Shorty and recognized him. "What is this, Powell?" he demanded thickly. "These men are outlaws."

You could see Gratney puzzling over it, trying to get the straight of it. Little Dick Powell looked uncomfortable. He didn't seem to know what to do about the situation. He had come in to put the sheriff in bad, and now he seemed to feel that he was in bad, instead.

Dan stepped to the sheriff's side, smiling. His hand was still on his gun. He drew the weapon slowly. "You're wrong about us being outlaws right now, Gratney. We're just gettin' ready to be deputized. Maybe Powell won't be as rough with you as I will. He hasn't got a price on his head yet. Unbuckle your gun an' let it slide to the floor . . . an' then swear us all in as deputies. You can explain to Leacock later how it all happened."

"I'll be damned if I will," Gratney refused violently.

Dan's smile grew broader. "Then you'll be damned, Gratney, and I'll do it with a bullet. Leacock might miss you, but I won't. Smile, man. I've laughed many a time when you've been after me with a posse."

Gratney was a brave man — but he was also a man who could face facts. He did not doubt that he was hearing the truth, for he knew Dan McNeil. His forehead grew moist.

"One minute is all you get," Dan warned.

345

Gratney looked past Dan to Dick Powell. "Are you going to stand there and allow this?" he demanded.

Powell rubbed his chin, and then shrugged. "McNeil is not one of my men," he said. "I wouldn't risk my skin to help you out of a jam, Gratney. You never were concerned about my troubles."

"Half a minute," Dan warned.

"Raise your right hands," Gratney surrendered hoarsely. "I'll swear you in, if you think it'll do you any good."

He did.

When it was over, Dan said: "Gratney, we have word that Rigby may bring his men into town in a little while looking for trouble. For your information, I'm not riding with the Rigby gang any more. For your further information, there ain't a man here who'd trust you to give him any benefit of law, if Leacock told you to hold off. Leacock's in this business, so we'll just keep you out of it. You'll spend the rest. . . ."

Dan broke off as a horse galloped over the courthouse yard to the front door. The rider's boots hit the ground, and he jerked the door open a moment later and yelled: "They're damned near to the edge of town already!"

Instantly all was confusion as the men rushed out to their horses. Dan jammed his gun in the sheriff's side. "I was goin' to lock you up!" he snapped. "But maybe you'll do more good with us. Shorty, Long Tom, Scantlin', ride herd behind the sheriff."

12

"NO MORE NOOSES"

They were coming from the southwest, over the broad, dry flats that surrounded Red Town. Gillian's little bunch of men was riding hard out in front — and less than half a mile behind them were more men, closing up faster after them. The dust they raised drifted up toward the hot, blue sky, and already through the thin, dry air the sharp crackle of gunfire was audible at the houses on the edge of town that hid the armed riders gathered behind them. The inhabitants of those houses had been warned to stay inside. The men were waiting with rifles and handguns, grim and ready. The sheriff's surliness gave way to interest when he caught his first glimpse of the chase.

"I thought you were lyin'," he admitted. "Is that the Rigby men chasin' after Hatch Gillian?"

"You've got eyes," Dan said. He was riding a little ahead of the sheriff. Long Tom, Shorty, and Scantling Deene were close behind them.

Gratney scowled. "Give me a gun!" he demanded violently. "They can't bring their hell-raising in under my nose this way!"

Dan grinned suddenly and passed over the sheriff's gun belt that he had brought along. "This may be a fool stunt, but I'm going to give you a chance to show that you mean that," he said.

Gratney did not seem to be aware of what Leacock and Colby had been doing. This was not strange, considering the nature of it. He had barely finished buckling on the gun belt when Hatch Gillian rode in past the first houses. Only five men followed him. Two had been lost.

It had been a hard chase. Their horses were lathered, tired. Their belt loops were empty of shells, and they were not firing back at the men who followed. Watching, Dan saw Gillian swinging his head in startled glances at the concealed men. Gillian's white teeth showed in his beard as he laughed aloud. He did not stop. Not one of the five men who came after him stopped. Riding hard, they went on along the dusty street, drawing the other riders after them.

Fully twenty-five men were in that string of riders who burst in between the houses after them. Jake Rigby was riding at their head, his black-bearded face outthrust in the eagerness with which he pursued. His gun was out, and he was firing every few strides of the horse. Costillo was close behind, and their men were following. Other men were there, also, riders from the Running J.

Rigby gave the attack signal himself. He saw the waiting men. Twisting in the saddle, he threw up a hand and shouted a warning. In the same instant, almost, his gun poured lead in between the houses he was passing. The attack rolled out on them from two sides.

Beside Dan, Gratney rode out against the outlaw invasion of his town. His gun joined in the crashing crescendo of gunfire that burst out all around them. Mad confusion gripped that stretch of dusty street. Men riding out from between the houses blocked the way. The chase piled up against those in front.

Guns were blasting; men were bawling oaths. Men who had emptied their guns clubbed them. One man swung a rifle by the end of the barrel. Another drew a knife. Others were trying to get free of the plunging press of horses. Men shot from their saddles rolled on the ground under stamping hoofs.

Dan spurred in among the trees. Billy Masters, by whose side he had ridden many days and nights, reined a plunging sorrel around on its hind legs and swung a six-gun at him. Billy Masters's square sweating face was contorted with anger. The past had vanished; only the present counted — and the present held death, if Billy Masters could bring it. Another rider behind Dan shot first.

Billy Masters swayed back in his saddle. Dan threw a quick look around and saw Shorty Pyle pressing forward. Shorty was not smiling now. Shorty showed no regret for that bullet he had put in Billy Masters. They had chosen their sides. They were living — dying by that choice.

Costillo was there. He turned his head and saw Dan coming. The dark, handsome face grew savage with hate, fear. Costillo's gun-muzzle streaked around toward Dan and leaped with the recoil of the shot, but Costillo's horse was plunging, and he was no better shot than usual. Dan felt the slight jar of the bullet through his hat. He grinned as he saw fear flash over Costillo's face at the miss. Costillo was unnerved. He knew what was coming. He tried to throw himself down out of the saddle. Dan was still grinning coldly as he released the hammer of his own gun. Costillo went all the way down to the ground, and his horse stamped on him as he lay limply there.

From the corner of his eye Dan caught a queer sight. Gratney, the sheriff, was standing in his stirrups, staring farther along the street. The sheriff's face was frozen in astonishment. Rising in the stirrups and following the look, Dan saw that Gratney was staring at the bold, red face of Leacock.

The sheriff had ridden out to fight outlaws. He had found them — and he had also found the man who had put him into office. He was stunned by the sight and did not know what to do.

A bullet struck Dan's arm, knocking him half out of the saddle. As he got his balance and felt the sudden, cold numbness of the useless arm, he saw Jake Rigby pressing close to finish him with a second shot. Rigby's black-bearded face was more threatening than Costillo's had been. His right hand was bandaged, and he was shooting with his left. Perhaps that had made him miss the body shot he had tried for. It was a fatal miss. Dan shot him squarely in the middle an instant before Rigby fired again. Dan's gun clicked on an empty shell as the hammer fell again.

Spurring hard against Rigby's horse, Dan clubbed the empty gun, but Rigby was already slipping out of the saddle.

The confusion in the street was breaking up as men fought out from it. Weary, caught off guard in a trap like they themselves had set at Leacock's ranch, the newcomers had little heart for such fighting after the first wild moments, especially the Rigby men. Gunman's wages were not enough to keep them facing men who fought for safety, for homes, and for families.

Dan rode over into the yard of the nearest house to reload his gun. From there he saw the sheriff riding toward Leacock, waving his gun as he went. Leacock burst out of the crowd just in time to see Gratney bearing down on him with a drawn gun. Leacock's bold, red face was snarling with fury. It was plain that he thought Gratney had arranged this trap. He did not hesitate as he threw his gun down on Gratney and fired.

Dan saw the sheriff give to the impact of the bullet. He saw the sheriff's gun fire from the hip — and Leacock fall forward across his horse's neck. Then Hatch Gillian and the five men who had come with him burst out between the houses and entered the fight. That was too much for the Rigby and the Leacock men who were left. They fled. A few riders followed them, but quickly turned back.

Hatch Gillian rode past Dan, his red beard bristling and his weariness forgotten. "How'd you get the sheriff in this against Leacock?" he called.

"Persuaded him," Dan said, grinning.

Blood was streaming down his arm. Pain was beginning to flash through the numbness, but he put that aside as he rode after Gillian toward the sheriff. Gratney was sitting dully in the saddle, looking down at Leacock, who lay on his back in the dust. Leacock was dead.

Gratney turned his head and looked at them stupidly. "I killed him," he said, as if he could not believe it. "He come in with the Rigby men, an' put a bullet in me when I tried to talk to him."

Hatch Gillian spat. "Good riddance," he said. "He and Colby were hirin' them to do his dirty work. We hung Colby this morning, an' you killed Leacock. There's goin' to be a heap of change around this county from now on, Sheriff. Soon as we get the wounded an' dead sorted out an' taken care of, you better make all this legal some way an' make the best of it."

"It's legal," Dan said. "Gratney swore us all in as deputies."

Gillian's look was startled. "All of you, McNeil?"

"All of us," Dan grinned. "Me, too. I got a sudden idea it might help later on."

"I'll be damned!" Hatch Gillian exclaimed. "You think of everything, young fellow. Hey, where you going?" he asked as Dan started to swing his horse.

"To get my arm patched up, an' then ride on," Dan told him. "Doesn't look like there'll be any more trouble on this range for a time."

"I'm takin' you all back to the Diamond A with me," Hatch Gillian said bluntly. "I need men like you. I reckon we can get the rewards taken off your heads an' make good cowmen out of you again. How about it, Gratney?"

"I reckon so," Gratney agreed.

"How about it, McNeil?"

Despite the pain in his arm, Dan grinned. "I guess so," he agreed. "There's a lot of unfinished business out at the Diamond A I'd like to tackle. I'm going to the hotel now."

"If you see my daughter, tell her I'm all right."

"I'll tell her," Dan said.

Hatch Gillian didn't know what he meant, but then it didn't matter so much. There would be time later to explain everything, Dan thought, as he turned his horse and rode toward the hotel. Lia Gillian would have to make up her mind about it first, and that might take time. But she would, Dan felt — he had thought of that, too, and he had a hunch about it.

ABOUT THE AUTHOR

T. T. Flynn was born Thomas Theodore Flynn, Jr., in Indianapolis, Indiana. He was the author of over a hundred Western short novels for such leading pulp magazines as Street & Smith's *Western Story Magazine*, Popular Publications' *Dime Western*, and Dell's *Zane Grey's Western Magazine*. He lived much of his life in New Mexico and spent much of his time on the road, exploring the vast terrain of the American West. His descriptions of the land are always detailed, but he used them not only for local color but also to reflect the heightening of emotional distress among the characters within a story. Following the Second World War, Flynn turned his attention to the book-length Western novel and in this form also produced work that has proven imperishable. Five of these novels first appeared as original paperbacks, most notably THE MAN FROM LARAMIE (1954) which was also featured as a serial in *The Saturday Evening Post* and subsequently made into a memorable motion picture directed by Anthony Mann and starring James Stewart, and

TWO FACES WEST (1954) which deals with the problems of identity and reality and served as the basis for a television series. He was highly innovative and inventive and in later novels, such as NIGHT OF THE COMANCHE MOON (Five Star Westerns, 1995), concentrated on deeper psychological issues as the source for conflict, rather than more elemental motives like greed. Flynn is at his best in stories that combine mystery — not surprisingly, he also wrote detective fiction — with suspense and action in an artful balance. The psychological dimensions of Flynn's Western fiction came increasingly to encompass a confrontation with ethical principles about how one must live, the values that one must hold dear above all else, and his belief that there must be a balance in all things. The cosmic meaning of the mortality of all living creatures had become for him a unifying metaphor for the fragility and dignity of life itself.